wilsan Harris creates a world where the events
+ people exist only [illegible]
+ the emphasis is f[illegible] [illegible]es'
tran pure ancestory [illegible]

Imagination: Cante [illegible]

JONESTOWN

Jonestown

WILSON HARRIS

ff

faber and faber

LONDON · BOSTON

First published in 1996
by Faber and Faber Limited
3 Queen Square London WC1N 3AU

Photoset by Parker Typesetting Service, Leicester
Printed in England by Clays Ltd, St Ives plc

Wilson Harris is hereby identified as author
of this work in accordance with Section 77 of the Copyright,
Designs and Patents Act 1988

A CIP record for this book is available from
the British Library

ISBN 0–571–17773–5

2 4 6 8 10 9 7 5 3

For Margaret and Sam
and to Zulfikar Ghose
and
Helena de la Fontaine

There was a man went out one night a-seeking for a soul
And oh he met a skeleton, a grim and grisly skeleton
A-sitting in a hole.

The man who was a gentleman and always most polite
Said 'since you're wise and old dear sir, I venture to be bold dear
    sir,
And ask your help this night.

I wonder could you tell me sir where I might reach my goal,
A place where I might hope to find a something for my peace of
    mind,
In short dear sir a soul.'

The skeleton looked very wise and rattled all its bones
And asked 'do you require the thing for beggarman or thief or
    king,
De Havilland or Jones?'

'Is that important?' asked the man, expressing some surprise,
'I hadn't thought of class before, it's just a soul I'm searching for,
I wouldn't mind the size.'

The skeleton disdainfully it looked him up and down
And said 'it's very plain to see you've no perception of degree'
And frowned a bony frown.

'The simplest thing that you can do is find yourself a hole,
And sit and watch the world go by and never mind the where or
    why
Or seeking for a soul.'

So down he sat for years and years upon a village green,
Until he was a skeleton, a very handsome skeleton,
The finest looking skeleton that ever had been seen.
                    Margaret Rose Harris, 'Skeleton Ballade'

The Maya Indians have been called an enigmatic people, and rightly so . . . How, where and when did this, the most important Stone Age culture, evolve? Why were all their cities, magnificently embellished by the most talented sculptors, abandoned? What is the message contained in their hieroglyphic script, the finest and most intricate of its kind known to us? . . . How was it possible for the Maya astronomers, the most outstanding of their time, to measure without the aid of any instruments the rhythmic movements of the heavenly bodies with an accuracy that amazes all the experts of our own day? Where were their skilled architects trained, and where did their sculptors learn the arts of carving? These and many other questions have as yet remained unanswered.

H. D. Disselhoff and S. Linne, *Civilizations of Central and South America* (Crown Publishers Inc., New York, 1960)

There are other aspects of the Maya philosophy of time . . . What had gone before and what lay ahead were blended in a way that is baffling to our western minds. Mysticism is not now fashionable, and so writers tend to stress the material side of Maya civilization, but surely it is precisely these (to us) strange aberrations of Maya mentality which pose the most interesting questions.

J. Eric S. Thompson, *Maya Civilization* (University of Oklahoma Press, 1954)

It means that . . . the future states of the Universe are in some sense 'open'. Some people have seized on this openness to argue for the reality of human free will. Others claim that it bestows upon nature an element of creativity, an ability to bring forth that which is genuinely new, something not already implicit in earlier states of the Universe save in the idealized fiction of the real numbers. Whatever the merits of such sweeping claims, it seems safe to conclude that the future of the Universe is not irredeemably fixed. The final chapter of the great cosmic book has yet to be written.

Paul Davies, in *Chaos*, essays edited by Nina Hall
(Penguin Books, London, 1988)

CONTENTS

Letter from Francisco Bone to W.H.

Trinity Street
New Amsterdam

Dateless Day

Dear W.H.,

I have learnt of your sympathies for voyagers of the Imagination and trust therefore that you will undertake the task of editing the enclosed manuscript or book.

I am the only survivor of the 'tragedy of Jonestown', which occurred – as many people know – in late November 1978 in a remote forest in Guyana.

The Longman *Chronicle of America* tells of the 'tragedy of Jonestown' and of the scene of 'indescribable horror' which met the eyes of reporters from every corner of the globe when they arrived in stricken Jonestown after the self-inflicted holocaust engineered by a charismatic cult leader, the Reverend Jim Jones.

In my archetypal fiction I call Jim Jones Jonah Jones. All of the characters appearing in the book are fictional and archetypal. In this way I have sought to explore overlapping layers and environments and theatres of legend and history that one may associate with Jonestown.

Not all drank Coca-Cola laced with cyanide. Some were shot like cattle. Men, women and children.

Francisco Bone is a disguised name that I employ for myself. I suffered the most severe and disabling trauma on the Day of the Dead (as I see and continue to see in my mind's eye the bodies in a Clearing or town centre in Jonestown on November 18). The shock was so great – I blamed myself for not taking risks to avert the holocaust – that though I was wounded a numbness concealed for some time the physical injury that I suffered. The consequences of such 'numbness' occupy different proportions of the Dream-book.

When I escaped I dreamt I was dead and gained some comfort from rhymes of self-mockery, from handsome skeletons, all of which helped to promote the theme of Carnival Lord Death in the

3

Book when eventually I began to write it. One such self-mocking poem – which I came upon when I arrived in New Amsterdam before I had started writing – is the first epigraph that I use. That poem helped me to offset the hell of Memory theatre for a while and to join strolling players on a village Amsterdam green. I relished the Jest that I associated with eighteenth-century Dutch plantation owners who superimposed structures and promenades upon the bank of the Berbice River in the vicinity of New Amsterdam. When I arrived in 1985 to write my Dream-book I strolled on a promenade called *village Amsterdam green* that ran from the township to a mental hospital. Patients and townsfolk tended to stroll arm-in-arm dressed in masks of Bone at Carnival time. I sought a pleasant hole to simulate the grave into which I should have fallen on the Day of the Dead. Why me? Why did I survive? It was this thought that drove me to write . . . Questions as much as thought! No easy answers.

I feared to write in – and be written by – a demanding book that asserts itself in Dream and questions itself from time to time (even as I question the meaning of survival) as you will see as you read. One overcomes the fear of Dreams, I suspect, for I did not stop writing or being written into what I wrote . . .

I was obsessed – let me confess – by cities and settlements in the Central and South Americas that are an enigma to many scholars. I dreamt of their abandonment, their bird-masks, their animal-masks . . . Did their inhabitants rebel against the priests, did obscure holocausts occur, civil strife, famine, plague? Was Jonestown the latest manifestation of the breakdown of populations within the hidden flexibilities and inflexibilities of pre-Columbian civilizations? The Maya were certainly one of the great civilizations of ancient America and the fate of their cities – such as Palenque, Chichén Itzá, Tikal, Bonampak – has left unanswered questions. Teotihuacan in Mexico raises similar enigmas. The unsolved disappearance of the Caribs in British Guiana is another riddle of precipitate breakdown. And there are many others. The amazing story of the Arekuna Indian Awakaipu is well documented in Georgetown in the 1840s. Awakaipu persuaded representatives from many Indian peoples to offer themselves as

4

a sacrifice at the foot of Mount Roraima in order to recover an 'enchanted kingdom'.

The Maya were torn by the notion of eternity's closure of time and another shape to time, blending pasts and futures to unlock closure or pact or plot.

The weight of charismatic eternity and a capacity to unlock closure became real and profoundly pertinent to me and to my age . . .

I drifted into what seemed an abnormal lucidity upon chasms of time. The price one pays for such voyages is far-reaching. One becomes, it seems, a vessel of composite epic, imbued with many voices, one is a multitude. That multitude is housed paradoxically in the diminutive surviving entity of community and self that one is.

All this emerges at its own pace in the Dream-book but the preliminary capsule that this letter is shows how vulnerable I still am some sixteen years after the Day of the Dead. The fabric of the modern world has worsened, it seems to me, in that span of time. The torments of materialism have increased . . .

It is essential to create a jigsaw in which 'pasts' and 'presents' and likely or unlikely 'futures' are the pieces that multitudes in the self employ in order to bridge chasms in historical memory.

To sail back into the past is to come upon 'pasts' that are 'futures' to previous 'pasts' which are 'futures' in themselves to prior 'pasts' *ad infinitum.* There is no absolute beginning, for each 'beginning' comes after an unwritten past that awaits a new language. What lies behind us is linked incalculably to what lies ahead of us in that the future is a sliding scale backwards into the unfathomable past within the Virgin womb of time . . .

The future brings terrifying challenges but it also brings foetal shapes, tender and young possibilities that enliven us to scan gestating resources in the womb of tradition that we have bypassed or overlooked or eclipsed . . .

As the severity of trauma began to break by degrees uncanny correspondences seemed to loom as I voyaged between Maya twinships of pasts and futures and the Mathematics of Chaos.

Chaos is misconceived as an anarchic phenomenon. Whereas it

5

may be visualized as portraying an 'open' universe. Continuities running out of the mystery of the past into the unknown future yield proportions of originality, proportions of the 'genuinely new' . . .

Composite epic is rooted in the lucidity that fractions or fictional numbers, fictional multitudes, bring. The walls of ruined schools and houses and temples and hospitals and theatres are full with presences and voices though apparently void and empty. Such is the mystery of Chaos. The weight of Chaos is sometimes apparitional, sometimes concrete. Such mathematics enhance an intact mystery in time. Because it is intact yet beyond seizure it acts upon us in apparitional Old Gods or Prisoners (dogma, ideology) locked into the gaols of the past; acts again in dismemberments of such Prisoners who walk on water or in space beyond fixtures or unities of place.

'Unity of place' is a dogma or an ideology in some quarters. But my apprenticeship to the furies acquaints me with a different topography or map of the Imagination that breaches the human-centred cosmos that we have enshrined. There are extra-human faculties and voices that bring contours into play to lift place into both familiar and unfamiliar dimensions which fall outside of presumed norms or absolute models of fact and fiction.

The trauma that I suffered in Jonestown may have imprisoned me absolutely in a plot of fate. But thank God! it aroused me instead to contemplate a hidden mathematics within the body of language . . . Language is deeper than 'frames', it transgresses against the frames that would make us prisoners of eternity in the name of one creed or dogma or ideology.

Maya 'twinships' between the buried past and the unknown future – which are regarded as bewildering to the Western mind – seemed of burning and invaluable moment to me in their bearing on factors of originality and living time. I had no absolute model on which to base my Dream-book except that I sought to salvage unpredictable keys to tradition within the terrifying legacies of the past. I sought to be true to the broken communities, the apparently lost cultures from which I have sprung . . .

A word about New Amsterdam before I close this letter. I

wandered for some seven years – sometimes in states of partial but acute amnesia – before I arrived there and began writing the Dream-book. I dreamt I was translating from a fragmented text or texts that already existed . . .

New Amsterdam is one of the oldest towns on the Guyana coastlands. It is a relic of the Dutch empire of the eighteenth century and was absorbed into British Guiana in the early nineteenth century. Its crumbling walls and roads witness to the erosion of townships and settlements and villages along the coastlands that stand as memorials to Spanish, French, Dutch, British colonization across the centuries.

Over the past half-century the population of Guyana has fallen from a million souls, it is said, to three-quarters of a million within a country almost as large as the United Kingdom.

This decline, which is due in large part to emigration, energizes the imagination into an apprehension of earlier peoples, Aboriginal ghosts whose presence is visible still in their nomadic living descendants.

Thus the mixed peoples of African or Indian or European or Chinese descent who live in modern Guyana today are related to the Aboriginal ghosts of the past of whom I spoke a moment ago: if not by strict, biological kinship then by ties to the spectre of erosion of community and place which haunts the Central and South Americas.

This over-arching Ghost throws some light on the play of 'extinction' within my Dream-book . . . I was driven in my flight from Jonestown to reflect on myself as an 'extinct' creature. I dreamt I had been robbed of my native roots and heritage. I suffered from a void of memory. I belonged to peoples of the Void . . . *But there was a catch, a shock of breath, in this sensation* . . . The *shock* of the 'peopling of the Void', the animals of the Void, the creatures of the Void, became so extraordinary that 'extinction' imbued me with breath-lines and responsibilities I would not otherwise have encompassed. I became an original apparition in my wanderings within over-arching Ghost in coming abreast of extremities of loss, in visualizing my own 'nothingness' as intangible 'somethingness'. Memory theatre was born in such

7

theatres of humility. 'Extinction' attired itself in many parts – as an actor may learn to play staggered roles and numinosities – it grew into bodily extensions, masks, limbs, prompted and sculpted by the comedy of ghosts within active traditions. A train of disturbing rehearsals and heart-searching conscience came into play . . .

Yet I was reminded that I lived in a world threatened by an explosion of numbers, *not* by declining populations. But this deepened, if anything, my inner experience of place and time. Without Memory theatre – and the art of self-rehearsed 'extinctions' in a series of stages upon which one retraces one's steps into a labyrinth of deprivations and apparent losses – the 'peopling of the Void' in all its extremities of *explosion* and *implosion* will not embody heart-searching conscience, heart-searching caveat, but will cement predatory blockages, predatory coherence.

Keys to the Void of civilization are realized not by escapism from dire inheritances, not by political glosses upon endemic tragedy, but by immersion in the terrifying legacies of the past and the wholly unexpected insights into shared fates and freedoms such legacies may offer. In the death of politics (however ritually or conventionally preserved in the panoply of the state) may gestate a seed of re-visionary, epic theatre rooted in complex changes in human and animal nature . . .

The mystery of the Virgin-archetype in the 'peopling of the Void' implies a form virtually beyond comprehension, a form shorn of violence in its intercourse with reality, but – as with all archetypes – it comes to us in its brokenness to activate nevertheless, it seems to me, a reach of the Imagination beyond all cults, or closures, or frames . . .

I suddenly realize that I should not close this letter without a comment on variations in the spelling of 'Guyana' or 'Guyanas' or Guianas' . . .

I appeal to your tolerance, W.H. – when you edit my Dream-book – to accept these deviations or distortions as meaningful in the context of partial amnesia and confusions that I endured in the great forest.

My fluctuations of memory, in my wanderings for seven years

8

in the wake of the 'tragedy of Jonestown', are rooted as well, I am sure, in the amnesiac fate that haunts the South and Central and North Americas across many generations overshadowed by implicit Conquest.

Hidden textualities of pre-Columbian and post-Columbian place are hinted at in the word 'Guiana' which British colonizers framed, for political convenience, when they came into possession of the Colony in the early nineteenth century.

'Guiana' springs from a variable Amerindian root-text which means 'land of waters'. It is as if one becomes aware of fragmented page after page in a volume or book long suppressed or hidden. How apparitional is 'British Guiana' or 'French Guiana' or 'Dutch Guiana'? How concrete are 'Guyanas' in vowel or innermost anatomy of flexible texts extending backwards into pre-Columbian age?

'British Guiana' became 'Guyana' in 1966. A link was implied with an older frame one may perceive in Spanish maps of the region encompassing the 'Guianas' and Venezuela and South Brazil. Cross-culturalities running through 'Guianas' and 'Guyanas' are invoked, it would seem, in the Dream-body of history, and in implications of the indebtedness of one convention to another through layers of space and time.

It may seem inevitable or convenient to submit to one frame or name but, in so doing, cultures begin to imprison themselves, involuntarily perhaps, in conquistadorial formula that kills alternatives, kills memory. Not only were Africans who came through the Middle Passage deprived of their names by slave-masters but in the twentieth century Arawaks and Macusis and Warraus and others have begun to adopt English or Portuguese or French or Spanish names and to suppress their native place names or animal names . . . There may be no harm in such adoption provided an inner/outer masquerade or Carnival lives in the imagination and is susceptible to many worlds, to parallel universes of sensibility, in Memory theatre. And what is Memory theatre but an acceptance of amnesiac fate that diminutive survivors begin to unravel . . .?

Long-vanished texts secrete themselves everywhere in Abori-

9

ginal, fragmented theatres of place, in living (sometimes mutilated) landscapes, riverscapes, skyscapes, apparitional at one
level, concrete at another . . .

Elusive El Dorado (City of Gold? City of God?), whose
masthead is consumed and refashioned on sacrificial altars in
every century around the globe, may have a buried harbour in
that compass or 'land of waters'.

Adieu my friend.

Francisco Bone

Virgin Ship

I lay in a clump of bushes like a dead man. Scarcely breathing. My head rested on a cushion of stone. I dreamt of angels ascending and descending into Jonestown. Jonestown was above me in the skeletons of the stars. No stars now at midday. Only the sunlit dead on the ground. How incredibly soft is stone when one fears flesh-and-blood!

Jacob

Jonah Jones was still alive with a gun. He would appear, I knew, at any moment in the Clearing.

There was a split leaf close to my nose through which – with slightly lowered head away from my pillow – I began to count the dead bodies on the ground. They lay not far from the rude church in which they had worshipped an hour or two ago. One swore one could hear their voices still rising into the heart of the South American Forest that seemed now in me, yet as remote from me, as the Milky Way blotted out by sunlight.

I felt a mental splinter sharp as the nib of bone; and voiced my own lament in tune with their vanished voices. The voice of bone was the art of the Word, of sculpture, of painting within the holocaust.

'Good God!' the bone sang.

The bone ceased for a while its tremulous, echoing tracery of scriptures of sorrow. It ceased yet never ceased for it continued to make silent pictures until the wordlessness of the sleeping choir of the dead in the Clearing welled up around me.

A woman whose name was Marie Antoinette was clutching a mystical cup or grail of music from which she had drunk milk and sugar and deadly cyanide. Her head lolled on the ground. Her torso wore the blind sunlight of Carnival. It was the sheer ordinariness of the cup against the lips in the head that struck me to the heart, the lips communion with Silence.

All at once the Reverend Jonah Jones, tall, commanding, came out of the rude Church of Eternity into the Clearing. His face wore an air of triumph like a general's on the field of battle. He stopped above the eloquent lips and head and the communion cup. There was a child beside her I had not seen before. A child I knew all at

13

once. *Me! Me* in another universe, a parallel universe to this. *I was in that parallel child*. Quantum hallucination. Quantum transference of psyche.

Jones stood in the whale of the sun, he knelt, he placed a gun to Marie Antoinette's temple that seemed in a state of divorce from the trunk of her body.

What curious memorials a bone inscribes, draws, paints, builds, sings in the mind, the exiled mind, the solitary mind and soul on the margins of doomed civilizations.

One is exiled when one refuses to obey the commandments of Conquest Mission, to think or write in a certain way, in conformity with the realism of Death. I was a sculptor of the bone in exile now, a writer of the bone in exile now, a painter, an architect, a poet of the bone in exile now upon the margins of the Conquest Mission established by the cult Master of Ritual, the Reverend Jonah Jones.

Jonah and Jones are common-or-garden names which have gained ascendancy in the Forest of my age.

I sensed the great danger I was in. I had deceived Jonah. I knew there was no persuasion or plea or dialogue on my part – dialogue I might have sought to exercise with him – that could have led him back out of the great white whale of the sun into which he was determined to go, sun or whale which he wished to inhabit as the throne of conquest, and in which he sought to secrete his followers. Could one begin to explain to him that such secretion, such a symbol of conquest, was a manifestation or a prelude to the extinction of all species within the insatiable stomach of eternity?

Was this the inbuilt nature of our civilization that we scarcely understood, that we had scarcely begun to question?

I had deceived him. I had been his comrade. I had been a close associate. But – at the last moment – had broken the pact in questioning my civilization, in questioning myself.

He was sure I had been obedient and was lying there amongst the dead. *I had disobeyed his command*. Would I pay dear for such treason? Would I be thrust into a wilderness? Who was I to disobey? Had I saddled myself with the traumas of an age, the traumas of disadvantaged peoples around the globe bewildered by the commandments they were instructed to honour?

At last the Reverend Jonah Jones was satisfied that the woman had been loyal. The subject of a revolution – in favour of the consolidation of conquest – that he wished to engineer, she had surrendered to his will, she had drunk her drink to the last drop . . . Or so it seemed . . . I was to learn differently later . . . No need to pull the trigger . . . He withdrew the gun from her broken body. Was it broken? Was it miraculously whole?

He raised the cold steel, the icy metal – cold as my pillow – to his eyes. I dreamt I was in his blindness. We were already dead. We had already pulled the trigger! But he was alive. *I was alive.*

Technologies and functions of life and death seemed the most ordinary things, banal commodities of conquest. And yet my fear was such I could have vomited. Vomited the stars! The moment had arrived – Jones knew – for him to join his flock. I could not help it. My limbs began to shake. Jonah and I had been close friends within veil upon veil of sun that hid us from each other even as we thought we knew one another. We were strangers. We were at war though we pretended otherwise.

We had debated points in the world's holy books, books of Rwanda, books of Palestine, books of the fall of Jerusalem, that bore on the end of Time.

We had chosen South America, we had chosen Guyana, for our Conquest Mission.

We had chosen – as the ancient Maya once did – the very heart of the jungle, in which to re-interpret the death of the arts, pyramidal epitaphs, painting-epitaphs, poetry-epitaphs. IMAGINATION DEAD IMAGINE.

We had chosen the rainforest hinterland for our Conquest Mission because the Central and South Americas were a theatre of enigma.

No place around the globe had so mirrored paradoxes of vanished cultures, abandoned settlements, from ancient Maya cities and causeways – long deserted, drowned, wreathed in jungle – to invisible Atlantean arches and bridges upon which migrating peoples had moved from the North to the South, the East to the West, and left behind but the morsel of a flute (as

15

though music possessed the secret architecture of ages after the collapse of frames in which conquistadorial priests of old sought to conscript the Imagination) – a morsel, a flute, a fury akin to the bone or splinter in my mind.

The Caribs ate a morsel of enemy flesh when the Spanish priests and conquistadors invaded their lands. They sought to know and digest the secrets of the enemy in that morsel. They hollowed the bone from which the morsel had come into a flute that is said to inhabit all species that sing.

Does music inhabit a quest for self-knowledge beyond all conventional frameworks?

Wherein lies the mystery of music in the densities of space, the live fossil solidity of music in the song of a blackbird or reflected rhythms and compositions in the mirrored throat of a South American apparitional mocking-bird? Did the bone in a wing of the mind, a wing of the brain, inhabit a treasonable space *beyond* fixtures which sanction extinguished species, poisoned landscapes?

Jones did not approve of such questions but he humoured me, he tolerated me. He occasionally elected me to serve on panels in the church. He was convinced of my loyalty to the Conquest Mission whatever my unrest of conscience. We dined together – Deacon, Jones and I – on the eve of the holocaust.

I was his left-hand man. Deacon was his right-hand angel. I could not deny it. We were associates. I was a traitor. I began to scorn the treasures of eternity in order to salvage a morsel of time.

News had reached us that the Police were on Jonah's trail. They claimed he had defrauded the Bank of America.

'The Caribs ate a ritual morsel,' I said, 'on the eve of battle. *You* Jonah know how important such ritual is to disguise bitter self-knowledge or bring it to light when our enemies – whom we would eat – bite into our own flesh. And now that we are on the eve of the holocaust, biter and bitten alike, priest and victim alike, time has become invaluable.'

'We shall all die rather than surrender to the corruptions and lies of the Police,' said Jones.

'Die?' I said.

'Yes, die,' he cried.

My throat was dry. 'It's astonishing to have such a conversation.'

My throat was dry but the Carib ritual morsel melted in my mouth as if I were consuming the flesh of a high priest to unravel the secrets in Jonah's constitution. Food on such a day tastes like the meat of one's commander or executioner, food at such a time brings terror, the terror of self-knowledge, the terror of knowing the greed in others in oneself.

It was impossible to dismiss Jones as a fanatic. He was too solid, too bloody-minded, bloody-minded normality. He was as sane as a Napoleon of finance. DEFRAUD BANKS? I did not believe it. Pocket millions, yes, in a crusade against violence that recruits the selfsame violence in pursuit of its ends. In the light of such symmetry, violence cemented into violence, the morsel I ate burned into my tongue. Was it poison, had I already consumed violence in the name of the people, in the name of a pact with Jones? NO! A worm may turn and puncture the pages of dogma. It was the fracture of loyalty, the disruption of loyalty, it was treason. I knew now – with the morsel on my tongue – how delicate is the balance between loyalty and treason; treason may involve faith in the action of truth, time's truths at variance with eternity's command.

I was joined to Jonah Jones in the delicacy of a bone – when one pretends out of fear to be one thing but knows one is something else – bone-flute music of anguish, a bone-morsel that I tasted deep as hell in heaven, heaven in hell, in the anatomy of linked pasts and futures.

I was joined to him in the splintered disruption of a pact with eternity that I had sworn to honour at his command. I was joined to him now in the fear that I sensed on the eve of disaster. I knew more searchingly and agonizingly than I had ever known before – with the morsel on my tongue – the perversity of the harmony that he inspired in his people, the perversity of symmetry and dread closure underlying the death of the arts.

Perhaps I had known it all along, perhaps I knew my age was dying. Perhaps that was why I joined the Jonestown Church.

17

What I had not perceived was the curious salvage of a Primitive morsel of time sprung from treason, treason's desire, *treason's a-symmetry* when one breaks a pact with authoritarian virtue and dines with the enemy in a fearful but true longing to consume fortresses of hate in him and in oneself, cemented bias in him and in oneself, cemented violence in him and in oneself.

'I thought they were bloody cannibals,' said Jones. 'These Caribs of whom you speak.'

I had forgotten I had spoken of them in my conversion of a Primitive morsel into a feast of terrifying conscience within the furies of history. I had forgotten that the Caribs were the authors of the American feast beneath the Virgin statue of Liberty, authors of asymmetric hospitality granted to aliens and strangers despite their suspicion of, and antagonism to, one another . . .

I had forgotten . . . Jones appeared to remember though he spat the memory on to his plate. He hated the Caribs. He tended to loathe the soil of pre-Columbian America though he was up to his eyes in it, in its species, whale and tiger and everything else, oil and gold and wealth. He would become, if not the Bank of America, a significant agent in the Bank of Memory when I began to shoulder the trauma I would experience the following day as I lay on my pillow of stone.

His face was curiously livid, curiously bland, as he projected his rage upon the vanished Caribs in thinking of the Police. So easy to orchestrate the law into scapegoats one would murder at the drop of a hat.

I turned to Jones with tears in my eyes but he did not see . . . My tongue was burning as well and I was unable to speak. The Dream-book anticipated the moment when I would start to write and spoke for me from the future –

'Are we not subject to the vocabulary of death-dealing regimes? Do we not need to consume that vocabulary and change it, consume the battle-cries, the marching songs, drums that counsel assault? Death coins every phrase that spells conquest. Death's vocabulary is rooted in human discourse . . .'

'*In counterpoint with the extra-human dissonances of the victim soul, the long suppressed, plaintive and wonderful music of the victim soul*

. . . ' said Deacon. He had been silent all through the meal as if he were nursing a bullet *to be fired at Jones* . . . The idea sprang into my head I knew not from where . . . A bullet, a morsel of a bullet in himself . . . 'Is it not time – when time seems to be ending – to unravel that counterpoint, varieties of counterpoint, between priest and sacrificial victim, between huntsman and hunted species, between lovers and Virgins of the wild . . . God knows it's too late for me, I have failed, *but you, Francisco* . . . ' He stopped. Was he laughing at me? Was he mocking me? Was Marie of Jonestown (with her dead child whom I was to identify with myself in a flashing moment on the morrow in the Clearing) a despoiled Virgin, a despoiled Liberty on the flag of Jonestown? I had helped to raise that flag on the day we began to build Jonestown. I was filled with anger at Deacon and at myself. I disliked Deacon then intensely as much as I feared Jones. Deacon was Jonah's right-hand angel. He was – I dimly felt at this stage – a signal for me of the riddle of the huntsman – in the book I was to write when I survived Jonestown (a book possessing its own life to be entitled *Imagination Dead Imagine*) – the riddle of the huntsman, the riddle of the hunted creature, the enigma or counterpoint of shared Passion between spoilers and despoiled, the riddle of the feast when one dines with enemies who are also one's close associates.

After the holocaust, when I fled Jonestown, his self-mockery, his mockery of me, gave way to truths I wrestled with on every ladder between heaven and earth, the truths of fictionality in enemy and friend, Virgin space and animal bridegroom, animal masks worn by heroes and monsters when civilization is in crisis.

He was to don the mask of the Scavenger or Vulture or Eagle. Jonah, at the point of death, *when Deacon shot him*, was to achieve guilt and remorse in the metamorphosis of the whale into a sun-striped tiger swimming in space.

But all that lay in rehearsals and stages in the Dream-book in the future. *In consuming such a rush of thoughts I am in the future now. I fear Jones but shall continue to wrestle with him. I dislike Deacon but shall continue to learn from him.*

A rush of thoughts takes me into the opening chapters of

Jonestown long before I begin to write. I see them, those chapters, in my mind's eye, as I quarrel inwardly all over again – in Memory, in my state of trauma – with Jones and Deacon on the eve of the Day of the Dead. An infinite quarrel from which one's pen is fashioned, heart's blood, the setting sun's ink on the eve of the Day of the Dead . . .

That coming Day already devastates my mind. I am driven to contemplate inconsolable grief, yes, *but within a context of rare Beauty*. Why Beauty? As though the dying of an age blends sunset in sunrise, inconsolable grief in Beauty.

WHY ME? WHY HAVE I SURVIVED? Dying ages do not entirely die when there are diminutive survivors.

Let me – in this opening chapter that rushes upon me with incredible urgency (am I already writing it, or living in it, being written by it?) – give a trace or a clue to the burden of inconsolable grief in Beauty . . .

Deacon had been abandoned as an infant child in the Courantyne savannahs of Guyana. A rice farmer (also a rearer of horses and cattle) and his wife adopted him. An infant, a peasant, fallen from the stars! Later he became the hero of the populace, a monster as well. He was inoculated by a medicine man of Mount Roraima with the venom of the Scorpion Constellation. He gained, or appeared to gain, immunity to pain!

But this was to prove the unmasking of the huntsman into the inner burden of unspoken grief suffered by victim cultures. The price of relief from pain, immunity to pain in a peasant angel, was to uncover all the more terrifyingly the helplessness of animals of fate destined to impart the rage of stone, or the venom of marble, into civilization for therapeutic, aesthetic purposes (it was alleged); the helplessness of animals of fate destined to labour in the promotion of privileges, but never to be accepted as equal participants in sorrow or joy or ecstasy of flesh-and-blood.

Did he (the infant peasant fallen from the stars, the infant angel of the precipice of civilization) bring the venom when he fell, does the venom lie in him or in despised creaturely souls that map the earth and the heavens in the intricacy of laddered feet, antennae, the intricacy of wing or feather or scale, the miraculous grotesqueries in masks of God, the terror of God, the instinctualities-in-numinosities in the mind of God?

Grief lies in creation when creaturely, apparently dissonant Beauty – in its infinite, webbed or cellular or corpuscular particularities and voyaging ramifications – is so despised, so outcast into spare-part methodologies, that it offers little or no solace, and the therapies it provides become functional callouses or tools. Immunity to pain, within privileged orders, comes to mirror functional callouses framed into animal destiny.

Grief lies in Beauty when the unmasked priest Jonah Jones, the unmasked right-hand angel Deacon, the unmasked left-hand associate (myself, Francisco Bone) discover their animal, archetypal masks within the hunted creatures each pursues in himself. We are hunted, we are pursued by repetitive catastrophes, repetitive Nemesis, and our insight into Beauty – which we may gain at the heart of terror – deepens the trial of creation to bridge chasms in itself.

Or else we will continue to perpetuate hierarchies of brutality sponsored unwittingly perhaps by Privilege, hierarchies in which each theatre of inhumanity is placed on a scale to measure which is less horrendous or more hard-hearted than the last, the symmetry of hell . . .

The angels in my Dream-book – playing on harps like stringed skeletons – brought messages I needed to interpret and re-interpret into infinity, into parallel universes that seemed at times to touch, to jar against each other like quake organs or plates within the earth's crust.

The music and the drama saturated my Dreams as I lay on my pillow of stone and the angels descended and ascended . . .

Yes, it was clear to me that dissonances in music lie in depth within all harmonies to acquaint us with unwritten relationships that disturb our Sleep. Or else harmony would consolidate itself into an illusion . . .

Jones withdrew the gun from Marie Antoinette's temple. She had been loyal, she had swallowed the last drop of poison. He pointed the gun at the space between his eyes. Time to join his flock on the *Day of the Dead*. I could not stop my limbs – as I lay on my pillow of stone within the bushes at the edge of the Clearing – from shaking. They shook so hard that a miniature storm, it seemed to me, arose in the leaves and bushes where I lay.

Jones stopped. His ears were sharp as claws. He could not see who actually lay in the bushes, but suddenly he roared – 'It's you, blast you Deacon. It's you – who else would dare to disobey? – hiding there. You thought to escape. I see it now. God damn you Deacon. You're dead.' He turned his gun and aimed at the heart of the shaking storm of leaves. He mistook the vestige of a garment protruding from the bushes for one of Deacon's cloaks. Indeed it was no mistake. I had borrowed it from him. It had lain beside the table on which we dined the previous day. Jones's ears seemed to pick up the sight of the blowing garment. They were sharp as a Tiger's seeing claws.

In that instant of miniature Chaos that made my limbs shake and tremble I seemed to fly or run back into primordial memories of Maya drawings and sculptures of Tiger-knights, Tiger-priests. And Jones's blind eyes but sharp seeing claws loomed above me in the Clearing. He was a Priest above his sacrificial victim, above an altar. Altar of death. My death? His death? His blind eyes gave me hope that he – in some unimaginable way – would collapse into darkness before he fired.

I prayed to the Scavenger of heaven that it would seize him in the twinkling of an eye before he fired. A Maya prayer!

His sharp ears however were sharpened as if the Tiger in the blind of his skull would win the Day after all, would claim me for Deacon on the altar of Jonestown; would claim me and encompass a circuit of enemy friendships around the globe. The trade in death, the trade in guns, was universal, friend competed ruthlessly with friend for the Tiger's share, the lion's share, in the marketplace or altar of industry . . .

I closed my eyes but continued to pray, to hope against hope . . .

And then I remembered the sensation I had had – at dinner on the eve of the holocaust – that Deacon held a bullet on his tongue or in his stomach as he ate. A Primitive morsel or bullet to be disgorged as a barn owl resembling an Eagle or a Scavenger disgorges a pellet . . . I remembered in the nick of time and my fingers clutched Deacon's stomach, pulled forth the bullet or pellet, inserted it into his hand and gun. Thus I appeared to complete the deadly circuit between Jones, Deacon and myself.

DEACON FIRED. Answer to my prayer or quantum hallucination of a deadly circuit!

Out of the corner of my eye I saw him standing at the other end of the Clearing. He wore the Eagle/Scavenger mask that duels with a Tiger's sun-mask in Maya Bonampak. Eagle, Vulture, Scavenger. He seemed all three in Maya, enigmatic triple portraitures, the mathematics of Chaos. Not one bullet but three pellets had been held on his tongue or in his stomach to be disgorged in a lightning flash.

The first bullet sent Jones reeling, sent the Tiger reeling. It blazed in the Tiger's blind eyes as if to confirm a state of Eclipse, miniature blaze, miniature Eclipse in Jonestown.

Deacon fired again with a pointed beak that overshot the Tiger's Carnival ammunition in the darkening whale of the sun.

How old is Jonah? How ancient is he? He was disgorged by the whale to launch a miniature atomic bomb in the rainforest desert of Jonestown. Does Jonah harbour unwritten oceanic texts – in paradoxes of sacred scriptures – when darkness envelops the sun in any corner of the globe, however apparently remote? Does a Tiger's remorse affect the threatened species of the whale when humanity dons archetypal masks, creaturely masks, and begins to dislodge the hubris of an absolute, all-conquering divinity?

DEACON FIRED A THIRD TIME. The third random bullet sliced two fingers from my left hand. Or was it my right? I was too numb to know or to care. I felt nothing at all. Nothing even as Jones seemed to rise over me again and crash back to the ground for good. He was staring at me. The sun darkened in the sky of his eyes that seemed to shine, to grow bright with sight, then to be veiled in a state of Eclipse when they seemed blind in the skull of an ancient Priest.

I lay in a miniature storm of leaves and bushes that shook as I shook. He lay in a miniature, darkening storm of the sky.

I had prayed for his death. Had Deacon answered my prayer? I felt my numb phantom fingers pulling the trigger in his grasp and firing and firing again and again at Jones.

Prayer had anticipated Deacon's random bullet as if my fingers were already sliced before they were sliced to lodge in his on the trigger of the gun. As though the future lived in bringing me insight into answered prayer that troubled and disturbed me immensely. *I lived. I survived.* But God knows . . . WHY SHOULD I LIVE? WHY SHOULD I SURVIVE ON SUCH TERMS? IS PRAYER A CONFIRMATION OF INTERCOURSE WITH VIO-LENCE? I had prayed for a weapon with which to kill Jones.

There was a sudden, wholly unexpected, cry from the despoiled Virgin not far from where Jones lay. It was music. Perhaps a bird had lodged itself in her throat. I saw her broken body, I felt myself in that breach, in that terrible womb, I was drawn out into the shadowy resurrection of the child beside her. ME! That child and I seemed now closely knit together, he lying there, I here.

We lay within another prayer or traumatic dream-text prompted by grave extremity when the mind trips into the body, the body into the mind: a prayer-text to live *but not through intercourse with violence*. That other prayer released one awk-wardly, with uncertainty, to visualize vistas stretching into 'pasts' prior to the genesis of violence, the genesis of conquest. An extreme prayer it was to the Virgin with a bird in her throat on the uncanny battlefield of Jonestown. An extreme prayer I dimly remembered now within the palimpsest of the womb, the intricate layers of the womb – more mysterious than the Brain's – half-erasures, half-painted new visibilities within the temple (temple it was despite everything) of a mother's, a bride's, battered body . . .

A prayer I dimly remembered now that lay on my lips, one half of my lips, even as the deadly circuit or plea to Deacon lay on the other.

Did the child's silenced utterance lie on one half of my lips? Did my call to his mother lie on the other half of his?

Such is the potency of language to make the dead speak through every diminutive survivor in the living body of humanity. Such language involves us in chasms that need to be crossed and explored . . . Intercourse with reality through the Virgin is shorn of violence . . .

Such is the impossible/possible womb of the Virgin from which Christ sprang, a womb that lay paradoxically in pre-Christian pasts, a womb prior to the genesis of history, the genesis of religion, a womb dimly perceived through a haze of hideous violence, a womb that encompasses – or responds to – a different prayer from circuits rooted in intercourse with violence . . .

The despoliation of mothers of humanity everywhere *augments* (what a paradox!) the necessity to *break* or *erode* compulsions to batter or rape . . .

To be born of the Virgin now, in a hideously violent world, is to glimpse within the numinous terror of the womb voices of hope that nest in the throat of the earth's bombed towns, or cities, or famine-stricken theatres of Mankind . . .

I tried to assemble some measure of meaning as I dreamt all over again that I lay on my pillow of stone at the edge of the Clearing in Jonestown. . .

What is the meaning of history, what is meaning? It is null and void until one sifts varieties of prayer, some perverse, some desiring revenge for evils one has suffered, others steeped in non-intercourse with violence . . . Not easy to put! Except to say that a capacity *prior to violence* makes one see how tribal are pacts or institutions founded on coercion and conquest.

To glimpse this abhorrent tribalism is to begin to question all one's premises and to look backwards into the mists of time for alternative creations, alternative universes, alternative parallels – so to speak – imbued with different weddings and marriages to reality.

'True I cannot deny the difficulty in such alternative parallels in the mathematics of the Soul,' I said to the Virgin as I prayed. 'Yet *you* intervene to break or erode the charisma of catastrophe built on intercourse with absolute violence.

'Such erosion, such intervention or breakage (however frail) of the forces of hell, may be all that we can hope for at this time . . .

'But it is priceless, the intervention of the Virgin is priceless. Such intervention never sanitizes cruelty. I know. It almost breaks my heart to learn of my own ignorance, my own obstinacy, to learn how necessary it is to transform my age. My grasp of the miracle of life is faint. Life may exist far out in space and may suffer within the womb of time when we direct a blow at others, strangers, aliens in our midst even as they would sacrifice us on the altar of their creeds . . .'

I stopped and then asked myself: 'What link then exists between us and strangers?'

I thought I heard a faint reply – 'In my body, in linked imprints, in still unwritten passages woven together from the brides and mothers of humanity! Build the Virgin Ship with the very instruments and terrors that plague you now, Franciso, but which you may convert into a new architecture born of profoundest self-confessional, self-judgemental nails and materials and fabrics . . .'

Thus it was that I drew my first nail in the construction of the Virgin Ship on which to sail from Jonestown into familiar strangers, unfamiliar friends in the body of the self.

First nail plucked from the sun, from the Tiger's killing weapon. Convertible nail into energies of the Imagination to cross barriers and chasms in time. My fear of Jones lessened and I reached into the Clearing and drew from him a fiery claw, an emblem of his remorse.

Was he experiencing remorse? Was I deceiving myself?

Remorse is difficult, it tests all cultures to the core, the core of myself, the core of Joneself. Jone's self, Bone's self.

The claw became a fractured Bone in me. It was sharp as living, re-constructive steel. It was sharp as living blood, a fluid nail through ancients and moderns.

Remorse and repentance are not easy. All of a sudden in the darkening sky, sunset over Jonestown, he became a tall cloud-Tiger draped in blackness. The moon had not yet risen. His anger overshadowed me as I lay in the bushes and he sought to clothe me in his outstanding Night. But the Virgin intervened as the sun set. She broke the overwhelming texture of the tall Night and plucked a Bag of Nemesis from it which she placed over me.

I knew I would have been utterly demoralized in Jones's tall

Night but I could sustain a portion of it, I could learn, I could see *in* it, I could see through it, I could see through the blind eyes of the Priest who murders in the name of love or loyalty.

The tall texture of catastrophe is eroded, in some degree, is miniaturized, in some degree, to make a re-creative vision possible, bearable, even at the end of time (or what passes for the end of time).

I rose from the bushes. But the Bag of Nemesis provided me with one more sighting of Deacon on the Moon, it seemed, that was slowly rising over the dead bodies in Jonestown.

My eyes were faint but I saw Deacon's wing and shawl, I saw him trail the wing in space, I saw its imprint on Moon-dust. Jonestown was on the Moon. It had levitated. It had become an apparition upon scales of past and future time, it was rising bright as a Bomb under the vast network of the Milky Way. It descended again, Jonestown descended again, in concrete measure. Jonestown's Earth, Jonestown's Moon.

Deacon skirted his way through the bodies around him. It was as if he had resumed his duel with Jones though Jones lay dead.

Perhaps he saw Jones through my eyes, tall black Cat, tall black Night. Bright Moon. Black Night.

He crossed the Clearing. He stood now above Jones. He placed a hidden boot under his wing upon Jones's skull in which the moonlight nested. He drew his boot along Jones's head and neck and spine. He rested his boot in a cushioned space beneath Jones's body. And then with a dancing stroke of the Scavenger's Eagle wing he kicked the body over and around. The eyes ceased to stare at me. They were drilling holes into the Moon. They were drilling a ladder to the Moon.

I turned at last and made my way through the Forest to the Cave of the Moon in a cliff above a Waterfall overshadowing the river of Jonestown. I climbed the ladder. The Virgin Ship was tied there and I knew I would embark upon it soon.

The ship took me back to my childhood in Albuoystown.

I sailed on the convertible claw of the sun as if I rode futuristic energy on the back of a Tiger.

A Tiger that could turn and rend me limb from limb in a storm but was harnessed in this instance into Virgin space within a mathematic possessed of the life of fractions to diminish the power of overwhelming seas in the sweep of time, black seas, uncharted regions from which the voices of nature goddesses broke into the human ear.

The ear mirrored a passage in the womb of space, the ear became a receptacle, a caveat, a curious vaginal receptacle instilled with the birth of consciousness to absorb and convert the music of the Sirens into guardian lighthouses.

Through the Sirens and the nature goddesses, and their linkage with the Virgin, consciousness hears itself in layered counter-pointed rhythms as never before, consciousness sees itself, questions itself as never before.

I could not entirely rid myself of ancient fear of such voices but their apparitional weight informed me that time would slide into concrete harbours within blended spirit and fact.

To learn to weather apparition is to arrive at a destination enriched with the voyaging wisdom of Spirit.

So easy to lose one's way as one sails back in time but the universe opens into unsuspected dimensions and I am back – yes, I am truly back – in Albuoystown: a child of nine. It is 1939.

'Albuoystown is linked,' I wrote in my log-book or Dream-book, 'to the former estates of an eighteenth-century French land-owner and slave-owner. They retain, to this day, the names he bestowed upon them: *La Pénitence* and *Le Repentir* (the latter a famous cemetery in Georgetown).' I paused but soon continued:

'An unsettling experience it is to return to the past from the bleak future, to return to 1939 from 1978.' As I stood on the deck of the Ship before I landed I saw a man darting through a crowd in a skeleton's costume. He was rehearsing for Carnival Night in Albuoystown. He could have been my grown-up twin. He was in his late forties, the same age as I was in Jonestown from which I had returned in a backwards sweep of time to Albuoystown . . . He had wrapped his head in a newspaper mask but I was able to read a skeleton headline, WAR COMING IN EUROPE. I was startled as if I had forgotten . . . I touched the Bag on my head that was invisible to everyone and felt it crackle like Nemesis newspaper.

I landed, aged nine, and made my way to my School in Albuoystown. Mr Mageye, the teacher, was giving a history lesson when I arrived.

'Ah Francisco,' he said, 'you are late this morning.'

'There's a new ship in the harbour,' I said, 'I was having a look at it.'

Mr Mageye smiled, nodded, as I took my place on a bench under the blackboard.

He had written there the names of the Frenchman's estates:

LA PÉNITENCE

LE REPENTIR

It was an old blackboard and I remembered it distinctly in the backwards sweep of time. There was a piece of chalk on the desk before me which I inadvertently rubbed on my face to acquire a slightly greyish unshaven look. A nine-year-old child with an ageing head on his shoulders within a Nemesis Bag invisible to all.

A jest that Mr Mageye appreciated, for he was laughing with me at the chalk-like apparition of a beard that I now wore.

I knew every dot and crack in the old blackboard. The School could not afford to purchase a new one.

Our ripple of mutual – almost ghostly – laughter subsided and Mr Mageye continued with his history lesson.

'The eighteenth-century French land-owner came to Guiana from France not long before the French Revolution. He was an aristocrat. He was desolated when news came of the revolution. The beheading of poor Queen Marie Antoinette! No wonder he bestowed the name Marie on several of his black mistresses. Your mother is called Marie. Is she not, Francisco? An embodiment of our history lesson.'

'I am told that the Frenchman is my great-great-grandfather,' I almost boasted.

'Quite so, quite so,' said Mr Mageye.

I was a trifle crestfallen. 'My poor mother claims that he's her ghostly protector. A kind of surrogate husband in the early twentieth century. You see my father died when I was two years old. He may never have existed. I never knew him.'

'We all have ghosts in this country for fathers,' said Mr Mageye. 'Fathers tend to vanish when their common law spouses (as it's now called in English parlance) conceive. It's a legacy of slavery. Mothers rear children invariably without help. And ghosts add a cubit or two to the stature of vanished fathers.

'One is born of several ghost-fathers,' said Mr Mageye, 'and a mother who wears a variety of masks. She's burdened with responsibility for a family of beggars, is she not? All sorts of orphans arrive from the street and cling to her skirts. She cries and she laughs, she is pathetic, she is sublime, she is nostalgic, she is practical, she is a saint, she is a siren, she is vulnerable, she is exalted . . . I sometimes wonder,' said Mr Mageye, 'whether this is why the Roman Catholic Church has such a hold on the masses in Central and South America. Within such a Carnival of history women suffer, but at a certain hidden level they are the true educators of a race that needs to judge itself, to breach a pattern of sexual irresponsibility. Such irresponsibility does violence to communities . . .'

Mr Mageye was looking at me with a quizzical look, a grave look, a jesting look, a serious look. 'Your mother, Francisco, serves beggars in her shop, does she not, as if they were her children, and they call her, do they not, the Virgin of Albuoystown?'

I was stricken to the heart for I suddenly remembered that my mother would die this very night. She would be borne aloft by beggars, she would be mugged and stabbed by a tall Cat of a beggar, an evangelist-beggar, a crusading beggar, in the Carnival of Albuoystown. I had returned not to witness her wedding to a tall Carnival ghost of a Frenchman but her death all over again as I had done as a child on Carnival Night in Albuoystown. I had returned on the day and night of her death. It was the 24th March, 1939.

'Why did the Frenchman give his estates such extraordinary names, *La Pénitence* and *Le Repentir*? Does anyone know?'

I knew but I was too grief-stricken to answer. When one returns to the past from the future everything is the same yet nothing is quite the same.

'His estates became memorials,' said Mr Mageye, 'to a tragic duel that he fought with his brother. He was sixteen, his brother was nine. They were playing with wooden swords in a garden on a moonlit night. The younger brother somehow or other dug his sword into the other's ribs. Not much pain but humiliation. Sword-play was highly prized. It felt like a national disgrace to be out-sworded, out-pointed, bowled for a duck. In a rage the older boy picked up a sharp stone and flung it at the nine-year-old boy. Flung it with venom and greater force than he had intended. The boy took the blow full and straight in the middle of his forehead. It was as sharp as a knife in the hand of a savage priest. He fell like a lamb in a crate or a boxing ring. Never moved again. Stone-dead like a statue that had toppled in the garden onto a bed of roses . . . The Frenchman never forgave himself. He brought a painter with him from France. Successive portraits portrayed him as he grew older, but his brother remained in each portrait as if frozen in time until by degrees they became not brother and brother but father and son.'

There was silence. Not absolute silence. I heard a clock ticking at the back of the classroom upon a wall with nothing but the moving fingers of time, my phantom fingers. They extended themselves into tracing a portrait on my mind's canvas, a portrait of father and son.

I visualized my mother's eighteenth-century protector and surrogate husband in the twentieth century. Would she break the mould of conscriptive protection in the end as Virgin animal goddess when she fell?

I visualized myself as his twentieth-century son. Fathered by my own painted slayer (as I was his painted son) in a game that became a battlefield, economic battlefield, sports arena battle-field . . .

Such is the paradox of imperial games and colonial sons, ornamental sonship, statuesque status, devoid of time's eruptive originality that breaches frame or plot.

'You do see, Francisco,' said Mr Mageye. 'Break the mould if you are to live and grow. And remember,' he added, 'this is a formidable task. But you can do it! It calls for daring, for profound imaginative truth. You are far older than your years, Francisco. You know that. I do not have to tell you. From the moment you arrived this morning we were enveloped in a fiction. The class melted into shadows on the wall. And you and I are alone . . .'

'I know. I know,' I said. 'It's as if we are rehearsing a play. I know but how do you know?'

Mr Mageye did not reply to the question but he continued:

'In breaking a mould, you sometimes break your heart, the heart's addiction to fallacious glories, and you enrich – curiously enough – your ghost-father's true heritage of Compassion. He was a Catholic, was he not? You lift that heritage out of subservience to another's style or will, out of base and opportunist compliance with another's cultural vested interests.' He paused and considered.

'Yes,' he said softly, 'equality between former masters and the genius of the new is only possible when originality is seen to be native as much to the powerless as to the powerful . . .'

'What is inequality?' I interrupted. 'Tell me Mr Mageye!'

'Inequality is habituated to incest, to persecution in the family, murder and incest. Murder in the ruling family projects incest upon colonized others to make all Mankind into a pawn. It is a terrifying lesson as we look around the globe, East, West, North, South. Yes, to teach history today is to entertain a complex vocation . . .'

'You are my magus, Mr Mageye,' I said impulsively.

It was a rash statement to make to a teacher in 1939 when School tended to be a rather authoritarian assembly. But not to Mr Mageye. I had not been a grossly favoured pupil by any means. For the records of the School show clearly that Mr Mageye had a reputation for freedom from bias. But there was a subtle understanding between us.

He knew of my curiosities with regard to shamans and seers and magi in the Americas. I loved maps of the Yucatán. I pored over legendary trade routes adorned with drawings of tumultuous forests and seas upon which dolphins and mermaids sat. South American rubber was used to fashion the ball in ball games played in ancient Mexico. Mr Mageye suggested that a brisk trade existed in rubber between South America and Mexico before the Spanish Conquest.

I loved charts of the Orinoco that were dated in the year that Raleigh adventured in search of El Dorado in Guiana. I had acquainted myself with books by the geographer Schomburgk and the anthropologist Roth.

Thus when I returned across a chasm of years – a nine-year-old boy (once again) with a bearded chalk-masked chin – my precocity heightened itself into a comradeship with Mr Mageye (unusual in that day and age). It heightened itself into the steepest, imaginary wave that I associated with the seas and rivers and forests that I had once consulted under Mr Mageye's wry but spirited approval.

In taking the liberty of appointing him my magus I affirmed the birth of consciousness in which one writes and is written into a Dream-book to come abreast by degrees of unsuspected dimensionalities in space.

Even as I took the liberty I was affected by the memory of a steep wave that had threatened to overwhelm the Virgin Ship on my crossing from 1978 disaster-ridden Jonestown back to 1939 Albuoystown.

Black and steep as Night over Jonestown, blacker than the blackboard at which Mr Mageye now stood.

He (Mr Mageye) loved to play pranks. He would arouse laughter in his class and then resume his history lesson. He dodged behind blackboard and wave. As the Ship was about to fall through the roof of the world he occupied a crevice in the blackboard and peered through it as if it were a telescope. At that instant I heard the bells of the Sirens ringing. The Ship righted itself.

I heard the voices of the Sirens through the magical bells declaring that Mr Mageye was a rare phenomenon, a genuine and a sacred jester. He stood there in the telescopic wave with the look of a gentle Sphinx. The expression passed from his features, he moved back to the front of the blackboard, and he resumed the history lesson.

'The Frenchman returned to France in the Napoleonic era but he

33

was unhappy with the state of his country and he crossed the English Channel and married a rich lady in Sussex.'

I held up my hand to ask a question. I was suddenly angry.

'Just a moment, Francisco, let me say first of all that the Frenchman left half of his considerable Guiana fortune to be used in the Colony on behalf of orphans. European orphans at first left bereft on the death of a planter or a slave-owner but across the decades all Guianese have benefited. Now Francisco . . .'

'A rotten shame,' I cried. 'He left my poor mother without a penny. What use such grandiloquent gestures and legacies . . .'

Even Mr Mageye was taken aback at my outburst.

'He left your great-great-grandmother without a penny! She was but a slave. He had many slaves, many mistresses.'

At first it seemed that Mr Mageye was dreadfully unsympathetic, dreadfully complacent, and then it dawned on me as I looked into his self-mocking eyes that he was testing me, pushing me to perceive the nature of conventional morality, the burden in language to grapple with disturbing factors in a society that takes cruelty for granted within the norms of the day. He saw I was puzzled despite my greybearded mask. And he spoke gently – 'I understand, Francisco. Synaesthesia!'

'What do you mean?' I cried with sudden tears in my eyes. I remembered that my mother would die that very night! I knew. I had returned to the past on the very day and night that her death would occur.

'The spontaneous linkage that you make between the organs of the past and the present (your long-dead great-great-grandmother and your poor mother today) is a kind of synaesthesia or stimulation of different moral ages and visions.' His face was grave, the gravity of a sacred Jester. 'The Virgin of Albuoystown, your mother,' he said, 'reflects synaesthesia – at the heart of the evolving theatre of Carnival – in her bones, her sacred bones: these lay beyond the pale of moral plot or cognizance in the Frenchman's day; now they offer shelter to beggars in Albuoystown.' He hesitated but I possessed the curious sensation that his hand lay in my hand in writing the Dream-book.

'The Virgin of Albuoystown stands at the core of a multi-faceted wave, however black, that threatens to fall on our heads unless we can break the mould of a complacent morality.

'A transference of psyche is at the root of all theatres of mothers of humanity, seers and visionaries. Think of the Virgin of Guadalupe in the capital city of Mexico. Pagan and Christian. Yes, your mother – I am inclined to say my mother now – is affected by a variety of masks which slide in the Waterfall of space into singing Sirens (that we *hear* differently from those who have encountered them in the past), warning voices, pleading voices. Thus is it that *you* Franciso and I (your magus-Jester of History) may begin to break the mould of the past and to release a creative/re-creative capacity to right ancient wrongs in the family of Mankind.'

I left School when the afternoon sun was still high in the western sky above the Virgin Ship in the harbour. I left with the heavy knowledge of my mother's coming death at the hand of a mugger. Mugger. Evangelist. Crusader. Carnival masks.

She had asked me to go straight from School to the leather Shop where she worked. There were to be many processions that night in Albuoystown. Some revellers wore newspapers on their heads, others were dressed as skeletons.

I knew of quiet alleyways we could take to avoid the pressure of the processions.

It was a dateless day to me (24th March, 1939) and when the Shop closed at night she would draw her last weekly wage before Death struck at her purse in the street.

Marie felt – my mother's name was also Marie Antoinette – that she could lean on my child's tall Lazarus arm as she made her way through the crowds after work. My Lazarus arm I had brought from the future and tacked onto my present/past body. I too was a creature of Carnival's reconnaissance of the past from a wave of the future . . .

When I arrived at the Shop there was a queue of shoemakers purchasing choice leather. Each shoemaker would take a sheet of leather, bend it, study its texture, pass his head along the rough edges of the sheet, taste it with tip of his tongue, bring it to his

35

nostrils and inhale the bouquet of the tanned skin.

It was a studied ritual. Leather was a Carnival ritual, a sacramental alliance with the dead, dead cattle transported from interior savannahs. In due course the leather was fashioned into shoes in which the living danced with the ghosts of cattle or rode on their backs.

With my eyes that had returned in a Nemesis Bag from the future I saw the ghosts of Jonestown purchasing shoes in Albuoystown. My sacramental treaty or alliance lay with them. As Jones's left-hand man had I not ridden them in my Sleep, in my unconscious? I had wanted to save them on holocaust eve (when flocks of sheep and horses and cattle were groomed to be burnt as a sacrifice to the gods in ancient Greece) but had succeeded in saving only my own skin with the intervention of Deacon, my own soul with the intervention of the Virgin.

The cattle lay in the Jonestown Clearing on the Day of the Dead. Cattle have human faces, tigers that burn in the sun have the faces of gods, horses weep. I could not help noticing the leather on their feet, the boot with which Deacon had kicked Jones onto his face in the Moon-dust until Jones's eyes drilled holes into a ladder between the Moon and the Earth, between the Moon (the Cave of the Moon) and my Virgin Ship. Deacon's boot and the shoes on the feet of the Jonestown dead reminded me of the leather in Marie's Shop.

In certain circumstances my poor mother might have made a Bomb in profit from tourists who came to Carnival by selling relics of Bone shaped as the Cross or saints fashioned from relics of leather. But thank God! she resisted the temptation.

The shoemakers bought the leather in the Shop, took it away, made shoes which they brought back to the very Shop to be exhibited for sale by my mother. It was a transaction that Marie understood and which she exercised with a rare and tender compassion, for I had seen her purchase shoes out of her meagre wages and give them to barefoot beggars. It meant her going without bread for a day at least every week.

I now realized that there were two intermingling queues in the Shop, one purchasing leather, the other buying shoes. Imprinted on the sole of each boot or shoe was a miniature Ship of Bread within a bubble or a fluid Shop, my mother's Economy, my mother's beggars' dead men's Shop on which she was sailing now (as each minute passed) to her death in Third World South America.

I had seen the imprint of trade unmistakably there, trade in bodies and souls across generations and centuries, in which my mother intervened when she fell in the street with a blow to her heart and was lifted shoulder-high by grey-bearded young beggars. Such is the legality of intercourse with violence, such is the trade between complacent life and matter-of-fact death in which mothers of poverty, mothers of humanity, intervene.

I had seen the imprint of trade unmistakably there on horses and cows that Jones had stabled along with the membership of the Mission whom he had provided with bunks and stalls.

Jones kept many horses which I had christened the horses of the Moon because of their glowing mane, their flowing mane, that encircled my brow and my head at times when I mingled with them.

And now as I recovered myself in the Shop to which I had returned from disaster-ridden 1978 to Albuoystown 1939 – heavy-hearted at the prospect of my mother's coming death – I inspected the crew of leather-purchasers and shoe-purchasers. If only I could seize the pendulum of the Clock ticking away remorselessly, as if it were a horse's cosmic phallus, phallic twisted ladder pointing to the Moon, or Venus, or Aphrodite, I might startle my mother's sobriety with the temperament of pagan goddesses.

'Don't leave the Shop tonight, Mother. Stay here until the full Moon drowns in the sky of dawn. The mind's anxiety-ridden full Moon on the darkest of nights. One lives in two universes at the same time. Apparitional full moon. Concrete Earth. I shall stay with you until tomorrow. Whenever tomorrow is! We shall voyage to the Moon at the bottom of the sky. We shall climb Jones's ladder. Blast him!' I spoke through lips shaped in a child's head upon a child's body that had nevertheless returned from the age of the future.

As darkness began to fall Marie began to close the windows

and doors of the Shop. It was a meticulous business. There were bars to be placed on the windows. Padlocks on the doors.

'I shall break through these one day,' my mother said with a laugh. 'How could we spend the night here, Francisco? It would be gaol.'

'Break through and go where?' I asked.

Marie looked at me sharply. She seemed to know I was testing her when I asked the question. I was seeking to confirm . . . What was I seeking to confirm? That the invisible Bag over my head was real? I had *seen* her coming death within the hour. But now I was unsure. Why should I not be able to stop her from leaving the Shop? How did one convert the gaol of fate into freedom? I wanted to say: 'If you stay here you will live.' But I was confused. Does the gaol of fate mean life or the postponement of death, freedom death or the beginning of unimaginable life?

There was a back door to the Shop that seemed to fall into a pit. An odd kind of sensation when one revisits the past! The door of space itself seems on the edge of falling out of its hinges. It is the knowledge one possesses – or dreams one possesses – that provides an inkling of a chasm in creation across which one voyages.

When one stood at the back door the Shop was tilted upwards, as on a wave, or upon a higher plane to the street below in which faces glimmered like spray in a deceptive sea of moonlight.

Faces glimmered up out of the pit. Black faces seemed white. They had acquired the prize of whiteness. They were white. A desperate whiteness. A desperate illusion of immortality or eternity. White faces glimmered black, a desperate illusion that they were being swamped by immigrants. Brown faces were stained with the salt of blood, neither black nor white. How red is blood, how pale or dark is salt beneath the Ship of the Virgin? Beneath the Shop of Bread?

We left the Shop through the front door that led straight into the silver blood of the Moon. I saw it all through the invisible Bag of Nemesis over my head. I saw my mother's coming death written into the sacred nerves and the fibre of her body, written into the shoes she wore that the dead woman, with her child beside her in the Jonestown Clearing, had worn.

It was as if I saw her walking above me on a wave as before I had seen black and white and brown faces walking below me in a pit. I saw the soles of her feet dance above me like bone in the mind clad in brown leather, white leather, black leather.

Then in a flash she was beside me again and we were walking in the street that led from the front door into throngs of passersby.

Funny the things one remembers! She had bolted the door securely behind her with a green, spongy-looking padlock and deposited the key in the purse with her weekly wage. The sound of a drum reached our ear with a curious ecstatic sigh and yet a funeral note. It was so muffled, so deep, so disturbing in low range yet ferocity of pitch I tried to seal my ears against it . . .

I clung to my mother's hand but the sound seemed to reverberate faintly in her peaceful, peace-loving body. It was as if I sensed her transition into a Blessed Fury . . . I placed my mind against the drum of her womb, so peaceful yet suddenly so mysterious . . . I thought I heard battle songs in the distance addressed however by the counterpoint in the Blessed Fury.

How strange, how terrifying, how disturbing are the ramifications of the birth of truth in the Victim Soul that my mother seemed to me in this instant . . . Was this a measure of the counterpoint of which Deacon spoke on the eve of the holocaust when he and Jones and I dined in Jones's house? He had confessed to his own failure as right-hand angel in the construction of the Mission. He had charged me to address the tragedy of Jonestown when he departed. He had nursed a Primitive morsel or bullet with which to slay Jones.

I heard it all in my mother's transition from peace-loving slave to Blessed Fury. I heard the music that Jones had sealed his ears against when he spat the Primitive morsel onto his plate.

That music had sounded again in the miniature storm in the bushes where I lay on the Day of the Dead with shaking, fevered limb . . .

Was this the very sound that Jones heard in the bone-flute, when we dined, even as he sealed his ears against it in order to prosecute the pact forged with the members of the Conquest Mission?

Easy to blame Jones, but with the birth of truth – as I lay against

39

my mother's body – I knew we had all been reluctant to open our minds to the Virgin Sirens in the pre-Columbian bone-flute, Virgin regenerative Sirens, Virgin regenerative furies that we hid from ourselves, denied ourselves, everywhere in nature.

Had Jones *listened* on the eve of the holocaust would he have named death in himself, would he have sought to cancel an equation between eternity and the conquest of all species that he harboured in himself as sacrificial victims?

'Death's essentialist vocabulary is conquest,' I thought I heard the Blessed Fury say, but I was unsure of everything. 'One needs to break the charisma of conquest in oneself if one is to build a new Virgin Ship.'

Where lay the roots of my uncertainty about everything? NAME DEATH IN YOURSELF.

Does the regeneration of oneself and one's civilization, one's uncertain age, lie through new translated rhythms of well-nigh unbearable counterpoint to complacent symmetry?

The Virgin is a blessed fury when she secretes her involuntary and pagan Shadow-music in the bone of Mankind and in the torso and sculpture of mothers of humanity upon every battlefield. NAME DEATH IN YOURSELF.

A terrifying commandment that breaks all commandments one associates with Privilege and Conquest.

Virgin Sirens! Bone-flute in the cradle of mankind.

How strange.

Regeneration through Virgin Sirens.

How strange to entertain the regeneration of oneself through the furies one has long feared. How steeped has one been – without quite knowing it – in uncanny dread of the masks one's dead mother wears, or has worn, across centuries and generations, the mystical wilds or wildernesses, the mystical brides? How profound is the fall in one's faint body at the heart of Carnival, one's fall that breaks such charisma, one's fall into a new birth of consciousness?

I held my mother's hand as I slipped in the throng and recovered my footing. I was suddenly faint. Suddenly apprehensive. Faint child's body, child of humanity beneath my greybeard, fallen from a wave of the future back into the past. Wave-labyrinth and stairway of the Brain, ladder of the Brain? Wave-labyrinth and stairway of Spirit?

I loved my mother, I stood in dread of her nevertheless, in dread of the masquerade of the womb, and its submission to death, even as she stroked my Lazarus-arm as a portent of a resurrectionary text in my Dream-book on my returning across a chasm from Jonestown to Albuoystown.

All this was pertinent to my love for my mother, my dread of my mother. Did she instinctively know more than I gave her credit for? I thought I knew the facts of her coming death, they seemed unassailable to me. Why could *I* not save her? I wanted to pray but was unable to pray. I had had no language, it seemed, no word or utterance of prayer when, as an infant, I lay against her breasts and drew the sustenance of milk from her. And this lay at the heart of my faintness, faint infant body that I dreamt I placed upon hers as we moved through the processions towards her death. Not processions towards the Cross (in Christian textuality) but inwards and towards the body of a mother of humanity in which/on which one lay.

When one names death in oneself, death the hunter, death the hunted, the processions begin. A tension mounts between the institutionalization of violence as the absolute premise of the hunt – hunter in slain hunted, hunted in predatory hunter – and a capacity in the body of mothers to portray (within a palimpsest of layered ancestries) an opening into the evolution of a hunter who saves creatures, who holds at bay the predatory logic of the hunt . . .

I held my mother's hand more tightly than ever.

She was leaning over me protectively. I felt her work-hardened, chapped hands upon the flesh above the bone of my arm. She had fought for me against invaders and tyrants – as an Amazon queen in a Carib mask – long before slavery began. Her limbs against mine trembled with paradoxical weakness, she was vulnerable, she was frail, she was ill (a doctor had said) with acute angina.

Her worn hands and fingers reminded me of the random shot that Deacon had fired which sliced two fingers from my left hand.

41

I had felt nothing at the time. But now the numbness throbbed with pain. I had come abreast of the wound. I knew the sharp, acute pain now that I brought from the future into the past.

We were in an alleyway within a procession that I had not bargained for. The Moon descended and stood over us.

A tall Carnival evangelistic Cat fell upon us. Had it succeeded in crossing the chasm of the years *in pursuit of me*? Was it the perverse resurrection of Jones? Perhaps it had spotted the Nemesis Bag over my head which I swore was invisible to all. *The blow it sought to direct at me fell upon my mother*. I was dumbfounded. The facts I had accumulated on Carnival night 1939 had made no provision for this. One returns to the past, the facts are the same, yet nothing is the same. *My mother saved my life*. I understood it now for the first heartrending time. In my Lazarus-arm – with its missing fingers – she perceived a faint portent of an evolution of the hunt – long eclipsed in traditions we take for granted, in facts that we enshrine as absolutes – about which I would write in my Dream-book . . .

She saved my life. She intervened and took the blow on her own head and heart it seemed. I had no memory of praying to her in her transition from peace-loving slave to Blessed Fury. Had I not prayed to Deacon in Jonestown and to Marie of Jonestown? Two different forms of prayer I knew. But now there had been no form of prayer. The language of prayer is sometimes hidden, incalculable, formless, in the birth of consciousness.

Giants of Chaos

Three days had passed since the Day of the Dead when I lay on a pillow of stone at the edge of the Clearing in Jonestown.

I had made my way to the Cave of the Moon at nightfall.

The shock of events had been so great that I remained hidden in the Cave above a Waterfall descending into the Jonestown river.

This was three miles or so above the Mission. I lay hidden but my privacy was soon to be breached. I heard the bell of the Church of Eternity tolling a requiem mass for the dead with the arrival of the grave-digger and his crew. They were accompanied by Mr Mageye (the magus-Jester of history), a Doctor (the magus-medicine man and God of poor people's hospitals), and an Inspector of Police (the magus-clown of the Law).

These were my three magi who were associated with the creation of a Dream-book or the cradle of Bone (as Mr Mageye called it).

The tolling of the bell may have been caused by my phantom-Lazarus arm when I sneaked into the Church the day they arrived but quickly withdrew back to my Cave. I was to discover later from Mr Mageye that no one knew who had actually rung the bell. There was talk of a high wind blowing the stench of dead bodies into the sky and invoking a chorus of bells or lighthouse messages. Some – who those were I do not know – swore they saw the great-great-grandmothers of the dead rise from the brothel of the grave to declare themselves nurses of infinity . . .

'A sacred jest,' said Mr Mageye. 'Slaves break every brothel in a sky of cloud, polluted cloud, in the teeth of their ancient masters to declare their love – despite everything – for their tragic, illegitimate progeny . . . Such is the vocation of a nurse in a poor man's graveyard or hospital.'

My choice of Mr Mageye as magus-Jester of history was crucial to the creation of my Dream-book (or cradle of Bone) in the years that followed the catastrophe of Jonestown.

He gave apparitional weight and comedy, for instance, to the way I dressed, the wretched Nemesis Bag that I wore over my head.

'Do you know Mr Mageye,' I said, 'you were at my mother's funeral (her coffin was borne sky-high by beggars) when three threads sprang from the Nemesis Bag and sprouted into three blades of grass, the colour of velvet, on my mother's grave? It was a relief, it was as if a ton had lifted from my head . . .

'When I arrived in New Amsterdam, took up my abode in Trinity Street and began to write I was virtually in rags. But I felt light as a feather. The year was 1985.'

'Yes,' said Mr Mageye, 'your mother's death in Albuoystown caused quite a sensation. I have a yellowing newspaper with me. *Carnival Argosy*, dated 1939.' He pointed to a headline which ran as follows: WOMEN OF THE BROTHEL AND BEGGARS IN PROCESSION TO GRAVE OF THE VIRGIN OF ALBUOYS-TOWN.

'I wandered in a state of limbo for seven years before I began to write,' I said to Mr Mageye. 'But all the time I was being written into the Dream-book with each thread that fell from the Bag on my head and from the garments that I wore. These became the substance with which to dress innermost Bone into the composite populace in my book. Is it my book? It's as much yours, Mr Mageye. I am not even sure of the Day or the year I began to write. The Maya speak of Dateless Days that become a medium of living Shadows in which history retrieves an emotionality, a Passion, to unveil the facts and go deeper into processions into the body of the womb. Think of the Virgin of the ancient city of Palenque. She died resisting a Tiger to save the life of her son. One of her arms was torn from her body. It gestated in space. It gestates still in forgotten traditions of fiction and grief in Beauty. There are many languages of the Imagination that affect us in the fibre of dismembered cultures that remain mysteriously whole in their resistance to the predatory coherence of fact that masquerades as eternity. The true fact is Love's intervention in blended times within dreadful circumstances I grant. The true fact is the undying originality of such interventions. Without this art is dead. IMAGINATION DEAD IMAGINE.'

Mr Mageye applauded my wild outburst.

Emotionality and passion gave substance to his apparition in

46

the Dream-book. It was as if one fed him with one's blood and flesh to make him live. And an irony, a paradox, flashed into my mind. Tigers seek to live on the flesh of women. No wonder Jones had been addicted to brothels in San Francisco when Deacon and I met him there for the first time in 1942.

Deacon and I had both been the recipients of scholarship prizes that took us to San Francisco College, where we met the young American. Our prizes had come out of the Fund that the ghost-Frenchman (my ancestral father) left when he returned to Napoleonic France in 1800. Jonah was two or three years older than we were. But he seemed even older. He intrigued us with fictions of whales, Moby Dick, whales that swallowed civilizations and threatened the Virgin Ship.

His sense of humour was broad, sometimes Whitmanesque, but threaded with anger and despair.

'Survivor Ishmael,' he said, 'hangs on Aeneas's Ship, on Jason's *Argo* as well. He hangs in dread of a brothel of history. Is Medea a whore or a Virgin Queen? Aeneas betrays Queen Dido. He had promised her fortune and then he abandoned her. He was a hero and a monster. Yes, Aeneas betrayed her,' Jones said and smacked his lips with a curious satisfaction.

A silence fell over us like a beam from the brothel of history. I nailed it nevertheless into the deck of the Virgin Ship.

Deacon was pensive. We listened to the young American with a sense of foreboding. Deacon was of Indian descent. His grandparents had arrived as indentured servants from South India.

'Mind you,' I said to Mr Mageye, 'I am speaking of his adoptive parents who were rice farmers and rearers of cattle and horses. No one fathoms Deacon's ancestry. He fell from the stars as an infant child. War in heaven, rebellions in heaven, it is said, in accordance with savannah folklore.'

Deacon was pensive. He had been affianced – in keeping with East Indian indenture custom – to the maiden Marie of his own age, when he left British Guiana to take up his scholarship. Would he betray her? Would he betray the young Marie of Port Mourant, the maiden, the Virgin Marie of Port Mourant?

'Three Maries,' I said to Mr Mageye, 'appear in the Dream-

47

book. Marie – this Marie – is destined to be Deacon's bride. When I saw her myself on visits to the Courantyne I fell head over heels in love with her. I would have married her like a shot. I hated Deacon. I was jealous of him. Hate is too strong a word. But the truth is we were antagonistic to each other. Racial antagonism? Racial antagonisms between East Indians and Blacks and people of mixed descent? It's rife in British Guiana. It's rife in the Guianas – Dutch and French as well. Surinam. Devil's Isle. Guyana.'

'Will he betray her?' asked Mr Mageye.

Deacon caught the drift of my silent conversation with Mr Mageye.

'Never, Never,' said Deacon. He bared his arm. On it was tattooed the Constellation of the Scorpion. 'This gives me immunity to pain,' he said. 'Why should I inflict pain on my bride?'

'All the more reason why you may,' I protested. I bared my arm. On it was tattooed an imprint of Lazarus.

Deacon glared at me. 'Heroes are saviours of the people,' he said. 'They build strong gaols and fortresses and coffins. But in the end they save the people, don't they? As for you, Francisco, fuck you! Lazarus eh? You are a ghost's ill-begotten son. I shall take you under my wing. I shall adopt you as brother and son. I shall even give you my Mask to wear in times of Carnival. Then everyone will think you are me and you shall be honoured.'

I shrank from him. I had not a word to say. But I pitied poor Marie. She was the adopted daughter of the Doctor-God of the poor people's hospital of Port Mourant. Her parents had died in a car crash on the busy road between New Amsterdam and Port Mourant.

'The Doctor is your magus-medicine man,' said Mr Mageye.

'Deacon has taken him in,' I said. 'Deacon has persuaded him that Marie and he will give birth to a true Lazarus . . .'

'But you,' said Mr Mageye, 'you . . .'

'I may have magi within my book but I am a surrogate of the cradle of the Bone that will flesh all races into genuine brothers and sisters . . .'

Deacon may have overheard my silent conversation with Mr

48

Mageye. He bit his lips savagely until blood came. Heroes eat the flesh of monsters in themselves to fuel life, to strengthen life.

The friendship, the curious enemy friendship between Deacon and Jones and me, was a phenomenon of the modern age, indeed of many past ages.

Jones's terrible moods of anger fuelled our resolution to face the world, to withstand insults, racial insults in America.

'All who aren't white are black,' said Jones. 'I shall protect you. You are all one to me.'

'Are Alexander and Genghis Khan one to you, Jonah? Would you have recruited them to sail on the *Pequod*? They were sons of gods, they were fallen angels like me. Brace yourself Jonah for a new peasant uprising across the Americas. All you need is one man who contains millions . . .'

'God help that one man,' I said, 'when he opens the door of the cell in which the Old God resides . . .'

'What Old God?' Deacon cried. But Mr Mageye put his hand to my lips. His face became grave as an Enigma or the Sphinx. And I said nothing. Indeed I was plagued by uncertainties and my allusion to a Prisoner upon Devil's Isle, or Old God, was rash in all the circumstances. Jonah was angry. Old Gods were useless unless they could bring time itself to a standstill.

Phenomenal as it seemed, peculiar in the light of common sense, a strange aspect of the fuel that drove us into forging a treaty or a pact – a pact between the white American Jonah Jones and racially mixed and uncertain ancestries within Deacon and myself – was anger.

Though I had said nothing when Deacon taunted me as a 'ghost's ill-begotten son' I was angry as much with him as with myself, angry with Jones as well in some classic, elemental way. Jones's antecedents had owned slaves, they had decimated the peoples of ancient America from the sixteenth century onwards. An astonishing factor in all this was that Jones appeared to be the most angry one of us. No wonder he revered Herman Melville's *Moby Dick* and Edgar Allan Poe's *Arthur Gordon Pym*. Such classics of anger seemed rooted in the cosmos itself.

Jones – in the Mask of the Whale into which he descended at

49

times – raged at the prejudices, the biases, the hypocrisy, that were visible everywhere. *His anger therefore appealed to us.* But it left me with a bitter taste in my mouth. I did not like the way he savoured anger as if it were the sweetest dish in the restaurants of San Francisco. Anger became the seed of his charismatic pursuit of eternity, eternity's closure of time.

I feared the gross enlargement of emotion, the enlargement or complex pregnancy of the male charismatic priest. He hunted women in brothels everywhere. He sought to fuck them, to fuck himself, and to become a pregnant decoy in a pulpit for the annihilation of his age through mounting apparitional populations, mounting apparitional numbers to be weighed on the scales of time, blended pasts and futures.

Anger at injustice everywhere could turn nasty and become an involuntary ape of imperial hubris rooted in the despoliation of the laws of conquered peoples. Involuntary apes are the 'ill-begotten bridegrooms' of deprived peoples led to the altar within military coups or rigged elections.

What was deeply alarming to me – in my crossing a chasm of years from dateless day in Trinity Street, New Amsterdam, back to San Francisco, United States, when the Japanese bombed Pearl Harbour – was that such Jonesian anger, such common-or-garden apehood of hubris, *appealed to us, fascinated us, fascinated both Deacon and me.*

True, it also aroused a sensation of foreboding and Nemesis. But the fascination remained. A fascination rooted in an addiction to holocaustic sacrifice and rivalry that ran deep in antagonistic cultures around the globe. Jones, poor Jones, was as much their pawn as they were his.

When the first nuclear Bomb exploded and sent its dread beauty, its fantastic mushroom, into the sky above an American desert, long-sunken ships and coffins of the dead arose from their sea-bed.

A fleet arose to greet the constellation of the *Argo* encrusted on Jason's head in the stars.

Mr Mageye held a Camera in his hand which he – as magus-Jester of history – had brought from the future as much as from the technologies in the past: a Camera stored with paradoxical archetypes, new-born yet old as the mysterious anatomy of time.

His apparitional figure stood on the deck of the Virgin Ship with the futuristic, ancient Camera in his hand.

He drew my eye to peer into the depths of archetypal oceans and skies.

'Do you see Francisco?' he asked.

At first I saw nothing but Chaos. I saw floating planks from the forests of King Midas, I saw floating cargoes of South American rubber bound for the Golden Man in the kingdom of El Dorado, I saw the mastheads upon broken slave-ships, I saw frail residue like the beard of Titans, I saw celestial mathematics written into rockets and sails upon space stations. An air of wreckage hung over them in the degree that civilizations had foundered but the fleet was now half-afloat upon ocean and sky.

'The Virgin Ship', said Mr Mageye, 'transforms the fleet, converts the fleet, into a cradle of Bone fleshed by resurrectionary mathematics.

'Bone is our innermost Cross that we scarcely countenance or understand.

'It is as old as time.

'On it hangs not only our flesh but the ragged flesh of populations and failed captaincies and heroes who are illumined nevertheless by the promise of a divine huntsman who hangs on the Cross in our flesh, our ragged flesh, to hold the Predator at bay when humanity is in the greatest danger.

'The Cross in the mirror of celestial mathematics is sometimes a net that salvages all wreckages of time in which to build the Virgin Ship anew.

'Remember Francisco there is a curious fragility to your Dream-book, the log-book of the fleet. But its true spiritual capacity lies therein. It wreathes itself in the collapse of high-sounding garments and punishments and glories to illumine Bone or Cross.

'Celestial mathematics of space! That is how I see the evolution of the divine huntsman in our ragged flesh. That is how I see a procession of brothels and wrecked architectures and wrecked fleets and marketplace cathedrals backwards into the stark Womb of the Virgin – shorn of intercourse with violence – from which the true, compassionate huntsman may yet evolve and arise . . . Remember all this, Francisco.'

Deacon had caught the drift of Mr Mageye's conversation with me. He seized upon 'celestial mathematics' as a platform for his own ambitions, his own perverse longing for glory.

'Celestial ambition,' he said to me and to the apparition of Mr Mageye, 'fires a peasant like me to perform great deeds, to fight unimaginable duels, to frame arenas for impossible (yet I believe possible) duels in space. Think of the Moon! What an arena for duels and commerce and sport. We shall fight on other planets, believe me! Buy yourself a ringside seat now, Francisco, before the price soars. Shall I – a mere peasant – dwarf Alexander the Great and Genghis Khan? Why not? I am born from the obscurity of the stars as they were! Poor Jonah believes in eternity. And that is why I have forged a pact with him. He will bring me the chance to duel with eternity. And if I fail then celestial mathematics will provide me with a ladder to climb back into heaven, to wrestle all over again with the Titans, the Tricksters of heaven. Yes – remember Francisco – civilizations fail and perish and begin all over again in some remote forest . . . As for you, Francisco, I shall give you a taste of my fallen angel's blood when or if I fail. I shall clamp my Mask into your head. I – and an Old God you shall meet (you love epic theatre, don't you?) – shall imbue it with conviction and lifelike appearance. Carnival's great Francisco.' He was laughing uproariously.

I said nothing. I was familiar with his taunts. I was familiar with his mockery of others and his self-mockery. Self-mockery was a moral fable, a moral truth, that fuelled peculiar underground sympathies between us though at another level we scorned or hated each other. Such self-mockery illumined hypocritical patriotisms, hypocritical loyalties, and it strengthened the pact between us and Jonah Jones. We seemed to eat our own mutual flesh in order to expose salutary lighthouse or Bone or Cross.

Mr Mageye eyed me with the oddest approval, the approval of self-questioning conscience, self-questioning imagination. He relished Deacon's joke – if joke it was – about Tricksters of heaven.

Sacred Jest! It appealed to him as a nourishing resource of comic flesh-and-blood: comic, yes, but curiously divine in flesh-and-blood's ambition to equate itself with Gods.

Such comic divine equation enlivened the apparition that he was in my Dream-book. He had died in Albuoystown the very year that I left for San Francisco to take up my scholarship. I recalled standing over his grave on the eve of my departure. He was my beloved schoolteacher, the wisest, strangest man I had ever known. He saw all his pupils as potential tyrants, potential liberators, potential monsters, potential saints. He roamed all texts, all worlds, all ages to help them see themselves as stripped of everything yet whole and majestic and comical (all at the same time). I visualized myself sailing with him into futures and pasts. I visualized the Nemesis Bag on my head. Three more threads fell from it and took root on his grave. This had happened on my mother's grave as well.

'I am no ill-begotten son of a French Catholic ghost,' I cried. 'I am Mr Mageye's South American pupil. He is my magus. I wish he were my father. But I – a nameless orphan really – must respect the wishes of my poor mother who saw herself on the Cross as the bride of a slave-owning, masquerading, divine imperialist.'

Having nourished itself on comic divine flesh-and-blood the apparition of Mr Mageye was able to feed my imagination in turn.

He stepped from his coffin into a classroom in San Francisco College and looked across the water to the famous prison of Alcatraz.

Why are prisons famous? What secrets do they keep?

Are they the abode of apparitions across the ages, legendary kings of crime, legendary Napoleons, Bastilles, legendary pirates knighted by queens?

My eye flicked into Mr Mageye's Camera and I saw the prison of Devil's Isle, French Guiana. A prisoner or Old God was housed there. He was as old as Quetzalcoatl (the most ancient king of the Americas), he was as young as the French Revolution.

'Kingship is a sphere within us,' said Mr Mageye, 'that dazzles and tricks our senses again and again. We hunger for romance, or chivalry, or knights in shining armour, or Scandal (with a capital

S), or pageantry (with a common p as processions line the streets).

'But all this is an evasion of the complex necessity for kingship. At the core of kingship resides a true embattled reality that we forfeit or lose sight of at our peril. Kingship witnesses to the agonizing problematic of freedom, the gift of freedom to ourselves within ourselves yet bestowed upon us by some incalculable design in heaven and upon earth . . .'

I raised my hand, but Mr Mageye rushed on, a rush yet a peculiar deliberation – 'I know, I know . . . Freedom is seen as the achievement of the common people . . .'

'Is it not?' I demanded.

'At the heart of the common people exists an invisible fortress in which a Prisoner or Old God or King is held as a guarantee, a half-compulsive, half-spiritual guarantee that some principle lives in the Primitive mind (surviving Primitive archetype) to sift the problematic resources of freedom.'

'I do not follow,' I said. But in myself I knew or thought I knew.

'The Prisoner or Old God places a question-mark against the extravagant gift of freedom. Is freedom anarchy? Is freedom reserved for the strong, does freedom nurture crime, does it come when we are not ready for it? At what age are we equipped to bear the burden of freedom? Do we need to cultivate wholly different philosophies of the Imagination to bring us on a wave of the future from which to discern how free or unfree we were in the past and still are in the present, how just or unjust to others we remain, how prone to exploit ourselves and others in the name of high-sounding lies?'

I could not help voicing a protest – 'Kings need to be forced, do they not, into granting freedom to their subjects?'

'And they pay a terrible price,' said Mr Mageye, 'their heads roll. Force – in such a context – may be an explosion of conscience in the King or Old God himself. He knows without quite knowing (he knows in the collective subconscious and unconscious) that he has failed in the problematic authority that he exercises. He is as much condemned as self-condemned. And without that tension of visionary, interior condemnation and trial by others at the heart of composite epic, epic populace, epic king, art dies, philosophy dies, faith in truth perishes. Freedom needs to weigh, examine, re-examine its far-flung proportions which radiate from a core of the Imagination, it needs to promote a variety of cautions in the body politic, freedom is not a gross or even a subtle indulgence of public appetite; or else it deteriorates into cynical diplomacy, it becomes a tool, a machine, a gravy train, a sponsor of a rat-race.'

I was appalled and aghast at all this. I felt as if I had been dealt a blow by an apparition, a solid apparition arisen from a coffin, the coffin of ancient kings that empowered the magus-philosopher-jester of history that Mr Mageye was.

'Where does it all start?' I demanded. 'If Old Gods and Prisoners are a sphere within ourselves, acting and running more deeply than the mechanics of political sovereignty, where does it start?'

'Deacon would say it starts with wars in Heaven,' said Mr Mageye. He was jesting but his face seemed straight as a bat in the hands of a weirdly gifted cricketer of genius. He had umpired many a game in Albuoystown. His apparitional nose seemed to have flattened itself. But then it grew again, it straightened itself into the colour of sculpted soil in Deacon's Courantyne savannahs.

'Let us,' he said, 'prepare the ground of theatre, the ground of folklore in the ancient savannahs. First the infant Deacon falls from the baggage train of routed angels. He falls to earth and is given a home by the savannah folk.'

I was angry. I was jealous.

'Is Deacon a bloody king?' I demanded.

'He is an adversary of Old Gods. He sustains on Earth an age-old quarrel in Heaven. When is the gift of fire to be exercised and bestowed upon humanity? When is the gift of freedom to be exercised and bestowed upon humanity? That is in large part the substance of the quarrel. Should humanity claim freedom? Perhaps it has with detrimental consequences on every hand! Should humanity claim freedom in the teeth of obstinate and uncertain regimes? Where does authority truly reside? We may think these questions are old-hat but they are not. They are more

55

savagely pertinent to human affairs than we care to admit. Should we pursue our adversaries, should they turn on us at every opportunity? Should we perpetuate forms of punitive logic to punish those who punished us when we rebelled? I tell you all this, Francisco, for it is pertinent to your visitation of the childhood of Deacon in the folklore, archetypal theatre of the Courantyne savannahs.'

The scales of blended times had changed in the half-apparitional, half-concrete fabric of my Dream-book and arrival on the Virgin Ship in the Courantyne River from which we made our way into the savannahs.

'Deacon had been affianced to Marie of Port Mourant before he left to take up his scholarship in San Francisco,' said Mr Mageye.

'Yes I know. He told us so.'

'But he met her for the first overwhelmingly intimate yet expansive time (that fires both love of art and science, and greed for fame) at the age of nine,' said Mr Mageye, peering into his Camera as if it were a computer of chasms in creation and visionary years. 'That meeting was the fulfilment of an age-old prophecy for the savannah folk. An infant child would fall from the stars in 1930. Carnival has its calendric humour, has it not, Francisco? The child – in his tenth year 1939 – would encounter a wonderful maid, a dangerous maid, a Virgin, in the savannahs at the end of a drought season when the first, torrential rains broke the walls of heaven.

'This would confirm the adversarial destiny of the angel fallen from the baggage train of the stars. It would confirm the venom of the Scorpion in his veins. The mark of a great hero . . .'

'Monster,' I cried.

'You need to see it happening all over again in your Dream-book. It is pertinent, believe me, Francisco, to a discovery and rediscovery of the depth of your own passion and emotion which you may have eclipsed or hidden from yourself until the tragedy of Jonestown brought you face to face with the accumulated spectres of years, the dread spectre of the twentieth century as it addresses the psyche of ageless childhood.'

I adjusted the Nemesis Bag on my head even as I looked into Mr Mageye's Camera.

'Deacon ran into the maid in the torrential rain. She seemed utterly changed from a child he knew! Had he not seen her before at school? Human magic dazzles the eyes of a fallen angel when destiny declares itself. Such is the precocity of love, the precocity of feud as well. Marie was known to be the adopted daughter of the Doctor at the Port Mourant hospital. Doctors are Gods to peasant folk in poor people's hospitals. But there was an ominous side to Marie's parentage. One report claimed that her parents had been killed in a car crash and that – above the debris of the car – an Old God, or escaped Prisoner, materialized. Escaped from Devil's Isle. The Inspector of Police seized him. Escaped prisoners from French Guiana were an occasional feature on the British Guiana coast. Carnival fastened on the event. *The Old God claimed that he was Marie's father and that the Doctor was not to be trusted.'* Mr Mageye was smiling.

'No laughing matter,' I said. 'Carnival is no laughing matter.'

'Indeed not,' said Mr Mageye. 'In the reaches of great wind-swept, rain-swept, sun-swept savannahs, the most ancient feuds between heaven and earth are revived in villages and upon roads that may seem jam-packed at times but are insubstantial and frail against an immensity of sky and land and sea that borders the coastlands. The peasantry and the people are native to, yet tormented by, such extremity. They long for a saviour, for authority, for truth. Where does authority reside? Does it reside in European empires whose presence they feel? Does it reside in the new power-hungry politicians? Does it reside in upper worlds, nether worlds? Tell me, Francisco. *Feed my apparition in your book.'*

I hesitated for a long while and then I found the confidence to speak.

'I would say,' I began hesitantly, pulling a loose thread from my Nemesis Bag and letting it fall to the ground, 'that all the ingredients of uncertainty that you stress, Mr Mageye, are woven into a car crash – as into the wreck of the *Argo* – into . . . ' I hesitated . . . 'into wars and rumours of war across the sea, into submarines and the shadow of fleets patrolling the Atlantic seaboard of South America. No wonder the Old God hovers in space only to be seized by the Inspector and placed in a cell.' I stopped, but then it occurred to me to lay bare my heart to Mr Mageye. 'That Prisoner or Old God wrestles with the Doctor and the Inspector to claim Marie as his Virgin daughter . . .'

There was much more that I wished to say, my desire for Marie even before I met her, my jealousy of Deacon, but Mr Mageye interrupted – 'Look! there they are.'

It suddenly occurred to me – as in a Jest of Dream – that my jealousy of Deacon had helped to flesh out the occasion, to give content to both Deacon and Marie in the backward sweep of years since I began to write. There they were indeed, large as life, within the raining, mist-filled savannahs in which Mr Mageye and I stood invisible to them.

We were I calculated halfway between Crabwood Creek and Port Mourant.

Deacon was naked. The tattooed Scorpion Constellation shone darkly on his child's arm. On the other monstrous, heroic arm stood the double star Aldebaran associated with Taurus, but the Bull had been overturned into Horses on the Moon. I was able to draw close to him with Mr Mageye's assistance and to read every pore in his body.

Deacon had abandoned his school uniform to come into his own as the masterful child-bridegroom who secures the Virgin of the Wild on her appearance at the end of every long, searing drought when the rains commence.

Deacon had paused as if locked into the thread of my glance. But he shot forward again in my Dream-book. Mr Mageye (Camera in hand) was out of sight – as on a film set – and I (in my Nemesis Hat) kept in touch (though I was invisible to him). Such are the wonders of technology and science within futuristic strategies of the Imagination.

He ran with a miraculous stride. Amazing to maintain his stride on the slippery path that he had taken. But the long drought had hardened the ground. The water table was low and it would take a day or two at least for the soil to change into an ankle-deep rich overflowing sponge.

The rain swept all around as if sky and cloud had been broken in cosmic theatre to provide a Waterfalling shower in the eye of the Camera down which Deacon had floated and come when he fell as an infant in space. Now he was in his tenth cosmic year and destiny was to equip him with a lasso to seize the Horses of the Moon and bring them showering and hoofing their way to Earth.

I saw the affianced child-bride in the corner of my eye. The rain swung into an encircling perimeter around her, the rain lessened, the ground acquired the look of a mirroring, flat wave as if a portion of the sky had fallen to the ground.

Deacon saw her now clearly. She was naked as he was. She too had abandoned her uniform, a child's nurse's uniform which the Doctor, her adoptive father, had given her to wear when she assisted him in the Port Mourant hospital after school.

Deacon stopped upon the perimeter. Carven into momentary astonishment. He had not seen her naked before. He knew her from school but she was not the same child that he took for granted when the Doctor-God and his savannah parents met to seal the promise of selves (savannah-self, Godself) in marriage.

His lithe body responded to hers by sheathing itself all at once in wings that blew around him as if a bird, an eagle, a fluid eagle, perched on his head in a fountain of mist as the rain appeared to boil around his ankles in the rising heat of the soil.

Marie began to dance on the mirror. She danced upon a portion of sky, skin of the shining rain on the ground. Her feet were suddenly and lightly and mysteriously laced with three threads that fell from my Nemesis Hat. They were the colour of velvet. Yet the springing grass of slenderest blades of rain were silver. The blades of grass from my mother's grave levitated and fell from the sky. The blades of grass from Mr Mageye's grave levitated and fell from the sky. Despite such beauty I was stricken by heart-rending grief. I felt the strangest foreboding. And I would have fired a bullet – if I had possessed one – at Deacon and swept his affianced bride into my arms.

Deacon moved and edged his wings into the mirror on which the Virgin of the Wild was dancing. A long plait of loose hair fell down her back from the nape of her neck to her waist. It was the colour of the mane of a Moon-horse that shook itself and encircled my head. Why me? How was I tied to her? By what fate, or trial of spirit, or torment of freedom?

Deacon seemed to glide and reach for her hair upon the fantastic mirror. He swept it from my brow even as – with a mocking glance – he seemed to nail it into the space where I stood invisible to him. The nail pierced me to the Bone. I cried for immunity to pain such as Deacon appeared to possess.

Marie swirled and the nail fell from my head into Deacon's wing. He may have felt no pain in the Shadow of the Scorpion but he stumbled and was unable to bind her to him in this instant of a doubling of stars in the sky or mirror on the ground, Aldebaran's twin stars in which I played an invisible role, twinned to a fallen angel.

The lessening rain and slightly clearing sky brought the pool of the Moon onto the ground. Deacon darted forward as if he flew or danced on water – his wing free again – and he held the Virgin's hair at last. But when he sought to draw her to him, in the theatre of the Moon, she dazzled him and thrust him away. They encircled each other, sometimes upon the perimeter within which they danced, sometimes upon an upright Wheel as though the flat circle or perimeter inclined itself into a vertical dimension, a wheeling dimension.

Step by step the Horses of the Moon materialized as a turbulent extension of the Passion of the dance. A haunch grafted itself into the archetypal momentum of cavalry of fate. Such apparently insoluble archetypes were native to ancient and modern civilizations and they drew Marie's Wheel in the dance.

Horses akin to Cortez's troop fleshed themselves into a scale of grafts within apparitions on the Moon.

Horses akin to Genghis Khan's hillsides rose into shoulders and necks around the edges of the Moon.

Eyes of flashing, poisoned gold sprang from the bodies of Alexander's infantry upon Darius's wheeling chariots beneath Marie's fleet foot.

From every corner of legend and history arose an assembly of the parts of engines of flesh, jigsaw cavalries, ribs, equine muscularities, bunched muscles, grapelike memories of blood, tanned, leathern proportions, giving substance to the terrible Horses of the Moon within which Deacon and Marie pursued each other in their dance.

No horses in Chichén Itzá but the dreaded Chac Mool possessed the countenance of a Chimera, half-human, half-horse. Chac Mool was a signal of militaristic atrocity in the Maya world and it foretold the decline of a civilization.

Who were the riders, who were the giants of Chaos upon such Horses? Were they Deacon's kith and kin in heaven and upon earth? Were they Marie's dangerous host and accompaniment of furies? Furies are omens, signatures of uncanny foreboding, and they tend to arrive hand in hand with Virgins of the Wilderness whose untameable spirituality in nature is misconceived for brute violence.

Were the riders princes of Carnival Lord Death's regime in theatres of history, were they dictators in South America, were they solid, stable riggers of elections in Nigeria and elsewhere, were they Amens or Amins, were they gagged priests, gagged popes, gagged bishops, bankers, statesmen, scientists, crusaders, evangelists?

Or were they shepherds from times immemorial, poor labouring folk in the savannahs of Guyana since El Dorado fashioned its whip to encircle the slaves who dug the earth, rode the earth from cradle to grave with an eye on the stars for the coming of a saviour, a saviour susceptible to miscasting in the theatres of Church and State, miscast as warrior-crusader-priest?

The poor, labouring, awkward folk seemed to Mr Mageye and to me to combine dictatorship and feudal features in themselves as they rode the Horses. They were also uncanny judges of themselves and others. They were submissive to Deacon now as they rode the Horses, rode the lotteries on the Moon, rode expectations of fortune on the Moon, but I felt – as though I were on trial – that they were capable of breaking themselves, melting themselves, reshaping themselves, in order to judge him in themselves, bring him before them on the Moon.

'Why the Moon?' I asked Mr Mageye. 'Why not the Earth?'

'In a Universe that quarrels with itself in Carnival sciences the

Moon is a ripe theatre, the Moon drifts to Earth, drifts into a sphere of incredible theatre and gravity, a space-station, if you like, within a quarrel of dimensions that plague us . . .'

Marie was now under the hoofs of the Horses ridden by controversial, pathetic, victimized, victimizing, paradoxical self-judges and giants of chaos. She slipped through them unhurt but saw the danger to humanity in the triumph of the warrior-angel that Deacon was. She was now betrothed to him as the dance confirmed. It was too late to turn back. She was destined – according to folklore legends – to bear him a child, the people's promised child that would herald his departure from her, in dread circumstances, to build a new Rome in South America in alliance with an American warrior-priest from San Francisco and left-handed Bone from Albuoystown.

It was a prophecy that was unclear to her. Unclear to me. I should have remembered the past in coming from the future but the trauma that I suffered in Jonestown had wiped a page or pages from my mind and those blank spaces or chapters filled my Dream-book with renewed foreboding.

'Am I left-handed Bone?' I cried. I should have known better than to indulge in self-pity. Mr Mageye did not reply. A Sphinx-like look came upon his face, a gentle hand on my brow . . .

Marie slipped through the Horses' hoofs even as she saw the danger. She saw – within her untameable beauty – the grief in the Womb of Space (when space quarrels with itself and becomes a potential series of battlefields).

I drew close to her and succeeded in helping her secure a triangular seat within the Wheel even as it spun. *I swore she saw me*. She turned her mysterious and wonderful and grateful eyes upon me. *She knew me*. But then I wondered. Did she mistake me for Deacon whose shadowy Mask fell upon her? Winged, Shadowy Mask? Black? Yet pale and silvery as the feathers around his Beak?

I placed my shoulders to the Wheel and gave it an additional push. It flashed. It flashed through the limbs of the great Horses and their riders. And she was gone in a flash. Back to her nurse's uniform in Port Mourant Hospital.

Deacon's venom rose with Marie's flight and helped to harden his heart for an enterprise that lay before him: the capture of the Horses of the Moon and their riders . . .

He had secured a long thread of hair from Marie's head. The rain had ceased and he would need to take full advantage of the respite to perfect the task on which he was engaged and the lassoing of the Horses.

Their necks gleamed as he lifted the glancing hair from the bride of the wilderness. That hair was curiously part of the topography of the landscape. It had been plucked as much from the map of his Brain as from the Virgin's body.

It glanced and stood before him as upon a draughtsman's sliding scale of uprooted contours and tributaries, the slenderest, coiling fabric of recalled rain coursing alive after the long drought through the savannahs.

Coursing alive along the Crabwood Creek in the moonlight pouring through broken clouds.

'I read in the *Carnival Argosy* in 1939,' said Mr Mageye, 'that engineers were contemplating diverting the tributary to the Courantyne River known as Crabwood Creek into an enclosure, or giant spatial lasso, so to speak, for horses and cattle to prevent them straying onto and grazing upon the rice fields.'

As he spoke to me I saw the extraordinary congruence of apparition and concreteness in the Camera of the mind within the Jester of history.

Deacon held the wilderness hair and lasso in his hand as if it were the sliding uplifted creek itself coiling upon its fragile, serpent's tail.

He whipped the serpent in the air with an engineer's bark, a peasant boy's ambitious dream and cry and prayer for the marvels of technology.

The wilderness lasso fell around the Horses' steaming necks in the moonlight. They shuddered and bundled themselves together uneasily but on the whole they were content to be mastered by an angel from the stars.

Mr Mageye studied – as upon a platform of invisibility separating him from the action of a rolling film – the amorphous, magical roles a child plays within the hidden uniform of a man already shaping itself into existence within him and around him. The amorphous magic in the psyche of a child is the sponge of growing pains, trauma, the trauma of deprivation, the trauma of acute longing for power, the power to rule, to execute gigantic projects that may symbolize glory or ashes in one's mouth unless one learns to see deeply into the cinematic theatre of cells and blood in mind and heart.

'Such a beautiful – however grief-stricken – theorem is the psyche of a child! Capsuled into childhood is the latent marriage of Brain and myth, feud and grace, terror and dance. Deacon's obsession (which may also be yours, Francisco) surely was plain to you as a lucid dream when he studied engineering and politics in San Francisco College.'

Horses and Giants of Chaos came towards Deacon now. He lengthened his tributary lasso, he pulled hard.

It seemed as if it would snap into Virgin blood on the Moon but it held.

He relaxed his grip into a wide-angling – almost gentle – invocation of space and drew animals and riders across the perimeter of the Moon into the river catchment of Earth and along the line of the creek. It was a remarkable procession that invested the heights of the Moon with the qualities of a watershed upon which distant falling rain escalated upon a mountainous cloud and then glided on both flanks into space.

Horseflesh flanking the Moon and the creek became the shadow of a wall, or a dam, as the procession advanced towards the Courantyne River.

The projected new polder, or diversion, materialized as a gift of passion inherent in his betrothal to Marie, reined-in animal passion, curbed and manifest in engineering, wilderness genius.

It was as if Deacon were intent upon converting the Wheel upon which Marie had fled into a simultaneous asset of culture, into gradients and stages down which he drew the Horses of the Moon.

Celestial mathematics!

He drew the Horses along the lassoing hair – *with or in* the lassoing hair – in the Virgin's body to the wide Courantyne River.

He came upon a box koker or sluice at the point where the tributary entered the main body of the river. The wide estuary was vacant except for a schooner on the bar and the Virgin Ship which Deacon failed to see.

In his child's mathematical, engineering, mythical eye, infused with wars and baggage trains and advancing, retreating armies, the box koker or Dutch culvert assumed the proportions of a giant coffin. He stood against it and lifted the lid. Then with a tug he propelled each beast and rider into its depths. The colour of new taxes he would propose (if he were prime minster) shone on each flank, money-flesh, political/economic flesh, ballot-box flesh, everything that was pertinent to the betrothal of a hero or a monster to the Virgin of the Wild. They were content to recline in darkness and await the fulfilment of his promise. He inscribed on the lid of the coffin Heracles strangling serpents – unleashing serpents – in his cradle and Hermes herding cattle, outwitting his brother Apollo on the day he was born . . .

Mr Mageye and I – even as Deacon propelled Horses and riders into a coffin – let our platform with its filming futuristic yet ancient Eye levitate in space. Such verticality, such a sliding scale, was native to blended time, past futures, future pasts. We saw Deacon's procession along the creek in a new fictional, factual light of peculiar irony and folk indefatigability and deprivation. Conversion of folk deprivation into glorious cradles allied to coffins and taxation in the grave ran hand in hand with mundane, plodding existences. We saw Deacon's processional wall in the lassoing of space change into apathy yet dogged hope.

The empolderment of the savannahs had been shelved when the War in Europe began in 1939. Money was short in the Colony. Posters advertising the Crabwood Creek Scheme (as it was called) began to loosen into tattered newspaper flags on the walls of buildings and in schools.

Deacon read the scraps and pieces nevertheless in his school. They flapped like wings of a noble scavenger or vulture or eagle that he attempted to draw within and around them into popular graffiti. One day he would come to power. One day his offspring would ensure an indefatigable cradle . . . Such were his larger-than-life thoughts as he led his plodding, smaller-than-life procession of horses from upriver Courantyne to downriver Crabwood Creek now that the drought was over.

Not giants in cradles to Mr Mageye and me on our platform and ladder in space but processions of hardy, ant-like creatures on the globe beneath us, as ant-like and enigmatic as the moving stars with feet in shadow above us.

Deacon's dwarf-like substance, the dwarf-like procession that he led – dwarf-like train of giants in the comedy of the wilderness – was nothing unusual in the life of the peasant folk. Peasants as young as Deacon were initiated into the savannahs virtually from the day they began to crawl. Mere lads – in the eyes of the Gods who contested the parentage of wilderness Marie – were skilled herders of cattle. It was a tough, dangerous life. As tough and as dangerous as it had been in ancient Palestine and ancient Greece where hardship was the name of the game.

Where were the new Biblical lands, the new Classical lands, but where exoduses and diasporas, and the threat of drought, of famine, prevailed in variable, unsuspected forms?

Where were the new ships, the new *Aeneid*, but in a web of ancient, conflicting cultures, modern Romes and Jonestowns overshadowing space even before they were built? Such overshadowing drove us forwards and backwards simultaneously into celestial mathematics. Deacon and Mr Mageye and Jonah Jones and Bone (myself) and the Prisoner and the Doctor and the Inspector and giants of chaos were witnesses to the diminutive composite epic that drove us into trial and error betrothal to fates and furies and dangerous maids, trial and error gestations in the Womb of space, infinite tragedy yet hope of divergence from absolute plot, absolute doom.

Deacon and his procession below us in the savannahs was a subconscious miniaturization of collective mystery, miniaturiza- tion of Classical Palestine, Classical Greece, Classical Maya in dwarf-like substance, true, unsuspected intercourse with com- plex, cross-cultural tradition . . .

Deacon had propelled himself upwards as he led his father's beaten horses, beaten by sun and drought, ribbed cages on which weak members of the family sat, from upriver Courantyne to downriver Crabwood Creek.

Propelled himself upwards into a Shadow beside Mr Mageye and me on the Platform of the Camera where we sat.

He was exhausted after the long journey. He seemed naked Shadow as I was naked Bone and Mr Mageye was naked spiritual Jester. We pushed him down again as he had pushed his train into the darkness of a coffin. He was exhausted. He settled in sleep on the lid of the coffin. The sigh of the river against the bank resembled buried souls in the wood of the box koker on which his head lay. Then he arose at last and made his way home.

HOME. Home is as elusive as it is real in Memory theatre. I remembered the Cave of the Moon into which I had fled from Jonestown on the Night of the Day of the Dead. It seemed home in a high cliff or bank from which a Waterfall fell beneath me into the Jonestown river. Was that Waterfall beneath me or did it spring from an opposite cliff or bank into which my Shadow reached as if it sought to bridge a chasm in creation? My stomach was hollow and I fed Bone with bread and rice and tinned fruit, tinned vegetables that I had stored in the Cave. Bone ate ravenously. So much so I was tempted to leap down the ladder of the Waterfall onto a rock far below shaped like a loaf of bread. Bone was universal me. I was universal Bone.

The holocaust is a vision of famine, the famine of the Soul imprinted on breath as much as bread that living skeletons bite or choke upon or devour . . .

I wanted to leap and forget everything that had happened . . .

But then I saw the faint outline of a body on the rock or loaf of bread. I broke my visionary teeth upon it. My pleasant rice and fruit in the Cave seemed straw for cattle.

Bone is tough, a spirited survivor in the wilderness of civilization.

Was it Deacon lying there far below?

Had he collapsed there and died after shooting Jones? Or was he asleep forever in the wake of the procession that he had led as a child?

His head lay on rock or seeming wood as mine had lain upon a pillow of stone. I resisted the temptation to fling myself down beside him and began instead to contemplate the construction of a Virgin Ship made of wood, of bread, stone, everything, times past and present and future.

Such a Ship begins to create itself upon a land and a sea of Limbo memory, Limbo chameleon memories upon which diminutive survivors such as myself feed in order to clothe themselves with the terrors of history that one may still convert into rare however flawed consciousness, indestructible hope. Such was my Limbo initiation into the writing of my Dream-book. I was to wander far and wide – uncertain of the steps I took – before I came to lodgings in Trinity Street, New Amsterdam.

Home is multi-dimensional space. And Limbo is the chameleon of home into which one reaches self-deceptively and endlessly in order to face truth when one comes abreast of the masquerades of the past that one has sustained voluntarily or involuntarily.

I left the Cave of the Moon and adventured into Limbo where I came upon the handsome, beautifully dressed grave-digger who had profited from the burial of the dead in Jonestown which he supervised.

'Did you bury them all,' I said, 'in a mass grave?'

In asking the question I could not help recalling Deacon and his child's heroic, monstrous incarceration of common-or-garden folk who were nevertheless giants and dwarfs, weak and strong, in the Eye of Mr Mageye's Camera. *They would return to judge me, to put me on trial.* Why me? Why not Deacon? Such are the paradoxes of judgement day, dateless day, theatre of Limbo – within the unacknowledged interstices of Purgatory, Hell, and Heaven – when one is recast to answer for another, when the embattled folk are recast into embodiments of self, oneself's trial is theirs, they are judges arisen from the living and the dead. One may know then under their terrible hand – considerate and inconsiderate hand – a flicker of the injustices inflicted by others upon their peers and subjects across the ages.

The grave-digger eyed me with a quizzical look: as if he were weighing every stitch I wore. My Nemesis Hat had deposited a few threads on my mother's grave, on Mr Mageye's grave, and on the Moon when Marie danced. The Hat or Bag was lighter now. It could be weighed on the scales of future pasts, past futures, radiating out from an apparitional core of composite self.

'Lost a few threads, Francisco,' he confirmed. 'Each could be auctioned no doubt for a bite of bread. I fancy sweet bread myself. Made from currants and lemon, Demerara sugar, and rich flour. I found quite a store in Jonestown. We split it between ourselves, me and the Inspector and that Doctor-God chap who is popular with the peasants of Port Mourant. They say he cares for the sick who lie on pallets on the floor. All well and good but your shirt and trousers are in tatters. A disgrace! Those would fetch nothing at all in the marketplace. I can see clean through to Bone, Francisco. Ah! but there's your shoes. I like those. Jolly good leather. I pulled off quite a few like yours from the heels of the dead in Jonestown. Gave me quite a turn. It was as if they were ready to run, to sprint. Well you can do it for them, Francisco. Just as well you got away, Bone. You're worth but a bite or two of meat and potatoes to me. Imagine my having to cart you into the grave for virtually nothing. I'm glad you got away.'

He laid out at least five hundred watches in the Limbo forest. He tied them to the branches of trees. He laid out earrings, women's purses, and men's linen shirts, men's vests, short pants and long pants and baby clothes.

A curious business, a curious self-addictive satire, a curious mockery and self-mockery rooted in despair, it was that the grave-digger conducted in charting his evolution into millionaire Carnival Lord Death.

The robes on his back had been borrowed from the dead and the living. The baby clothes seemed dead baby clothes too small for the giant of Death. Who knows how small or large Death is? He possessed a scarf, on the other hand, around his neck that had been mine. I had wrapped it around my hand when blood oozed from the wound I received and left it on the bushes beside the Clearing. Nothing! I felt nothing at all when I lost two fingers from Deacon's random bullet . . . Carnival Lord Death wore the bloodstained scarf now with style that was a wonderful gloss upon numbness.

What was bizarre and charismatic in his style was the strangely lifeless but majestic, ritualistic folds of his dress. He possessed the aplomb of an astronaut on the Moon in Limbo theatre.

This was fascinating stuff. Charismatic aplomb was in fashion. Tradition bouncing on surfaces but bereft of depth, Brain shorn of mind or philosophy, life shorn of unpredictable Spirit or originality.

The array of goods – far beyond the range I have described – confirmed his majestic skills as an entrepreneur *par excellence* of Limbo Land.

But there were other considerations and moral fables in Carnival Lord Death's pitiless barter of the numb word, numb lips, numb ears and eyes for treasurers that he pulled from the pockets of the living and the dead, from their running feet, or reluctant hands, from their frames and bodies, to adorn his kingdom.

The quality of Justice! What sort of Justice did Carnival Lord Death administer? He was a just man: as just as any man could be in the Mask of Death. What are the foundations of Justice as the twentieth century draws to a close?

I looked around but there was no help from Mr Mageye in this instance. Carnival Lord Death loomed over me as I uttered a silent prayer, an unorthodox prayer that was more an awkward statement than a request for enlightenment.

'To feel nothing,' I dreamt inwardly, 'except the possession of privileged immunity to famine or to hell, to feel nothing but a licence that is granted in Carnival jump-ups and crusades, in an age of the mechanical death of the soul, *is* justice. Justice is the tautology of the death of the soul. Justice is the prosecution of spare-parts methodologies, spare-parts bodies. Or so it seems everywhere. I know for mechanical ornamentation, buttocks and breasts and all, in pleasure palaces, is the structure of a wound that forgets it is a wound.

'God forgive me (as I pray awkwardly) but I know. I was shot in Jonestown and lost all feeling in my hand. It became a tool, an insensible tool.

'Perhaps Lord Death (you are in my prayer, for who knows

what Carnival omens Death employs in an age of the death of the soul in the machine?) were you to permit me to reach up and unloose the scarf around your neck, feeling would invade my absent fingers at last which were blown like cigarette ends in the wind.

'The scarf or noose is mine. That very rich scarf that you wear. Poor man's, beggar man's, thief's, scarf of kings! It sings of soul's blood and the genesis of pain all over again. It sings of an apparitional or phantom grasp of reality that may resurrect the elusive lineaments of the Soul.

'And this brings me to the mystery of injustice that the Soul expresses in my wounds. To suffer injustice is to see the Soul within every small creature that cries out for pity against pitilessness. Can we fathom the enduring, insubstantial cry of pity? Pity's sake can neither be bought nor sold. Compassion is beyond price.'

Another form of prayer it was that involved me not in a plea for justice but enduring, creative capacity to suffer the mystery of injustice if the Soul were to live, phenomenal fellow-feeling, despite predatory games and uniform insensibility to crisis . . .

I feared Carnival Lord Death but he appeared to acknowledge – in some recess of himself – the mystery of prayer and he returned the scarf to me.

'You poor devil, Francisco,' he said, 'if it gives you some comfort have the bloody scarf. It went well with my daring dress. I came upon the eighteenth attire I now wear in Jones's house . . .'

I wanted to tell him that this too was mine. I had loaned it to Jones for a fancy dress occasion in Jonestown. It was a kind of heirloom or legacy that I had been given by my mother.

The travail for me in the grave-digger's evolution into a capitalist and into Carnival Lord Death lay in the chasm it illumined between mechanical Justice and the extraordinary numinosity of Injustice and in every trial one is called upon to endure at the bar of time. How to come abreast of the past one believes one has forfeited or killed is more self-searching than knowledge of current affairs. For if one fails to come abreast of dead time (or what seems to be dead time) a Predator in the future will destroy us. And time past, the living texture and spirituality in time past, would have become too weak to stand at our side and assist us.

Limbo Justice involved an equation between numbness and immunity to hell. To be just then in Limbo Land was to serve one's vested interests absolutely, whether pleasure or profit, to sublimate or suppress or eclipse one's wounds in favour of strengthening a wall between oneself and the inferno that rules elsewhere in many dimensions of one's age.

Injustice, on the other hand, bore on a coming abreast of wounds one has suffered in the past through which one knows pain in oneself and others, pain of mind that revives the Soul of Compassion beyond all machineries of the law of Death or of the state of embalmed institutions.

Without the mystery of Injustice – when one suffers with others to whom the world is unjust – the soul would vanish entirely and leave behind the mechanical futility of knowledge in the besieged Brain in the crumbling Body . . .

I had never meditated on morality in this light and I needed to emphasize and re-emphasize, rehearse and rehearse again, what I had learnt from my encounter with the capitalist Carnival Lord Death.

I needed a Dream-book that would take nothing for granted within the prayer I had attempted to address to an unfathomable Creator of worlds and universes. I needed to embrace 'pity's sake' though such an embrace of the Word made me infinitely vulnerable.

I was now convinced that Limbo Land was a trap from which it was unlikely I would ever escape to view the open cities of Paradise. I had failed in building a new Rome in Jonestown's web of abandoned and lost cities arching back into pre-Columbian mists of time.

All well and good to have escaped from the holocaust into Limbo Land but a variety of enormous and subtle dangers now encompassed me. Foremost amongst these was the menace of the Predator who lurked in the giant forests of Day and Night.

I was infinitely vulnerable. How could I withstand such a

72

menace? In a sense I felt easier with the grave-digger now – when I ran into him in my wanderings after the Day of the Dead and prior to my arrival in Trinity Street – I accepted his new role (with the death of the conventional Church) as Lord Death. Perhaps he and I possessed a secret understanding about the omens of Carnival.

Nothing however could forfeit or erase the scent – the backwards, forwards scent – of the Predator. I knew I was hunted, pursued, or stalked in Limbo Land. Stalked as a commodity to be devoured by mighty institutions, great Banks, great systems that ransacked and devoured privacy: but such systems were but one feature in the unnameable menace of the Predator.

I wondered, *as my mind tended to lapse and to lose reflection in the bark of a tree to which I clung, in shed leaves of memory here and there or cracked branches of trees into which I occasionally climbed (as my Carib or African or Arawak ancestors – runaway European antecedents as well – had done in the sixteenth century when slavery and persecution ruled the Americas),* whether the Predator was Carnival Lord Death after all despite our secret treaty or understanding. A part of that understanding was to inform him of flying or running strangers in Limbo Land.

I had no intention of doing so but I humoured him, especially when he assured me that the Inspector would take me to see the Prisoner or Old God of Devil's Isle who claimed to be the father of the Virgin of the Wilderness, Marie of Port Mourant.

BUT NO! The Predator was older than Death itself. The Predator possessed a curious weight that lay beneath gravity's Skull, beneath every falling or fallen creature, a curious *violence* that subsisted on nuclear deadlock, or perversity, or cosmic devastation, on meteorites colliding with Jupiter, on the manipulation of elegant mathematics into spectacles of beauty that kill, random bullets in space, or from space, that strike the Earth from time to time. The Predator's craft and skill and range in Limbo Land was immense and I felt his breath (unlike the breath of resurrectionary organs of Compassion) rearrange the grain of the hair on the back of my neck.

The tickling sensation of the hair on my neck and head aroused in me a contrary sensation to absolute fear that the Predator sought to instil in me. I broke my Nemesis Hat or Bag into two containers. One I retained as a Hat and this I replaced on my head. The other I adopted as a Bag. I retraced my steps in Limbo Land and collected the fallen leaves of memory from cracked branches or trees into which I had climbed. They possessed the numinous texture of a book and I promised the three Virgins (Jonestown, Albuoystown, Port Mourant) that I would write a Dream-book should I gain Trinity Street in New Amsterdam . . .

How much did I know, how much remember – within composite epic – of ages prior to Death, ages in which the Predator's regime of violence seemed both immanent and transient, ages in which nevertheless the Womb of Virgin Space seemed shorn of violence, shorn of intercourse with reality that was violent?

Within that implicit and terrifying opposition how wounded were the parameters of genesis – the genesis of the Imagination to cope with terror and grace – how wounded the Virgin herself as she broke into a trinity of Masks, the three Maries?

I scanned each leaf as I placed it in my Bag. A variety of inscriptions appeared upon leaf after leaf. Faint light-year vistas . . . Were they progeny of the Virgin driven by a quest to minimize violence in a world in which Death had appeared? Were they progeny of the Predator to augment or absolutize violence in a world in which Death had appeared?

Such vistas lay beyond absolute translation into certainty.

They were resources of uncanny drama, resources of uncanny rehearsals of the genesis or unfinished genesis of the Imagination . . .

The Scorpion Constellation shone in the eyes of the Tiger-mask of the sun. Which blinded which, who whom, it was difficult to say. The Scavenger swooped. The Eagle dealt the Jaguar a blow on the Moon and on the walls of abandoned Maya cities. But all such manifestations were curiously hieroglyphic: self-deceptive and true within the partialities of genesis. They bore on the mystery of injustice that runs hand in hand with the resurrection of the Soul of Compassion for all wounded creatures whether born of the Predator or of the Virgin.

A further complication lay in another well-nigh indescribable imprint, a huntsman who seemed to stand within the Womb of Virgin space. I sensed that he had no illusions about the might of the Predator. As I listened to the whisper or rustle of each leaf within my phantom fingers I dreamt that I heard his voice seeking to instil the strangest wisdom everywhere, into creature and constellation, however prone these were to linkages with the Predator, into heroes and angels, however prone these were to linkages with monsters. I sensed his tread at Night in the footprint of the Predator.

The gathering menace broke into a Storm and I felt it was useless running from the Predator any longer. My desire had been to destroy him by hook or by crook. So much so that unconsciously, subconsciously, I was driven to contemplate poisoning the air everywhere that he breathed, the seas and oceans and lakes and rivers in which he swam, the environments and places that clothed him. 'Kill him even if it means killing yourself,' Carnival Lord Death had said to me. Death's freedoms encompassed the advocacy of Suicide. 'Walk with a Bomb of environmental disasters under your shirt to blow up the globe.'

But the huntsman in the footfall of the Predator – close on the heels of the Predator – possessed a different tune.

'Leap,' he said (in the gathering menace of the Storm), 'into my net and help me to hold the heart of the Predator at bay within rhythms of profoundest self-confessional, self-judgemental crea-tivity. The leap into space I grant is dangerous. It is a kind of surrender to an unfathomable caring Presence that seems absent in a cruel age. It is the leap of the unfinished genesis of the Imagination that may bring to light unpredictable resources in an open universe that nets, in some paradoxical way, creature and creation. LEAP . . .'

But I was unable to do so. Nevertheless my desire to poison or slay the Predator loosed its grip on my unconscious, unconscious motivation, motivation of disaster. I settled myself on a tree-platform instead and created a pillow with the Bag of memory leaves and pages. The Storm blew a further volume of leaves upon me. The Predator knew of my lofty hiding place. He knew of my inner Dream-pillow or book. He knew of the outer volume that the Storm had granted me, the raining blanket of leaves in circulation, cross-circulation, rehearsal, re-visionary momentum . . . I was lost. I was convinced I was lost. It was finished. I lay in the Predator's bed and he knew.

And then the huntsman threw his net. I knew without knowing how I knew that the net fastened itself upon the limbs of the Predator even as it appeared to release me, leaving me still to leap . . .

'I cannot leap,' I said. 'Not now. But thank you huntsman for saving me from madness, from being devoured by an appetite for violence that grows everywhere.'

I wondered in a flash of lightning whether the huntsman would now seize and destroy the Predator forever. I listened and my heart virtually ceased to beat. BUT NO. The huntsman held the Beast at bay, he lifted him in his net. And I was privileged to gain, with another flash, a glimpse of terrifying beauty. I was bewildered, confused. Heartrending grief arose in myself at the sight of such stripes of beauty. Such was the inimitable hide of the Predator. As the huntsman turned in the lightning Storm with the Beast in his net I dreamt I was free to surrender myself at last, *not to leap now* but to contemplate surrendering myself to an omen of Beauty that I needed to turn inside out for hidden graces, hidden sorrows, in creatures one despised because they appeared to lack the might, the power, the charisma, of the Predator.

The Storm passed and as the Moon descended on my tree-platform it shed a striped visor over my Nemesis Hat: an astronaut-knight above Limbo Land. One version of Limbo seemed charred, another version appeared to have been pierced to the heart, still another glowed, intricate, lovely, beauty translated into inside-out, marvellous graces and sorrows. It was the vulnerability of the Earth, planet Earth, that made me weep.

Once again I wanted to leap but instead I flung my visor into space. Skin and Bone throbbed where the shield had grazed my countenance and I was conscious all at once of punctures on my head and neck and shoulders. Holes had been imprinted there. The subtlest holes into which futuristic nails would lodge as if they were new bones to uphold another Mask of flesh-and-blood in Memory theatre. Perhaps the huntsman's net in its range and sweep – as it bore the Predator away – had inflicted wounds from which new bone would grow to uphold the Mask when it came . . . I was confused and bewildered by the prospect . . .

Dawn light brought me to the ground again. No visionary leap this! Problematic descent, problematic feet . . . I felt faint and leaned against the trunk of the tree. I placed the Bag of leaves over my shoulder and set out for New Amsterdam.

Problematic feet implied problematic stages of implicit surrender to the huntsman's net. But the hiatuses and gaps in Memory theatre remained to be reconnoitred afresh in my Dream-book, the fears, the uncertainties, of pilgrimage, of departure, arrival. Who was I? Where was I?

Were there perverse resurrections, death-dealing regimes and crushing labour, that one would need to re-vision and come abreast of, in order to break a numbness and paralysis of the Imagination everywhere?

Were there amazing truths of unfinished genesis and resurrectionary consciousness that one would glimpse through the Wheel of civilizations within the turning globe in the Womb of space?

Hospitals, El Dorados, colonial possessions, Dutch, French, British, within a web of ancient vanished empires in the Americas, apparitions of the dead-in-the-living (of all races) in the wake of imperial Limbo and Jonestown, banqueting halls, circuses, would haunt me as I wrote. Yet from their debris I became a diminutive cosmic architect of a Virgin Ship and of Memory theatre. All were stages for, and initiations into, my trial at the bar of time.

Foundations of Cities

I tipped the leaves from my Dream-pillow and came upon the hieroglyph of the betrothal of Marie and Deacon in the savannahs, their dance on the Mirror of the Moon ... It should have occasioned me joy – however tinged with jealousy – but it brought me sorrow.

Inscribed into the dance were re-traceries of horses and cattle that Jones had stabled in Jonestown (or Jonah City as I was inclined to name it).

Jones, Deacon and I had been the architects of Jonah City within the huge, forested belly of South America, the new Rome afloat upon sea (a sea of leaves) as upon land branching into space.

Marie, the Virgin of the wilderness, fled from the dance on a Wheel, and I followed her into Port Mourant hospital. Marie was but a slip of a child. She extricated herself from the Wheel in which I had lodged her. She was naked, wet, dripping with the glass of rain through which she had run. So it was a miracle that I salvaged the imprint of the Wheel on a leaf. It was less a question of running and more of securing herself in the Wheel like a reflection of time: the Wheel of civilizations that corresponds to the Virgin's circular leap in space!

Fractions and circles are profoundest mathematics that one needs to weigh and reassess with the greatest care in returning to the foundations of lost cities: riverain fondations, falling or rising whale's belly Atlantis, Plato's Cave, light, space, earth-cradle foundations, sky foundations that dripped on the Virgin Marie's body.

Four-square leaps, triangular leaps, vertical leaps, horizontal leaps, are a measure of the dance that one equates with lost, revisited cities, villages, homes ...

The sky dripped through the leaking roof of the Port Mourant hospital into which I had come with Marie. Hospitals and Ships within the Wheel of civilizations are symbols of the globe. The dance of the Wheel brings one intimate knowledge of bombed villages and churches and hospitals and houses.

Jonestown. The sky dripped upon Limbo and upon Jonestown.

Jonah saw himself in the belly of the White Sky or Whale of American legend as a saddened Aeneas afloat upon coffin and cradle.

'Do ghosts cradle themselves in tree-tops above their graves? You lucky devil! You survived, Francisco.' I thought I heard his voice in my ears in Port Mourant hospital as I stood amongst the sick on pallets on the floor.

I had been one of Jones's lieutenants, his left-hand man. In the 1970s when we were busy erecting the new Rome, afloat on the back of Atlantis in the South American rainforest, I used to play music on a Maya drum. I possessed five fingers then.

But in my sorrowing resurrection backwards in time from 1978 to 1939 Albuoystown, Crabwood Creek and Port Mourant, I found myself with only three. Yet I continued to play with two phantom fingers as a memorial of Soul, apparitional grasp, apparitional reach into Soul, Soul's design of invisible triangles, parallels, and spaces.

Memory theatre has no fixtures. One exercises a riddle of proportions as one writes of time and times, in time and times, through time and times, as if blended times are the solid and elusive foundations of holocaustic Jonestown . . . The lives and limbs of those who have perished need to be weighed as incredible matter-of-fact that defies the limits of realistic discourse. Fallen angels become engineers and architects on the death of a child to whom they build citadels and memorials on earth and in heaven. Babes such as Marie are replete with the eloquence of the Virgin. Fiction's truths are absurdity's common sense, absurdity's revelations of composite epic heart in the ancient and the modern.

Deacon occupied a privileged station when we began the construction of Utopian Jonestown in the 1970s. It won the approval of the head of state in Guyana. Jones appeared to cherish Deacon. He was the great evangelist's right-hand peasant angel and engineer. No one knew (and I myself forgot within lapses in my Dream-book) that he nursed a fear of the Predator after the death of his son Lazarus born of the Wilderness Virgin Marie in December 1954. One forgets. One remembers. Such lapses and bridges between memory and non-memory are native to the trauma of cultures . . . No one knew that he nursed a fear of the Scorpion Constellation that brought him immunity to pain and wealth and fortune with which to build a memorial township to Lazarus.

Jonestown was a memorial to Lazarus, a memorial of deadly fortune that was to catapult me into space in due course. As if dream-rockets are sometimes founded on the slaughter of infants or twins or brothers. Had not the eighteenth-century Frenchman's fortune – founded on repentance that drove him overseas to El Doradonne Guiana after the slaying of his brother (whom he nourished in his imagination as he aged as a composite son, composite slave and son) – granted me a scholarship to San Francisco in the twentieth century?

Had not Herod's slaughter of infants – when Christ was born – cemented a resurrrectionary Bank of Fortune in Christendom?

So does civilization question itself, in dread at its foundations, through composite epic survivors of feud, or conflict, or genocide, or death-dealing regimes.

Composite epic parents itself, parents its Gods, parents humanity, in order to answer at the core of the self for the shape of things everywhere. Yet the apparently random choice of diminutive being, a frail Imagination here and there, to bear this burden of multi-faceted collective, multi-faceted community, is unfathomable . . .

I was a South American Utopian in the 1970s. It was a peculiar burden to carry. Utopia was less an absolute place, absolute society, absolute theatre, and more a Bridge festooned with ruins . . . Utopia signified a Bridge of collective genius, yet dread for me, from the coastlands of Guyana (into which people are chained) into the hazards of capacity within the interior of the South Americas: a wholly different architecture, a wholly different Imagination from the politics and the institutions of economic fixture and habit.

Were the oceans to rise along the South American coastlands in future generations they would play havoc with the coastal shell of settlements already beneath mean sea level.

Sea defences and walls and foundations of villages and cities would be shaken to their innermost core.

Utopia was therefore a way of turning a world (while time was still an ally of creative possibility) into perceiving itself from within its future, shaken core of self: perceiving processional expeditions from one ocean to the North (the Atlantic) to another ocean to the South (the rainforests). Except that the latter ocean – however deep it seemed – was far above the reach of the Atlantic plundering tides that had once blossomed into pirate and conquistador.

Now the time had come to move ... Depth was uncanny proportionality of Memory theatre, Memory's lift, Memory's height, upon which to view impending events, failed events, lost causes, futuristic ruins, as well as past events that are native to the wastelands of the future, past events that one may have buried in conventional complacency within the present moment that continues to ignore the Shadow of the future ...

Jonestown was now a ruin in Memory theatre. It was rubble and wasteland on the Utopian Bridge from the coastlands of Guyana into the interior of the South Americas. Its leaking roofs and ruined or flattened walls became an imaginary station to be revisited through other imaginary stations and ghost trains in time.

In returning to 1939 (Marie's childhood, Deacon's childhood, my childhood) I stood on the Wheel of civilizations, and the Utopian Bridge, as upon a stage on which to assemble the poor people's hospital, and its pathetic walls and leaking roof, that invoked the wastelands of 1978 in Jonestown. The sick who lay on their pallets on the ground were true Utopian characters in the Carnival of the future. Lord Death was already amongst them making a tally of their possessions as the grave-digger had done (or would do) above the pit or mass grave in Jonestown and theatre of the burial of the dead.

How does one build new architectures out of the rubble of traditions and out of diasporas across millennia?

Marie was weeping her heart out on the floor of the hospital in 1939.

Poor Marie. Rich, wilderness Marie. Virgin Marie. Queen Marie. Princess Marie. Peasant Marie. Child's ancient heart. Bride of humanity. Mother of Gods. Child of Gods contesting their parentage of her. Biological magic? Adoptive, spiritual, medicinal magic?

Marie was weeping ancient tears until they formed a mysterious pool on the ground, or sea, or ocean. Refugees swam from Cuba and Haiti, climbed the Utopian Bridge, and began their futuristic trip into the heartland of the Guyanas. 2050? 2025?

Hungry masses pressed against the wall of the Mediterranean seeking entry into an overcrowded Europe. Jobless Mexicans fought to cross the border into lands once theirs now part and parcel of the United States.

The dying and the sick – assembled in South America from every race around the globe – lay on the floor of the hospital within the Shadows of the past and the future. They were masked actors of El Doradonne Utopia, a new Rome to be founded by apparitional Aeneas, or Lazarus ascending from the rubble of Troy; such founders were in my blood, and in Deacon's blood, and in everyman's blood within experimental nuclei of epic, resurrected consciousness.

I dreaded the mark of Lazarus tattooed on my arm as much as I dreaded the bite of the Scorpion on Deacon's arm.

Deacon's infant Lazarus – born of Marie in 1954 – was a deadly fortune or role that I would inherit in Memory theatre.

That fortune would unfold in Dreams long before it was conferred upon me. It would unfold in absurd, even humiliating, ribaldry, when Deacon taunted me in San Francisco. It would unfold by unforeseen stages into a honeymoon with bliss. I would be appointed – when Deacon vanished after Jonestown – to return in Memory theatre to his wedding feast. I would be appointed to read or scan the intricate, terrifying seed gestating in the womb of the Virgin of the Wilderness. I would be appointed to play the role of her bridegroom in order to know in myself how worthy, or dreadfully unworthy I was, to plant the seed of Lazarus once again across millennia in the womb of space . . .

Yes, I knew of the news of my appointment but it tended to

fragment in my mind, it tended to slip from my mind as I awoke and wrestled with the Dream-book . . .

The patients in the hospital in Memory theatre 1939 (when World War Two lit up flares across the Atlantic which alighted on the Utopian Bridge) may have seemed divorced from Jones's flock of the future in the 1970s. Divorced from Bosnia, or Rwanda, or Ethiopia in the 1990s . . . They were different at first glance but the fires of war lit up Carnival mirroring blood in feature and mask.

The finest cast of actors one could assemble to play at war, war with famine, war with plague and addiction, in the twentieth century. To play at holy wars, religious wars.

They ate cherries of blood in hopeful, hungry mask, hopeful, hopeless lip. They ate cherries of hope in the 1970s decade when Jones, Deacon and I visited the head of state in Guyana, obtained a generous lease, gave them their lines to read in the tragedy of Jonestown. They were our sheep. Brilliant actors on the world's stage.

They ate cherries in 1939 when they lay on the hospital floor.

Each cherry – planted in the teeth of Masks, Bridges of Bone across generations, centuries, millennia – was a rounded thread coiling in Marie's hair, upon Marie's Wheel.

'The unfinished Wheel is my father's gift to you,' said Marie. 'Even as hair grows in the grave but vanishes on an infant's brow.'

I felt no surprise at such an utterance. Marie was the queen of ghostly children as tall as Bone who flit in the Shadows and the Lights of wildernesses since time began.

Her tears were genuine. A dog resembling a lamb arose from the bedside of a patient on the floor and lapped at the pool as if it were milk.

I dived from the Utopian Bridge – on which I stood with Mr Mageye and his ancient, futuristic Camera imbued with elemental proportions of comedy and tragedy – into the pool of milk.

POOL OF MILK was a private joke between Deacon, Jones and myself when we were in San Francisco College and tended to swim in a hothouse, atmospheric, veiled pool not far from the Golden Bridge that arched across San Francisco Bay.

Men and women consorted and swam there in the misty, milky,

hothouse, fleecy light that the theatre of the bath provided . . .
They all seemed naked in the Camera's Eye and immersed and
preoccupied with sexual, underwater intercourse, instant milk-
and-coffee. Black and brown bodies loomed in the milk to give
coffee pigmentation to the scene.

'It's not true,' I said to Deacon (as I arose from the Pool and
joined him at the edge of the Milky Abyss, the consumer abyss),
'it's not true, they're innocent actors abroad, surely no sexual
games on Sunday in broad daylight. It's a trick of Mr Mageye's
futuristic Camera.'

'This isn't broad daylight,' said Deacon, 'it's the Milky Way, the
white tears of the Virgin for every lamb or dog and for Leviathan.
Look! the White Whale rises festooned with Ahab's doomed
voyagers.' He was laughing. Jonah was displeased. I was
unhappy.

'Have a glass of rum, Francisco,' said Deacon. 'Rum mixed with
poison. Or is it milk mixed with cyanide? No idea how the
ridiculous thought flipped into my skull. Memories of the future
when we build Jonestown! Where in God's name is Jonestown?
I'm drunk.'

I thrust the poisoned drink from me. But it was as if Deacon's
prophetic eyes stood in my head now and Ahab's doomed
voyagers were being toppled by a misty grave-digger into a
mass-media pool.

I pulled the eyes from my head and flung them into the Pool.
Carnival Lord Death snatched them up and popped them into his
mouth. He held them there for a moment or two as if to test their
immunity to poison that Deacon had inherited from the Scorpion.
'They're worth a million dollars at least,' he cried. 'Indeed much,
much more. Insurance for dead or living actors' eyes is priceless.
Perhaps not as high as a dead footballer's legs or a punch-drunk
boxer's wrists. Role models – who knows? – may fetch a billion on
the Day of the Dead.'

'What's that? What's that?' cried Deacon. 'Whose voice is that?'
He glared at me and the sockets in his head – with their Eagle's
glare – seemed wonderfully hollow. Jones was slightly mesmer-
ized. It was a brilliant performance on Deacon's part. He slapped

me on the back. 'It's a rotten world, isn't it Francisco? Can you play the role of a saviour?' I shrank from him. He was mocking me. He was mocking himself. He was mocking role models.

He was pointing to the tattoo on my arm, the tattoo of Lazarus shaped like a T inscribed on Bone.

'Play a surrogate Lazarus Francisco in the Milky Way, in the Virgin's Pool, cohabit with innocent brides in the misty Pool, all in anticipation of the birth of my son when I return to wed Marie. She's but a slip of a dancing thing now – a princess in my eyes – on a distant coast.'

It was as if the skies had fallen in on my head.

No, No, I wanted to scream as the naked misty-bodied throng jostled together in the grave of the Pool. Had I not seen them in that light (though I had forgotten it all) on the Day of the Dead when I lay on a pillow of stone at the edge of the Clearing?

To be survivor Lazarus – even in Jest – to play such a role is to know that the part involves an inner marriage to a resurrectionary Womb, inner eyes in a resurrectionary Womb, inner organs in a resurrectionary Womb, inner intercourse with Virgin, wilderness space, that may bring new birth to the Self (within a Sorrowing humanity); to contemplate such a role is to tap resources of forgotten initiation into a bridegroom or a fool as much as into the foetus of a saviour in order to acquire the strength to stand at the bar of time . . .

Mr Mageye saw my distress. 'See the funny side of the sacred, Francisco,' he said. He spoke softly for my ear alone on the Bridge with the Camera. 'See the funny side of Deacon. Alas he knows that from birth, and his exposure in the savannahs, he began to play the role model of Fate. *You* have been tied to him as a Fool to be taunted and insulted and reviled. You (and the society to which you belong) must suffer his bouts of arrogance, and drunkenness, and bad behaviour. It's Fate, it's the role model of Fate, in the theatre, in the duelling arena, in sport, everywhere, when a civilization is addicted to violence as ours is. Only a Fool may absolve Deacon of the burden he carries . . .'

Mr Mageye saw my incredulity, my dislike of the label Fool . . .

'Look at it this way, Francisco. You are an apparition in time on the Bridge above the Pool. You stand beside me. You are an apparition in time down there beside the Pool. So you may entertain the comedy of having many fathers. The Frenchman's Catholic ghost for instance. Your mother's great-great-grand-father and husband. Carnival theology. And why not? Such surrogacies break the spell of divine human incest and bring us into the mystery of freedom ... Freedom confesses to the partiality of all parenting dogma which it entertains as sacred, human theatre ...

'When the sky falls treat it as manna from heaven and crumbs from the bodies of role models (Jones is a cult model, isn't he?), the heroes, the monsters, that we feed upon in our gluttony for abuse at the hand of Fate ...'

I was filled with fear, comic fear, uncanny fear, the fear of creation, of the possibilities of creation, the possibilities of fiction. Models of fiction cemented in the eighteenth and the nineteenth century are sacred in the twentieth. Sacred eighteenth-century, nineteenth-century linearity. But I was attempting to rewrite the past from the funny side of sacred, imperial time, from a futuristic angle that breached linearity. One drew one's characters from the grave of time, they migrated backwards from the future never-theless into the past, susceptible to one's knowledge now (however flawed) of the past futures to which one belonged. The funny side of time in the future. Such is the resurrectionary, comic consciousness of the Fool Lazarus whom I sought to invoke in my texts though I knew without a shadow of doubt that Church and State showered him with fortunes and riches to keep him safely dead ... This was the substance of my fear, my uncanny fear, as I wrote my Dream-book, as I sought to build Memory theatre ...

There was no way around such fear except divine comedy and the acceptance of Fate, the abuse of Fate, the abuse of Prejudice, the abuse of Predator.

'Is Lazarus – you call me Lazarus Deacon – a Colonial Fool in a so-called post-colonial, post-imperial age? I do not know. If he is he must die and die again and again and each resurrection will prove abortive ... Unless ... Unless ...'

Deacon was outraged. He had been drinking rum and Coca-

Cola all afternoon at the swimming pool with its misty embracing bodies.

He had also caught the drift of Mr Mageye's conversation with me.

'Fuck the Frenchman's ghost,' he cried. 'Fuck you, Francisco. You are a Fool. Your mother was a Fool.'

'It's the Frenchman's fortune which brought you here on a scholarshp in the twentieth century.'

'I am the peasant, legendary father of the Americas. Folkloric father. Ask Marie to whom I am betrothed. We need a different Economy . . .'

Jonah Jones had had enough. He knit his brow like an ancient thunderer and struck the frame of the Milky Way until it shuddered as if to the rumble of an earthquake.

'Nonsense Deacon,' he cried. 'Blue-blooded puritans are the fathers of the Americas. I am your father and every fucking bastard's.'

He had been drinking too and swallowing the women in the Pool with his drink. Their reflected bodies sprawled on the glass in his hand. His rage melted and he laughed in Deacon's smiling teeth.

'You Francisco, you Deacon, are my sons. Together in the New World we will forge a new pact and build a new Rome unlike the Pope's Rome. I nearly said Poe's Rome. Poe was a racist. But never mind. He's a genius all the same! Would you not agree, Francisco? Troy, believe me, has been sacked and Rome turned its back on the Jews when Hitler marched into Poland. Berlin and Paris and London have suffered bouts of racism and fascism. Fascism is the death of the Imagination. IMAGINATION DEAD IMAGINE.'

I wanted to shout to him from the Utopian Bridge. I wanted to shout a rain of questions at him as he swallowed the women in the Pool. I wanted to shout across a chasm of generations but my tongue froze, and his ear – for all I knew – was sealed.

I wanted to shout within my own grave of memory – as though I too lay on the sick bed of civilization in Port Mourant hospital. But I was a diminutive survivor and my voice was weak and small. Though I sailed into the past with knowledge I had gained from the future, the queer and the funny side of knowledge served to show how much – beyond reckoning – I still had to learn.

I wanted to shout to him – within my own grave of memory – as though I too had died in Jonestown: 'Have you, Jonah, rid yourself of the disease of fascism?'

I wanted to shout: 'I know little or nothing except that I survived . . .'

'How is it,' I said to Mr Mageye, 'that one knows so little yet dares to write fiction's truths, the hardest truths to garner?'

Mr Mageye laughed. 'Fiction is not tautology. Fiction,' he murmured, 'must diverge within itself from itself to be true to itself. Or else it becomes the mimicry of fact, the shell of fact . . .'

'How do you see my Dream-book, Mr Mageye? You are my magus-Camera Man, you transcribe my Dream-book into cinematic dress, into ghost-theatre – you are a ghost yourself – but I have no idea whether it's simply a technological or cannibal appetite in ghosts, capitalism's ghosts, when they swallow fictions indiscriminately; or whether there's more, there's freedom, there's liberation for fiction in the Camera.'

Mr Mageye acquired his peculiar air of the Sphinx with which I was familiar. But this time a new element tended to emerge. I perceived an almost calculated look of interwoven spectres upon him as he placed his hand upon the Camera.

'Who can say what may prove to be the role of the Camera in future ages?'

'But yours is a futuristic Camera . . .'

'Ancient visage of time as well, Francisco, in hidden chambers of the heart and mind where figures peer at us dressed as mystical astronauts. That's in my Camera as well. Deacon would call it celestial mathematics.'

I was startled by the Jest which gave me food for thought as one glimpsed a rare temple of the human body . . .

Mr Mageye was smiling with a deceptive gravity, a kind of inner levitation of the imagination lifted his features as if his smile took him up into a laurel wreath above his grave in Albuoystown.

'But to be serious,' he continued, 'the Camera is possessed of an organ that cannot – in all honesty – encompass all the textualities

91

of your Dream-book. It measures its limits nevertheless – I speak now in purely technical terms – within those variable boundaries. It pictorializes concrete happenings but imbues these at the same time with far-reaching and meaningful hiatuses and gaps that *speak* for themselves. The tears that the Virgin weeps, for instance, in poor people's hospitals become an eloquent pool of milk at which dogs lap and in which rich men and women swim. Eloquent pool! Not straightforward eloquence. Dogs lap, their teeth flash into famine-stricken multitudes that we harbour in our unconscious. Feed my sheep. Feed my dogs. Even as you gorge yourselves on sex. Do you recall the creation of loaves of bread and fish in the Gospels from scraps and crumbs? A multitude was fed. The wonders of mystical science and hungry spirit, hungry ghosts, that can take many shapes around us and in our bodies, shapes that breed excess, or shapes that address us within the gaps of self-centred technology.

'A hiatus lives within all models of technology. A chasm exists. We tend to turn our backs on this within patterns of realism that we reinforce into absolutes. But the hunger of the spirit grows, the hunger of ghosts everywhere, and excess may turn by degrees into death-dealing prosperity . . .'

The Pool of Tears – into which I had dived – faded and I was back in the poor people's hospital.

Marie was dressed in a nurse's uniform. It was too large for her and her head rose above it with the eagerness and pathos of living, carven wood from an El Doradonne tree, wilderness flesh-and-blood child and twentieth-century peasant child. It was the custom or inbuilt tradition of the Golden Man or King of El Dorado to open doors in the oxygen bodies of trees (this was ancient El Doradonne Cinema) and to sculpt emerging Shadows into the retinue of his court, his civil servants, the members of his family, the labourers in the fields . . .

Marie was playing a princess of ancient El Dorado in a hospital play. The patients were enlivened by the sight of a nurse's uniform as the robe of royalty.

I was overjoyed to see that her tears had ceased. The dog had lapped the milk and retreated to the side of his master who lay on the floor. The incongruity of the over-size uniform brought the occasion alive as though the princess's large dress sheltered a multitude of workers who were kith and kin to royalty.

Such was the game of El Doradonne Cinema, ancient, modern synaesthesia.

There was a cradle on a table beside the chair in which Marie sat. The cradle was empty save for a beautiful toy, a wheeled chariot (each wheel one-eighth of an inch in diameter) within which lay a minute cherry from a flake of blood-wood in a Christmas tree.

'The Wheel is the gift of my father to civilizations,' said Marie.

I was invisible but a part of the Play and I spoke aloud from a corner of the hospital under the Shadow of Mr Mageye's Camera.

'El Dorado never possessed the Wheel or the Christmas tree. Labour was hard as nails. Bare hands pulled rocks and stones into pyramids.'

The Doctor-God arrived on the stage above Marie.

'It's true,' he confirmed, 'I am the ghost of an ancient medicine-king in olden times. My voice is scarcely heard nowadays. I am a king, a ruined king, yet I am worshipped in this hospital as a free spirit. Science is a free spirit. The Wheel remained a toy in my ancient kingdom. I never found the means to make it available to brutalized labourers. Indeed the labourers in El Dorado may well have been on another globe or planet. Cherries and Circuses were my promise to them, bountiful drugs and prescriptions and harvests and games to come. But alas the gap between heaven and hell continued to widen. Why this was so I could not tell. I knew there would be an uprising sooner or later. El Dorado was paradise on earth, it was heaven . . . War in heaven and upon earth! But I brushed this aside as rubbish. And even if it happened the cradle remained my enduring hope. It would fly through the air on hidden wings, hidden wheels. Yet I remembered I had reduced the cradle and the Wheel to a toy that the princess played with. I had never found the means to employ them differently. And future generations, it occurred to me, might do the same. Thus it was that I grew a blood-red Christmas tree in El

Doradonne forests. Are not ghost-kings – such as myself – the true originators of Christmas? They appear in your Dream-book, Francisco, as magi of medicine, of law, and of the Camera. My dream now – which you may share in this hospital (I do not know) – is that medicine (the science of medicine) may extract the venom from brutalized species and brutalized labour through intercourse with the Scorpion Constellation. That venom would be converted into a serum or a medium of inoculation to achieve immunity to pain.'

I shook my head in fervent disagreement. But his eyes were upon the Princess Marie. Was I visible to him, to his X-ray eyes? A shudder ran through Marie's frame. She clutched the cradle to her heart. No tears in this instance. Yet hollow tears of Beauty are sometimes the most heartrending of all.

I felt her anguish in myself. It was bitter as hell. I loved her with all my heart. No tears, in this instance, scalded my eyes. No tears, in this instance, were consistent with an inner, unconsumable fire in the wilderness Virgin, a fire one could understandably misconceive as hell. Not hell but a mirror reflecting *uncrushed* Spirit in the teeth of adversity. Uncrushed Spirit and hell sometimes seemed to walk hand in hand in the wilderness Virgin . . .

I sought to hide my eyes, and hers – as if they were wed together – in the Shadow of the Camera. Was this a heretical wedding? Had I taken Deacon's place? A Dream. Nothing more.

One sees but is blinded in seeing . . .

'Blinded less by Beauty than by what the apparition of Beauty begins to signify for the age in which you live, Francisco,' I thought I heard the Virgin say. 'Beauty can easily be framed by mass-media churches and states and cynical marketplaces. But when fire weeps yet does not seem to weep it breaks the frame. That breakage is misconceived as hell. For it plunges the world into mental anguish, it disrupts planetary hypocrisy, it disrupts the trade in commodities of framed Beauty, commodities of pigmentation that mask a void. God is dead! God is a Prisoner on Devil's Isle. The truth is that the Apparition of Beauty within the hollow eyes of a child brings innermost fire that may sustain

94

us to question all frames, all partialities, all literalities that we enshrine as absolutes . . .'

At last she arose from her chair draped in the Shadow of Mr Mageye's Camera. I dared not feast my eyes upon her terrible, childlike loveliness.

I seemed to gaze upon her within the fragmentation of my own composite, epic body. She approached the framed cherry tree in the kingdom of the Golden Man of El Dorado. She moved upon the Utopian Bridge into that ruined kingdom. The tree was wounded, her Apparition was wounded, her eyes were wounded, the numinous child in the cradle that I could not see was held by her to her breast in the game that she played with the Gods in her nursery in El Dorado.

I could not bear to look but I saw it all nevertheless through Mr Mageye's fragmented Camera with its ancient, futuristic lenses.

She moved in her apparitional, royal nursery to another tree.

This resembled the ornamental branches in a Japanese garden. I swore now that I saw Prisoner-Gods, Prisoners of War hanging from it. Were they weak, were they mutilated? They held the Atom Bomb in their fingertips. At last she moved to the Christmas tree. She placed the cradle of a sick God beneath it. Was it possessed all at once of the lineaments of the patients in the hospital?

I bowed my head still further but I could not rid myself of the Virgin's eyes, the Virgin Princess's childlike fiery eyes.

They burnt a hole into the Camera.

I had sailed in that hole into the vanished kingdom of El Dorado. I had sailed East, I had sailed West, I had sailed North, I had sailed South, to sight the Golden sick Man in a village hospital in Port Mourant.

'Marie,' I cried, 'the king at your breasts whom you rock invisibly in your arms has left the stage and become a child in your arms, a child at your breasts. A sick king. A patient in this hospital. What a bridge across ages! If only I could tread upon it. So many bridges to cross. *There he is!* The Doctor is back. Your father is back. He does not perceive the game that you play. He thinks he is well. He leans over the patient with the dog

95

resembling a lamb lapping milk. He does not see that you have pooled his reflection into the North and the South, into the East and the West, into a collective desire for gold everywhere, gold without pain. He does not see. Do I truly see? Do I truly understand? Let me lift him from your imaginary cradle and address him as the ghost of gold and medicine and science.

'Doctor,' I cried, 'you are the Virgin's son and father in this riddle of theatre. She sees you playing many parts, she sees me playing many parts, she sees us with the eyes of *uncrushed* Spirit.

'Doctor,' I cried again, 'you are blind, you need her eyes to see in this hospital. Her eyes are the fire of *uncrushed* spirit.'

I held up my left hand with its phantom fingers. They were possessed of music even as the Virgin's childlike being was possessed of ancient wisdom. Had I not heard her speak in an impossible tongue that had long vanished from the face of the earth?

The Doctor turned his back on me and made his way off the stage. Was he displeased with his daughter? Words seemed pointless now against the displeasure of a God. To whom should I pray?

'Pray to uncrushed Spirit in every newborn child with whom you share an apparently empty cradle,' said Mr Mageye. 'Pray to the heart of the Wilderness. Pray in silence, pray to invisibility's wounds. All wounds, all stigmata, carry a silent and invisible counterpoint in the orchestra of ages. Silence speaks nevertheless, invisibility surfaces nevertheless, through you into a community of selves. One knows yet does not know one's wounds in all their range and particularity; yet they are stored in some private mystery or theatre of music that animates oneself to come abreast of deprivation and numbness in humanity across the ages. One sees it in some unforgettable moment or glimpse into the temple of the human body as much as in the forlorn possessions in Carnival Lord Death's Limbo marketplace. One strikes an exquisite chord or lament in the orchestra of ages with absent fingers upon a piano in a pawnshop, or on a beach against a golden flood of hollow materialism, or on the wave of a desert. The apparently irredeemable structure and plot of a civilization breaks . . .'

I waited within what seemed the displeasure of God (or of the Doctor-God). And it dawned on me to my astonishment that my unspoken prayer to uncrushed Spirit had been answered within the net of the Virgin's hair.

Marie – the nurse – in her oversize, slightly ridiculous uniform, had turned from El Dorado in Guyana to the patient with the dog. I turned myself to Mr Mageye in further astonishment – 'Is it possible?' I cried. 'He holds a long strand of her hair in his hand. Not to employ as a lasso for the Horses on the Moon as Deacon did or as Alexander the Great may have desired to do when El Dorado was an empire. No – look Mr Mageye – he coils it into a net. Have I not glimpsed that net before? In Limbo Land! I remember. The huntsman and his dog! He saved my life.' I stopped to consider the extremities of response to unspoken prayer in wilderness theatre, wilderness orchestra.

When music and unspoken prayer animate language, all proportionalities of being and non-being, genesis and history, are subject to a re-visionary focus.

The Wilderness comes into its own as extra-human territory which unsettles the hubris of a human-centred cosmos that has mired the globe since the Enlightenment.

The interrelationships between the sciences and the arts – that ancient humanity may have sought to nourish within its crises and difficulties – address diminutive survivors of holocausts (such as myself) all over again in new and startling ways.

I voiced these thoughts to console myself. I was bewildered by the sudden dawning light on the countenance of the sick patient in the Port Mourant hospital. He was arising from the floor now with the net in his hand. I was bewildered . . . . How could I have seen that net before in Limbo Land – when he flung it around the Predator and saved my life – if he had suddenly acquired it now from the wilderness nest of the Virgin's hair?

Was it the same net? Was it an old net? Was it a new net?

Such are the paradoxes of musical chords that compose a net in the language of fiction.

Was it possible that a deeply sprung chord of music is unique and untranslatable fiction and therefore both old and new? Was it possible that the strange density of the net – arising from the universal wilderness unconscious into the subconscious and the conscious – was of quantum linkage and differentiation and thus what was old was new, what was young was ancient, Virgin was child, child was ancient mother of humanity in the live fossil nursery of language?

I was so bewildered that I had no hesitation in setting forth my thoughts as if to plumb some tracery, however elusive, of the depths of unspoken prayer . . . I prayed to a disembodiment and an Apparition and an Abstraction that I felt I perceived in the sick man's Christ-like face.

Why sickness? How sick was my *projection* of sickness, the archetype of sickness, *into the huntsman* in whose dawning light upon his face I dreamt I saw Christ? In such sickness I saw a dying age (though when that age would die, if ever, I did not know). Still it was implicitly dying and imbued with new elements of a re-visionary genesis of the hunt . . . The sickness of slaughter for slaughter's sake was subtly evolving beyond fixtures of cruelty into a net to save me and hold the Predator at bay.

An enormous theme this was that I needed to ponder upon again and again and again.

'Is it an insoluble net, Mr Mageye?' I asked.

'You must seek to understand,' said Mr Mageye. 'You must seek to visualize its tracery or traceries everywhere in Memory theatre. Remember, Francisco.'

'I remember Limbo Land when I thought I would be crushed by the Predator but was saved by the huntsman. I did not see his face then even as I dream I see it now in a patient arising from a bed . . .'

'You were caught in the same net that the huntsman used in bundling the Predator away . . .'

'Why did he not kill him, make an end of him? Would not that have solved everything, Mr Mageye?'

'Ah! Francisco, have you forgotten that in desiring the Predator's end you were compulsively drawn to him . . . ?'

'*Me*? Was I?'

'Yes, you! You were fascinated by his magnetic charm and

terrifying beauty. Try to remember. A beauty that you compared – do you now remember? – to the marbled hide of the globe seen from the Moon. Indeed the Predator has no qualms in wearing the elements of earth and sky on his back. It's not so astonishing. You, Francisco – and I for that matter – wear shoes of leather, the occasional fur hat, the occasional skin of a creature. Though nowadays conscience pricks.'

'Are you suggesting,' I cried, 'that the Predator and I are equal prey – or shared prey (an odd way to put it) – in the huntsman's net?' I stopped and considered as Mr Mageye riveted his glance upon me. An odd kind of broken, uneasy conversation we had been having . . . 'I remember,' I said slowly, 'that in desiring his end my heart grew faint as though his end could prove to be mine as well.'

Mr Mageye smiled as though to hearten me afresh in my fear of self-induced closure within the magnetic compass of the Predator.

Then he cried: 'Surely you know, Francisco, that there are no endings to a Dream-book of creation animated by music . . .'

'I know nothing. Not a damned thing.'

Mr Mageye suddenly grew grave. 'I understand your pain, Francisco,' he said. 'But consider. Here's the crux of the net. Crux – I can hear you saying – is an odd word to associate with a fluid net. There is no ending, no closure, to the *text* of the prey in which you reside, the text of the Predator that you abhor and admire. Mind you! I am guessing in the dark. For there's a hidden text of elusive differentiations in Predator and prey that lies behind all "beginnings" and beyond all "endings". That is one awkward way of putting it. But I must be honest. Those hidden texts may never – I would say will never – be absolutely translated. They are wilderness music. They infuse an uncharted realm, a mysterious density, into every chart of the Word. They infuse immense curiosity and vitality as well in empowering the vulnerable prey (such as ourselves) to seek for endless translations in time of differentiations within ourselves between prey and Predator.'

'What am I to make of the huntsman's intervention when he threw his net and saved my life?'

'Spared the life of the Predator as well! Each creature tends to prey on another.'

'Where then lies the difference between me and . . . ?'

Mr Mageye held up his hand. 'The difference lies in prayer.' Prayer? I was stunned but I understood. I understood the jest or pun.

'Unspoken prayer matches hidden texts. One prays that one is free to offer one's body to another in sacramental love. One prays for such freedom.'

'And the Predator?'

'The Predator draws blood, the blood of lust. The Predator sometimes seems invincible. The prey *knows* he is vulnerable and even when he prides himself on being unscathed in the huntsman's net his blood nourishes the sun. All this is susceptible to extremity as we saw in the late Mayan world when men's hearts were *literally* presented to the sun. Hidden texts teach us to breach such frames, such literality . . . The ghost of the prey in ourselves, the vulnerable prey, that we offer to the sun, is an unfathomable inspiration of grace, hidden grace in all subject creatures, that transcends frame or literality or predatory coherence or plot. But may I remind you, Francisco! Dream-books are translations of the untranslatable. It is a vocation that may well take us through and beyond the stars into life's blood on other planets.'

'Why did not the huntsman intervene and save the people of Jonestown?'

Mr Mageye riveted his glance upon me again.

'Come, come, Francisco,' he said. 'You know – you must know in all that you have confided to me in your Dream-book – how odd, how varied, divine intervention in human affairs is. It's not easy to read the signals, to respond to the warnings. Our minds are often closed . . .'

'Was mine closed?'

'Of course it was. Habit dies hard. I speak of myself as well. Educators such as myself need to be re-educated . . .'

'But . . . But . . .'

'I know, Francisco. I am in your Dream-book and I know that your mind cracked a little in Jonestown. Your mind-set that is! But consider how charged and peculiar was your apprehension of intervention. You were driven to weigh and assess the shot that killed Jones in the nick of time, your own phantom hand on the gun, the pain of self-confession, self-accusation, numbness, numbness that erupts from one's wounds, one's traumatization that is built unwittingly into past weaponries, future weaponries, technologies . . . Yes, it's all there in your Dream-book and still you are challenged to consider and reconsider the ground of experience.' He was laughing all at once but I could scarcely fathom his humour. Was he laughing with me, at me, with himself, at himself? 'Intervention by the divine cannot be entirely divorced from laughter at oneself, one's refusal sometimes to read the signs until it is too late or almost too late.' His expression was grave, half Sphinx-like again. I was aware of his lightning shifts of mood.

'Take your own case again, Francisco. The gun that Deacon fired seemed to flash into your mind as if it had been built out of the concretion of your own trauma, your own numbness. *There*'s a warning from which civilization recoils! Perhaps it is unable to read the signs! It refuses to countenance its own predicament in the light of technologies that are – at a certain level – an extension of the trauma of an age: *a trauma that is building a void into sensibility*. New technologies should bring into play profound and new literacies of the Imagination. They are sprung in part from ourselves, our defects, our deprivations however novel they seem. They may appear to be our slaves, our servants, but as in the Virgin's El Doradonne cradle (do you remember?) – the play in the hospital – they are already becoming toys for the privileged wealthy, or well-to-do areas of civilization, privileged nurseries, toys that we are unable to translate into the genuine service of humanity. The signs are there, the necessity for a different comprehension of the language of reality. The signs of intervention, the intervention of divine furies, are all there, but are we responding? Will our response come too late? Will it ever come?'

Mr Mageye had stopped but his glance was still riveted upon me. Suddenly I wondered if it was he, my beloved teacher, or whether it was an extraordinary eye in the Camera beside him. Had his apparition frozen into a parallel spectre of technology? Was I witnessing a species of dual technology, apparition and frozen spectre?

Was this an intervention in my Dream-book to be weighed and sifted in returning to Jonestown in Memory theatre?

I recalled the Day of the Dead when I lay on my pillow of stone and arose at nightfall in the bushes. I recalled my half self-accusatory, half self-confessional response to Deacon's intervention and to the Virgin's intervention in moments that seemed my last on Earth.

I knew then how ill-equipped I was to fathom intervention *through* the masks of fallen angels and Gods and Virgins (all of whom themselves are surrogates of an unfathomable Creator), *through* hidden texts that I needed to consider and reconsider again and again and to match with unspoken prayer . . .

'Intervention by divine powers,' I said at last to Mr Mageye, 'is a challenge to the responses it seeks to invoke.'

He sensed my bewilderment as I faced him, two-in-one dual being he seemed, apparition and frozen spectre, frozen into solidity.

He said darkly to me: 'I shall break, I shall break into many extensions, I shall appear to dissolve, a necessary trick.'

'No, no,' I cried in desperation. 'I need you, Mr Mageye. What would I do without you?'

Mr Mageye gave his warm and magical smile. 'It's not yet time for me to depart from your Dream-book, Francisco. A warning that's all. We have much still to do together. Have we not? We are still erecting a Memory theatre.'

'But why break, why leave me?'

Mr Mageye touched me without appearing to touch me. He was deeply moved in himself by my need of him.

'One guesses in the dark, Francisco, about the nature of the Creator as a subject to be taught in the history of creation. Should we not perceive creation itself as an extraordinary fiction susceptible to varieties of hidden texts . . . ?'

'Translations of the untranslatable that move us to look through and beyond ourselves?' I could not help laughing at myself.

'Quite so, quite so, Francisco. Without a sensation of uncharted realms, extra-human dimensions, I am inclined to feel that one is destined to freeze or burn in an absolutely human-centred cosmos inevitably promoting dominion and lust as its hidden agenda. It's simple really, though some will insist it is difficult. The paradox of extra-human characterization in your Dream-book which brings surrogate Gods, surrogacies of a Creator, is that the surrogates (kings or Gods or angels or phenomenal Jesters or Judges or whatever) may appear to stand on platforms in space, to walk on a wave or a vortex, or whatever, but they surrender a hidden agenda of dominion in fiction which takes its cue from uncharted reflexes built into space. Those reflexes are akin to the wilderness music of the Word. Thus the agenda of absolute command over all species and things breaks, and surrogate Gods – whether they are fully conscious of it or not – disperse their apparently broken limbs into supportive organs of disadvantaged cultures and a sick humanity everywhere.'

I was so excited I could scarcely speak.

'It seems to me, Mr Mageye,' I said at last, 'that there is a sacred Wound built (if I may so put it) into the Creator, a confessional deity-Wound which matches the reflexes of uncharted space. The Wound is so mysterious that it cannot be measured . . . But it is this which authorizes at some level of hidden grace – in counterpoint to orders of dominion – the dismemberment of Gods into supportive organs everywhere.'

For some uncanny, emotional reason – some uncanny wound within philosophy that brings ecstasy and pain – I found myself laughing with Mr Mageye. But laughter ceased and we began to consider terrorizing and terrorized regimes, cruel natures. How does the intervention of the Creator apply? Can we read or translate such intervention within the dismemberment of Gods?

'One is in the dark, Francisco. But I would venture to say that this is a question that runs beyond all man-made frames or realisms or commandments. We need to adventure into intangible graces in counterpoint with terrors in nature. Not beauty for beauty's sake, or realism for social realism's sake. These are often disguised kingdoms of dominion that we would chart in nature and in history. There are intangible graces that we cannot seize but whose tracery exists in a web or a vein or the music of a bird or some other creature. These may suddenly illumine the intensity

objects or definite ideas, but Harris denies this
standard model + combines the word with another
meaning: indefinable and transitory. The word
isra which holds it's meaning in being seen, is hidden
one critic suggests that language is emptied + that images

and extensity of a shared Wound within live, fossil realities of space, the *psychicality* of the living fossil . . . Such traceries are of immense archetypal significance and they break through absolute predatory coherence or plot . . .'

I glanced around within the chasm of space, in which the Earth revolved, and back through veils and intangible resources into the Port Mourant hospital in which the sick man was arising from his bed with his dog or lamb at his heels.

'Shared Wound! I understand, Mr Mageye. Tell me more please! Is the imprint or tattoo on my Lazarus arm an aspect of that shared Wound?'

'If it is,' said Mr Mageye warily, cautiously, 'it means that *you*, Francisco – as you wrestle with the severity of trauma – need to revisit Jonestown. You cannot do so without the horn of the huntsman and the sound of the flute. The huntsman wears the mask of Christ. The horn and the flute are branches of the archetype of a numinous and pagan Christ who summons Lazarus from the grave. That summons will take us through the Wheel of Virgin space. Your fate – if I may so put it as I read the signs, Francisco – is to venture into the music that addressed Lazarus, the music of the womb of space, the music of remarriage – in your case, Francisco – to the people of Jonestown. How can one break the trauma of the grave and not find oneself involved in a remarriage to humanity? I do not envy you the task. It is a terrifying embrace to remarry a perverse humanity, a bitter task, a bitter threshold or re-entry into Jonestown. *And yet it has to be done.* I can promise you a genuine ecstasy nevertheless, before I depart, and the trial that lies before you – however tormenting – will prove a liberation . . . I cannot say more for, in some ways, as I read the signs, I am as much in the dark as yourself, Francisco. Let me say however that *your projection of sickness upon the Christ-archetype* is an unspoken cry for help, a cry from the grave into which you dreamt you fell when you lay on a pillow of stone on the Day of the Dead.'

How could I feel anything but sorrow and anguish in the light of such remarks? And yet I would not have relinquished the challenge even if I could.

2. The juxt. of words 'elu '$\overline{104}$' f' followed by 'w' + 'v' illustrates Harris's project which sets the concrete + the apprehensional side by side. The word foundation is associated with concrete +

'None can respond to your cry, the unspoken cry of humanity, save the Christ-archetype upon which you project the sickness of an age, a sickness rooted in an eclipse of orchestrated imageries that bear on the enigma of the hunt, the enigma of genesis, the enigma of birth, the enigma of savage numinosity as much as phenomenal summons through dissonances and consonances to the dead . . . LOOK! THERE HE GOES, FRANCISCO. The horn sounds in the branch of a tree. The flute cries in creatures that we consume. Do you hear, Francisco?'

'Yes, I do,' I said quietly. 'He also bears the net from the Virgin bride's hair. And he holds a door ajar in the Wheel, a door between worlds, between ages, between times. That door cannot be seized. It is untranslatable space . . .'

Mr Mageye and I followed the huntsman through the door in the Wheel into Jonestown, early 1978, tropical Spring. We heard the noises of the town, a living town, unconscious of being hauled up from the grave in which it lay since the day of the holocaust.

'I remember clearly,' I said to Mr Mageye. 'Would you believe it?'

'Believe what?' said Mr Mageye matter-of-factly. 'Believe that the huntsman accepted statistical pay when he was employed by Jones around this time? *This* time! When one voyages back from the future into the past it is not just time that changes, it is the spatialities inserted into time that are different. He accepted statistical pay to mask himself as a Nobody.'

Yes, I saw now in Memory theatre that there had been something odd about the huntsman when he accepted the job in Jonestown back in the future from which I had returned to this Dream-book changed spatiality.

I remembered now the way his hands moved to articulate a spiralling touch upon the dollars that he received. He touched his pay as if it were sampled money in a pool of numbers justifying astronomical rewards to the managers of privileged companies and religious, sweatshop pay to someone like himself. Statistical justice in the pool of the marketplace! On occasion I had seen him come to the Carnival Circus that Jonah sometimes sponsored. I

105

had seen him wave a single dollar in the air and convert it into a huge bunch of fluttering pieces of paper.

Was it a statistical hoax, or caveat, or illumination of the fraud perpetrated on the Bank of America of which Jonah Jones was accused by the Police?

Eventually Jones's suspicions were aroused that the huntsman was some kind of underground agent. He sent him packing straightaway. He did not relish such a warning to his flock. I had not understood or perceived the warning myself – executed it seemed now with a curiously dismembered hand – until I followed the huntsman through the door in the Wheel . . . The dog or the lamb at his heels invoked the invaluable life of the species of genesis. Nobody's dog, Nobody's lamb, imbued the huntsman's pace, the latitude of his grasp, with a watchful eye for all species, care, scrupulous measure of instinct to put numinous flesh in the shape of living masks, plucked from Carnival Lord Death, upon the Bone of wasted lives that survivors of holocaust harbour in themselves.

Space was intrinsic to re-visionary narratives of changed time. I followed the huntsman and his dog or lamb in the music of space into the elusive foundations of Jonestown which lay, I knew, in the hidden vistas of modern and pre-Columbian civilizations.

We were walking in two forests, parallel forests, parallel universes. I shook myself at the thought of such trespass.

We were on the margins of Jonestown (or Jonah City) . . .

I concentrated on the silvery-grey bark of tall, skyscraper greenheart out of which the Port Mourant hospital had been built and which we employed in the construction of Jonestown in the 1970s up to 1978.

A delicate balance needed to be struck, a delicate clock of space, ticking space. The Reverend Jonah Jones was insistent that the treasury of the lofty trees – in which Jonestown was set – must be nurtured even as we made use of it. He had – to give him credit – issued the strictest instructions of which Deacon and I approved. For a Forest is akin to a Bomb. When it blows apart birds cease to sing.

'It is Spring 1978,' I said to the huntsman. 'The prospects look bright for the new town.'

The giant leaf of parallel ages shivered under my feet, whispered.

The shadow of the grave with its rubbled door through which we had come cracked a vein in my mind within the music of the raining, sun-bathed leaves settling on the ground like a pillow resembling stone.

I heard the shivering leaf again and remembered how I had ignored it in the future from which I had come. I had ignored its intervention in seeking to warn me of the poisoned cup against the shattered lips of the woman in the Clearing; in seeking to warn me of the shaking bushes as well in which I hid from Jones.

The Forest opened all at once and we had arrived at the edge of a sawyers' pit. Stalwart sawyers they seemed in the raining shadow and light of the leaves as they sliced limbs and planks from the fallen living body of trees.

I felt the sawyers' living breath upon me in the lungs of the trees.

There were three pairs of active sawyers in the long wide pit to which I had come. Each pair operated a formidable saw with rhythmic precision.

A faintly mesmeric and profound shadow of music – sprung from the huntsman's horn in a tree – enveloped the sawyers and myself.

Mr Mageye whispered that this was a portent of my remarriage to the people of Jonestown.

The sawn timber echoed the sound and dismemberment, the depth of dismemberment, of ancient tree-gods in the service of humanity.

They (those tree-gods) shone with the mysterious, alarming light of aroused flesh-and-blood, trembling flesh-and-blood wood that steamed, it seemed, as it arose from the pit.

The light in the incalculable glow and gloom of the Forest seemed to boil everywhere within the pit, within the noises of bustling Jonestown that one could hear through curtains of leaves, bustling Jonestown arisen from its grave; it floated within and above the implements that the sawyers used like a mist in vein and artery to be traced in trunk or tool or body. It seemed to differentiate inwardly and outwardly – as it <u>flocked</u> within the sawyers' arms – a range of perverse resurrections within an alchemy of true resurrections in our apprehension of the daily tasks that we perform and the materials that we use . . .

The timber and limbs and sawn material stacked beside the pit possessed an uncanny patience. Yes, they were the gift of the tree-gods to Jonestown. One legend has it that the Creator created Man from dust.

Dust – when it arises into archetypal bodies and branches and horns and flutes – embraces tree-god wood as much as live, <u>fossil</u> stone or pillow of rock. Beds, chairs, desks, walls, windows are patient receptacles for flesh to lie upon, or move within, in its arousal from dust. Thus the equation between tree-god wood and flesh (animal and human) is shaped upon intangible frontiers between inanimate and animate, legendary worlds and ages . . .

Those frontiers secrete different pulses, different rhythms, and <u>the pulse of the inanimate</u> (however apparently remote or hidden) is as real as the pulse of animal creatures . . . One is possessed by shock when one flees from the dead and discovers a measure of disguise they possess in instruments and furniture that one had long ignored as passive features of nothingness. That shock is implicit in the shadow of music upon frontiers of being and non-being that begin to levitate and change places. I remembered the Day of the Dead when I arose from the bushes and fled into the Night of the Forest.

I remembered the bodies piled everywhere from which I fled.

I remembered their effort to dance to shadow music in the leaves of the whispering Forest, shadow orchestra of dust, as they half-crouched, half-lay, half-stood leaning against a wall, half-knelt with their head in the flattened bowl of the sun.

I remembered the black-lit grave yawning at the heart of the Night when I came upon the sawyers' pit. The sawyers had fled. There was a glowing lantern in the pit or I would have fallen headlong into it. I paused at the edge with beating heart. Tools, garments of all shapes and colours, were scattered helter-skelter in

108

the pit. The bodies that I had seen in the flat bowl of the sun lay here as well in the circling lantern light as the wind blew. Their heels were chiselled, their ankles were bolts and nuts, and their brow of the sun – the windblown, flattened, shadowy, bowl of the sun – addressed them as awakening lantern light, in the pit, anticipating my return to bustling Jonestown in the middle of the day.

I could not however quite rid myself of the memory of the grave into which I had come so close to falling in November 1978.

I could not quite rid myself of 'middle of the night' November 1978 – when I came close to falling into the sawyers' pit – though I knew I had returned to 'middle of the day' Tropical Spring in the selfsame year. I stood on the frontier between shapes of time, past future, future present.

I prided myself that I had not fallen in the 'middle of the night' and yet on that frontier between 'middle of the day' and 'middle of the night' I sensed another shape to myself that had fallen.

That shape was a key I felt to unlocking another door into Jonestown, a key that the huntsman provided. He had been there in that 'middle of the night' and had caught the other shape of myself that fell.

'Your skeleton-twin!' Mr Mageye whispered. 'You need that twin to orchestrate Bone – the Bone or survivor that you are – into the Carnival news of a further re-entry into Jonestown.

'On that day of the holocaust you survived, Francisco Bone, but something integral to the fabric of yourself remained behind within the trauma of the grave. A skeleton-twin! You saw it fall though you did not fall! You saw the gleaming net (or perhaps it is visible only now in the "middle of the day") that held it as it fell. Held it to return it to you as a companion-key to coming events (or past events?) as you tread a frontier between shapes of time.'

'Turn the key of Night and Day, built into yourself, and enter Jonestown.' It was the huntsman who spoke but the voice may have been a whisper in the horn of a tree.

I hesitated. The nakedness of my skeleton-twin made me wonder if I (Bone) were naked too.

But then – as if to reassure me – the huntsman waved his horn.

A cloud of particles arose in the 'middle of the day' as the sawyers sliced into the flesh of wood. Their rhythmic slicing spread a carpet of golden-white dust upon the ground from the spoil of the trees. I was clothed in that cloud in flesh or fleece. The dog at the huntsman's heel became a frisky lamb.

I now slipped into the bustling throngs of Jonestown. Clouds rose overhead. A blue sky. So blue it seemed porous with the memory of Night. So easy it seemed, as people brushed past, to embrace everyone; to love everyone, to lose oneself in everyone. I stood still in the slow raining curtain of the sun's blue shadow instinct with a coming Storm, a faint premonition in the dome of space, inner flesh of the middle of night I still remembered in counterpoint to fleecy cloud.

My skeleton-twin was beside me now on the rude pavement of the new town. It was a holiday in Jonestown. He was wheeling a bicycle on which were stacked two columns of newspapers, one on the saddle, one on the handlebar. I reached out to embrace him but he thrust my Lazarus-arm aside with a jarring rebuff.

It was so unexpected I was seized with chagrin. Was he not my twin? Was he a stranger?

I sought to cover my pain by pointing to the newspapers.

He interpreted this as an unspoken question.

'The *Carnival Argosy*,' he said. 'You should know, Francisco.'

I said nothing.

'Let me jog your wretched memory, Francisco. Yes, I shall! When I broke from you and fell into the pit I took part of your memory with me. Memory is archetypal. It is shared between fleshed Bone and twin-skeleton. Thus it is sometimes that a society sustains itself. One is in blessed ignorance of what the other suffers. I kept you going. I made survival a shade of flesh easier for you. But now it's time. I have been in hell. And it's time you knew. Every charismatic cult breeds hell. You were Jones's left-hand man and close associate. To give you credit in an age of lies you have never hidden the fact! So when I broke out of your fleeing body on the day of the holocaust I took the rap. I took my hell with me to give you a Limbo chance to grow flesh upon our mutual grave. You see Francisco the truth is never static, it needs re-visionary momentum in all proportions of narrative convention or conviction, the truth can never set us free unless we are multi-faceted and able to face our indebtedness not only to surrogate Gods but to obscure twins in the family of Skeleton and Bone . . .'

I was shaken. I was appalled. The assault took me by surprise. I thought I had been coming along well in my Dream-book. But I knew now that I had scarcely begun. I needed to dip into hidden texts of the grave to achieve some measure of translation of the hell that I had – perhaps unwittingly – helped to build when I joined Jones's charismatic cult.

And the newspapers on the bicycle! Had my skeleton-twin taken them into the pit when he fell and left me at the edge of a lantern-lit Night in the darkness of the Forest?

'I lay under the *Carnival Argosy*,' he said, 'until now. News-papers were my perverse Virgin Ship, Francisco. I lay under them in the pit. A pillow of earth and stone and leaves under my head. Rich juicy scandal. The Virgin press is wed to bridegroom Money.'

He gave me his faint lightning smile that was harnessed to underground distant thunder.

'We arranged, Francisco – you and I – when we planned a Carnival celebration for Jonestown to take place in the Spring, *this* Spring, to ride with the *Carnival Argosy* on our head upon a bicycle, distribute it to the cult membership of Jonestown, and pass Jones's copies to him in his house at the edge of the river. I see you have forgotten, Brother.'

I tried to pretend I had not but my skeleton-twin, or brother of the grave, was sharp as a nail, a seeing nail in a hollow socket.

'Let me jog your memory again, Francisco! Jones acceded to our request to stage the celebratory RETURN OF THE LIVING FROM THE DEAD such as is staged in Maya folkloric villages, South American settlements, and in Mexico City every year. As for another title . . . well, we debated several. Remember? UNDER THE CAVE OF THE MOON (into which you fled Francisco). UNDER THE STORM OF THE MOON. We even considered UNDER THE VOLCANO. But abandoned that . . .'

His tone was lighter perhaps, self-mocking, jesting. Perhaps he had glimpsed Mr Mageye. I was more drawn to him in this instant

111

*their relationship to character. Flock is a christian image of . . .
Another example is*

and I cried: 'Good God! Did Jones really agree to such a Carnival? I remember he was totally against such pagan Memory theatre!'

The Skeleton's Carnival lips crackled into a blissful smile riddled nevertheless with accusation.

'You do remember something after all, Francisco! But let me continue to prod – is that the right word? – into the archetypal recesses of Memory theatre. Jonah felt that to give you what you wanted was to encourage you to keep your head well below the parapet of memory. Even as I kept mine in the pit. He knew that you could raise hell if you wished. And so you shall! But Jonah bargained on giving you a licence for hollow ritual. Carnival resurrection might become an end in itself, a hollow ritual in itself, hollow theatre in itself. The best thing he felt was to give you latitude for hollow Carnival year after year. You might then come to forget what it was all about. Play dead, play resurrection, to your heart's content, until in the end the banner of conquest in his hand would prevail and seal hollow resurrection into the death of living memory, living archetype.

'Yes, Jones's brand of religion, Jones's split between the dead past (so-called) and the future (so-called), Jones's irredeemable universe, can prove a killing dogma, a killing manifesto directed at the heart of originality . . . Pity him by all means, Francisco, love him, yes, if you can, he is (or was) your associate – indeed a friend – as human as you are, as human as all fallible establishments. But remember it is hell that springs from the grave of memory where it has long slumbered and cries out to be portrayed in its true colours of intolerance and tyranny within dogmatic and charismatic cults.'

I was stunned but the ramifications were clear. The Christ of the conquistadores possessed a twin in the sick man who arose from a hospital bed and whom I followed through the Virgin's Wheel into Jonestown. Sickness was a skeletal aspect of the hell into which Christ had descended. Health was flesh on the Bone within the split materialistic/spiritual mind of my age. *Numinous paganism was a gleaming web or net or medium of a true resurrection of archetypal memory.* It was a net in which to salvage a broken world and reclaim its bearing on a living future . . .

Ideology: carry into catastrophic event
devastation
concrete events – bk concerned with
imagination
cosmic relevance

Hell was around the corner but we rode through heaven into the Carnival crowd which made way for us. My skeleton-twin held the *Carnival Argosy* on his head. He sat on the towing bar of the bicycle that ran from the pole of the saddle to the pole of the handlebar. I pedalled on the saddle and achieved a miraculous balance with a column of newspapers on my head. We distributed them into the crowd with amazing Circus sleight-of-hand.

The huntsman and his dog ran as lithe as Spirit beside us.

We were all upheld between parallel cloths and elements and were spinning along on surrogacies of the Virgin's Wheel within blossom that rained on the futuristic grave of Jonestown, the futuristic grave of the globe.

1. Blossom and cloud and the foam of the sea were parallel Sleeps and Wakings.
2. One novel element lives dies, another dies lives . . .
3. Spring springs eternal but it is broken in the subtle and changing, quintessentially flexible organs of time.

Such are the harbours and investitures that I wear with my twin.

Blossom, sea, river, land, space are Bone's flesh that I wear in a Skeleton's waking heaven arisen in the grave of space.

Spring and Bone voice together the rhythms and veins in the music of a tree. Time is the precipitation of sleight-of-hand eternities in masks and sculptures, the masked, etched bloom of forests, the winged traceries of cloud, blending, re-forming, reshaping into unfinished web, unfinished catastrophe or unfinished regeneration, heaven . . .

Heaven was an omen. It could not be taken for granted. Beauty was heartrending mystical truth. Every idyll carried an edge of harshness to awaken the palate of memory. I had travelled in the very processions on the road – largely unseeing then in the future from which I had returned to the past-in-the-present – towards the holocaust that lay across mist-ridden, wonderful vistas into the heart of the town. Now I knew (or thought I knew) the rhythms of a universe rooted in unconscious and subconscious interventions of grace that stimulate a tapestry of response possessed of its ominous grain as well as its primordial ecstasy.

P.C. context – Harris writes beyond the actual + personal events of history, and uses the idea of imagination, an inter-national space to express humanness.

I had been akin to a soldier marching through a living, paradisean landscape embroidered in the labyrinths of the rainforest. A paradise that was to assume with hindsight the fabric of a terrifying, haunting, indeed monstrous beauty in that one was marching into horror, into gunfire, into murder.

The fabric of catastrophe dwelt in Carnival heaven as paradoxical intervention of grace that prepared me now to respond at many levels within the composite epic imagination in my Dream-book. I steeled myself for my encounter with the formidable solid ghost of the Reverend Jonah Jones in my return from the future into the present-in-the-past, return from futuristic winter 1978 to spring 1978 and the crowd of Carnival ghosts through which I rode to Jonah Jones's house at the edge of the Jonestown river.

I arrived with Jones's copies on my head of the *Carnival Argosy*, covering the news of a fortnight and more.

Jonah had been swimming before I arrived and had received a glancing but heavy blow to his head from a hidden log just under the surface of the stream.

He felt like a log himself. The twin-wood or log which struck him may have slipped into a tributary to the main Jonestown river, a tributary that ran close to the sawyers' pit.

It had floated into the main river, notched and broken in places, a phallic organ, a phallic tree or ladder, such as South American legend associates with the body and cell of a great Prisoner in Devil's Isle, French Guyana, bordering Dutch, British, Spanish, Portuguese Guyanas. One could place other titles and masks upon them if one wished – Surinam, Brazil, Venezuela . . .

Jonah Jones was the Prisoner's perverse twin-brother! Unconscious twin-brother to the great Prisoner as he descended into the river beneath his house.

I had never dreamt of this far-flung archetypal relationship before but was prompted into doing so by my jesting Skeleton-twin who stood on the river-bank with the bicycle rattling slightly against his bones as a gentle wind blew.

I had never seen Jones in this Carnival light until now – until this revisitation of Spring, Tropical noonday Spring.

114

The Prisoner was possessed of the hell of memory, budding, frozen, scorched, reviving memory in Spring, the hell of a descent into elements that chained him to an eternity he loathed, chained him into misgivings of the reality of freedom in an irredeemable universe. Yet he wanted to reach out to his fellow prisoners everywhere and bestow freedom upon them through the dismemberment of his limbs that would gain them unsurpassed agility. A Dream! Nothing more. It was a risky matter when Prisoner-Gods entertained the gift of freedom in themselves, a gift from an unfathomable Creator. Such a gift seemed *whole*, but it *broke* in its passage through the barriers and walls of circumstance, the prisons of circumstance, in its passage into an unresponsive and perverse humanity. All archetypes are broken in their intercourse with humanity. Broken yet *active* . . .

Jonah was the other side of the fabric or the coin that charismatic Gods may bestow upon Mankind. He had settled for non-redemption for outsiders. Heaven was barred against the damned even as it locked into itself the saved in all eternity. Freedom of soul or body was a blood-soaked mirage.

Charismatic Jonah Jones had indeed suffered a close shave, he had narrowly escaped drowning in the river beneath his house. That was historical fact. What was not historical fact was his unconscious and awakening subconscious, tormenting glimpse into the Prisoner-God in himself as he rose upon a net or current to embrace the log and pull himself up by the dazed skin of his teeth in nail and hand.

He suffered a mystical dismemberment but was largely unaware of it. Still a seed of remorse, repentance, uncertainty was born, a seed he sought to disperse into nothingness.

His house stood on the bank of the river as if grounded yet floating in its reflection in the river.

It possessed a fine view upriver and downriver.

One could even glimpse – through Jonah's ghost eyes – as if one eye remained in the log in the river, the other rose above into a window in the house – rippling sun-shadow slipping around a bend (at least a mile away) beyond which, another couple of miles or so, stood the Cave of the Moon high up on a steep bank or cliff.

'Francisco, I am morally confused,' Jonah Jones said to me, when he came to the door, upon my knocking, and led me into the house, as if we were conversing on the bed of the river yet high up on reflected timbers, within reflected walls, architectures, in hell.

Difficult to record what he was actually saying.

Did he say 'morally confused' or was it 'mortally confused'?

When one revisits the past from the future memory does not conform to fixed patterns of space. Memory troubles the pit of conscience in which prisoners and living skeletons lurk, in which a phallic ladder lurks secreted with messages of the split mind of an age, moral confusion, mortal confusion.

I was fully into Jones's ghost-fractured house now, I was in the river, I was above the river.

Spring was a fracture in the phallic log or ladder to which Jonah had clung. But the question of the net remained. He had climbed up to the floating head of the log glancing down upon him through a rippling belly of water: glancing down upon him as if it were a severed, sexual eye drawn from his own head or global stick with which to beat his cult membership.

The house had become an extraordinary seminal bubble. I saw the calculating grave-digger, digger into the flesh of the earth, whom I had met in Limbo Land, reflected in it. He swore he had pushed the house into the river when he arrived in Jonestown three days after the Day of the Dead. He had ransacked the house for ticking bombs, watches, explosive money, twisted earrings of gold that Jones gave to his mistresses. He had come upon an eighteenth-century suit or heirloom that I had lent to Jones. He had put it on his own frame intending to return it to me.

I saw Carnival Lord Death's administration of hell in the grave-digger's cunning politics.

'The river here is safe as you know, Francisco,' said Jonah Jones all of a sudden. The house shook. The grave-digger's hands were upon it all over again though Jones had surfaced and gained a respite.

'No electric eels or perai hereabouts. Higher upriver perhaps but not here. That is one reason why we chose this site. Do you remember, Francisco? As I sank from the blow I received I had the sensation of a bullet in my head and my limbs grew heavier and heavier.'

He stopped.

'My brain ceased to function. And yet I remember sinking into a wilderness of currents, a kind of chasm, a Virgin Ship from which a net descended.'

'You were dreaming my Dream of survival,' I said quietly under my breath. 'There's room to accommodate hell and a passage to heaven on the Virgin Ship.'

'What's that? What's that, Francisco?'

'There's freedom of the press and of the Word on the Virgin Ship when charismatic establishments repent. So my mother used to say of the eighteenth-century ghost of a slave-owner whom she saw in her shop in Albuoystown.'

'Believe it or not, Francisco, a net of light fell around me. Talk about the game of space and constellations. Your talk, not mine! But now I'm unsure as we meet again in the light and the shadow of a running stream. Forgive me, Francisco, I'm dazed after the blow. All that stuff *you* talk about. It's as if you're dreaming me or I you.' He was glaring at me accusingly.

'Damned if I know, Francisco.'

'Damned if I know,' he repeated, 'how one returns into a book – such as you're busy writing – and into language that transgresses against one's vested interests, one's desire to seize time in the name of tradition and bring it to an end. Have not great prophets desired the end of the world? I am rambling again. It's your fault! How did it fall, that net of which I speak? A blend of currents perhaps. Strange things happen in these South American rivers that bear the ghosts of Atlantis. Circumnavigation and all that by drowned ships upon the bed of oceans. The rebirth of Conquest in the sixteenth century may have possessed its root in a map in Plato's cave.'

Strange utterance to put on Jones's ghostly lips in my Dream-book. *Ghosts of Atlantis*! But they were a form of hell's truth.

Hell's truths are branded into the mystical dismemberments of charismatic leaders when one revisits them in shapes of fractured time within the Spring of the year preceding the Winter of the holocaust.

They speak in the active, reactive, speculative, aggressive, uncertain tongue of shared ghost-psyche within writer and written that one inhabits with them. Repentance required a new language, a new archetypal tongue in a century of abnormal cruelties inflicted by humanity upon humanity.

My repentance as well! I had been Jones's left-hand man and close associate. When he received the blow in the river I felt that I had received it too in composite epic. Except that I had survived the holocaust and the burden of hell's truths was inscribed into me.

Jonah and I fenced with each other in the Dream-book, in a new Circus, New World, New Carnival of savages and heathens, pre-Christian resurrected paganism that Jones despised in his charismatic Church of Eternity. He had almost infected me with his prejudices.

He and Deacon and I would eye the Arawak and Macusi women who passed through Jonestown occasionally. Jones eyed them, one eye in the belly of river beneath the reflected timbers of his house, the other in his bedroom window . . . Save their souls, embrace their bodies! Hell's missionary truth.

Were they not – these women and their silent menfolk – ghosts of Atlantis? Had they not come precariously close to extinction across the centuries since the Conquest? Had they not seen their pre-Columbian continent, South and Central and North, fall into a veil akin to an oceanic grave as their bones, their cemeteries, their sacred places were pillaged, uprooted, cast aside? Atlantis was here in the Americas, North, Central and South. It was in the belly of a veiled ocean within the forests, the mountains, the valleys, within the dry land and the rivers.

'Heathen savages,' said Jonah, 'you may think what you like, Francisco. I am liberal enough in my School here in Jonestown to teach them good English when they send their children to me out of the Bush. Teach them to read Charles Dickens and Jane Austen and to write in the same true vein . . .'

'But when we were in College in San Francisco you told me,' I said, 'that you loved the American classics of anger in which the heathen – as you put it – feature so strikingly . . .'

'True, true,' said Jonah. 'The heathen are a stick with which to beat my cursed society. Use the heathen savage as a clarion call when you wish to upbraid your civilization. Pretend to be black or red or yellow. Say you understand what black South Africans have suffered under apartheid regimes. Eskimos, South Sea islanders, whatever. I was addicted to classics of anger. I am an American charismatic preacher. But let me tell you this, Francisco. Human nature never changes. I never doubted that the heathen savage is damned. I preach salvation to the saved who must forsake time and aim at eternity.'

He spoke to me, his close associate, as if I were not there. I was no savage! I was invisible in my Dream-book.

How peculiar are the proportions of the split mind of my age, hell . . . How peculiar are the challenges ingrained into original epic, modern epic . . . My invisibility – his difficulty to see me for what I was, who I was, neither damned nor saved but drifting somewhere between the two realms in their archetypal intercourse – was the price I must pay to suffer the anguish of addiction to American classics of anger that ran through my mixed ancestries and his puritan logic. I was linked to him in self-understanding within my Dream-book because of the humour, the elemental humour, of savage gods and goddesses though he was unaware of it.

I could see Jonah in myself, suffer him in myself, with a dark humour. I could write him into organs of fire and water even as he sought to mould me (or my heathen kith and kin) into liberal Dickensian flesh-and-blood. A liberality that made me invisible to him and ripe therefore (who knows) for salvation! Such is the predicament of savage conscience in seeking to lay bare the transgression and transfiguration of anger that I sought to achieve in my Dream-book, the transgression of anger's compulsive frame to damn and use others forever; transgression and transfiguration into a mystical dismemberment empowering a Virgin Ship, that I had begun to build, in order to cross (or contemplate crossing) every divide in hope of a third or fourth or fifth dimension beyond pure salvation or pure damnation . . .

Hell's truths make us wary of complacency in ourselves and in others, wary of charismatic institutions, wary of fascism in any disguise within ourselves, within others.

It was a complex, yet profoundly simple, self-revelation . . . But simplicity often signifies difficulty to the bloody-minded heart. So I needed to state again, from another angle, what I had been saying about the 'proportions of the split mind of my age'. I was so prompted by my Dream-book . . . The Reverend Jonah Jones (I wrote) conversed with me in hell – which I have revisited with my Skeleton-twin on this Carnival Day – about heathens and savages. He seemed blind to the fact that I am descended from such savages, that my savage conscience *knows him so intimately in itself* it endorses his predicament, his anger, even as it seeks to breach such endorsement, to transgress against categories of absolute damnation, absolute salvation . . . This riles him for he thinks he is offering me a great prize in making me – or electing me – into a pawn ripe for salvation.

His championship of me, the erstwhile savage, is a 'liberal' exercise in which 'liberalism', or 'conservatism', becomes a medium to upbraid his civilization for the impurities it houses. Likewise he harnesses heathens who have not yet attained my invisibility, who have not yet shed their savage pigmentation in his eyes, by sleeping with their sisters and mothers.

He sleeps with heathen women (in brothels and elsewhere) in order to gain through intercourse a vicarious measure of consanguinity with the age-old blood of the savage that he has forgotten he carries in his veins. Such forgetfulness is the bliss of eternity that he espouses. His tool of blood is intent on exercising a sanction that nullifies mixed ancestries, mixed origins. It is a privileged tool, privileged technology of sex, that violates women into a collective map of place to be conquered, to be saved, to be purified.

Sex therefore for the charismatic missionary Jonah Jones is purification and an atrophy of origins by way of eternity which kills time. It is a ritual and practised laceration of hollow flesh, it is a map of blood.

Poor Jonah Jones is tormented in hell that he has elected for others! Sex is closure in his eyes, it is a frame, it is the predicament of mixed ancestries, animal ancestry, human ancestry, divine ancestry. Mixed races as well! His addiction to brothels therefore is a demonstration of his privileged status. He is privileged to loathe and to enjoy the promiscuity he condemns. How else would he gain experience of what he preaches . . . *Eternity's closure of time in the brothels of civilization, doomed time* . . . Such is his sermon.

I saw all this through Jonah's eyes with tears in my eyes. We were both mixed in the spirit of hell and heaven and earth and other nameless spheres of creation. I saw his subjection to anger, to a kind of authoritarian fixture of wrath, as the hell he had created for himself and for me in this Carnival moment of my return from the future to the past . . .

Except that I dreamt of converting such anger in him and in myself into transgression against the forces of absolute damnation.

Was I capable of creating freedom within the content of visionary losses I had endured?

Was I capable of converting such losses into chasms of the self that would take me beyond the split mind of my age? Was I capable of leaping into the arms of Love, Love so terrifying (in height and depth and range) and all-inclusive it imbued me with dread? Was I capable of dying yet living in order to sustain a vessel or vessels of living time, living ghosts, Memory theatre . . . ?

Was I capable of such staggered fiction, broken trauma, in the hell of remembered Jonestown, revisited Jonestown?

Memory theatre indeed! I laughed with tears still in my eyes. I had forgotten so much.

I looked out of the window upon my Skeleton-twin. I was chastened. A column of fire arose on his Carnival skeleton head. It matched other columns upon the Carnival masquerading queens of Arawak and Macusi women whom Jones had had in his bed.

'There they are, Jonah,' I said at last. 'Spring's hotting up.'

'Heathen savages,' said Jones.

'Perhaps they would like to tip you, Jonah, into a labyrinth of fire such as you experienced . . .'

'Tip me? You are at sea in the elements, Francisco. I experienced a labyrinth or net of currents when I struck my head in the river . . .'

'Rivers burn in South America today, Jonah. Fire spouts rain. Charisma and hubris, human-centred cosmos, despoil our planet. And yet the omens are visible. Fire's speech lives in its counterpoint with rain and river. There are other voices, extra-human voices in angry living landscapes that we refuse to hear or see. To hear what one sees erupts in the senses and what is other than the senses in a language of counterpoint . . .' I spoke from a depressed mind and heart.

But then I was utterly startled, utterly astonished, to see a woman, named Circe by Jonah, standing in the crowd of ghost-revellers beside the ominous Jonestown river. I could not believe this.

I knew her now.

I had seen her on the Day of the Dead with her child in the Clearing but had not recognized her as Circe. Marie Antoinette. I knew her by that name. The Virgin of Jonestown. What a transgression of boundaries one takes for granted. What a transfiguration of animal goddess into Virgin.

Yes, I remembered in hell. Hell's truths . . .

She had been Jones's mistress in San Francisco. He swore – when he returned from one of his drunken orgies – that she had tattooed his face and his penis on her buttocks, he was her whale, her submarine, her tiger.

A terrible sadness invaded my heart and mind.

Memory theatre in hell bites deep.

In the games that we played – Deacon, Jones, and I – Deacon had claimed me as his Carnival Lazarus-son in order to project upon me a bewilderment in womb and tomb (as he used to put it). Who were his parents? He had been exposed as an infant-child in the Courantyne savannahs. He could easily have died there. His adoption by cattle-farmers and horse-rearers was a kind of resurrection, a buoy to which he clung. *I* had been born in Albuoystown. I was Bone and Flesh upon which to project his state of orphanage. He seized me as a canvas upon which to paint his bedevilled condition of a fallen angel, fallen from the womb of space, arisen from the grave of the earth.

Orphans tend to play at parenting the globe, the grave of the globe, the cradle of the globe. Orphans tend to play at parenting other orphans. I was his Albuoystown orphan upon whom he was tempted to place his father-mask, his sonship mask as well. Composite epic!

In the same token – as if to appoint intangible distinctions and crossed frontiers as well in composite epic – Jones claimed that *he* was the puritan father of invisible savages – invisible to him and therefore ripe for blind salvation in his Church as orphans. Heathens and savages and colonial peoples were damned but once converted into orphans they could be claimed by any parent, or state, or university, and baptized afresh: indeed baptized for the first time in wasteland fire and water.

'Circe's your foster-mother, Francisco,' he used to say when he returned from one of the brothels that he patronized in San Francisco. 'She's an animal goddess from Rio, Brazil in the United States and I shall take her with me wherever I go. Like a fucking masthead on a bloody ship. Fire in her veins that spout to heaven. She resembles you, Francisco. Epic nonsense in a Christian age. A dash of French blood perhaps, English, German, *and* tainted African and Arawak. Let's claim that when I fuck her I save you Francisco from taint. I recruit you in her into the Church. It's the sanctification of the beastly brothel, is it not? The art of colonialism. Give every Colony a civilized foster-mother, foster-son face.' He was drunk as a lord, drunk as an aristocrat, drunk as a conquistador. But I was bitterly crestfallen. I was bitterly ashamed to confront such theories in hell, seductive theories of the conversion of colonials and bastards within a liberal, charismatic, imperial backcloth.

How to transfigure, metamorphose such a backcloth into a sail upon the Virgin Ship! Not by social realism obviously, which is blind to the mystery of orchestrated imageries of parallel universes of the Imagination and to counterpoint . . . Blind to the music of counterpoint in fiction . . .

The thought of such transfigured histories flickered in my mind but I was so downcast and ashamed that I blotted out the face of the animal goddess from my mind, from the wilderness of the mind. *Not entirely, for I knew her*. I knew that I needed to speak to her, to hear her voice, to attempt to translate her replies within a Dream-book susceptible to some degree of the convergence of the unconscious, the subconscious, the conscious . . .

But Jonah Jones's voice continued for the time being to ring in my ears.

'She chucked me out of her bed, Francisco,' Jonah said. 'She chucked me out one Spring day. Imagine that!' He was laughing and yet I sensed genuine disbelief in his mind. I sensed he was confessing within the pages of my Dream-book to something that he rarely acknowledged and of which he infrequently, if ever, spoke. A mystical riddle lay on his tongue, that a savage woman was capable now of thrusting him from her bed. Alas it was too late. Or was it? Would such an apparently inconsequential gesture – directed at Churches of Eternity – save doomed colonies, doomed cities, doomed landscapes, from charismatic gunfire, charismatic closures of time, charismatic fires, charismatic floods?

Jones continued: 'She (that bitch) said she felt pity for me. Imagine that! A whore and a bitch.'

I could not resist taunting Jonah. 'Was Helen of Troy a whore and a bitch when she chucked the king her husband out of her bed?'

Jonah stared at me –

'Helen was no *animal* . . .' he cried. 'You go too far, Francisco.'

'What was she then?' I asked. 'Are not queens and princesses royal animals to teach us how invaluable is the Circus of civilization?'

'Damn you, Francisco. You are not listening to me. Circe said she felt *compassion* for me. She said she was ready now to become a *human* animal. What the devil does that mean? She said she was ready to bring a re-visionary vista into the Circus. A protectress of animal species from every quarter of the globe. Such she claimed was the new legacy of queens! Or else the Circus would collapse around our ears.'

'That's why she's called the Virgin of Jonestown. She tells of the hidden extensions of past doomed civilizations and of the fate that may await the entire environment of the Guyanas if we continue to be as blind and deaf and *numb* as we have long been.'

Jonah was outraged. 'I do not need her pity, or her wisdom, or her compassion. Who is she to tell me what I should or should not do? Who is she to transgress against the frame of my Church? She is no Virgin. Who is she to tell me I am a pig?' He stared at me in disbelief. But then – to my astonishment – he could not help laughing. 'She said I was a threatened species and that I needed protection if I were to remain visible to posterity. Pigs she said were in danger of becoming a threatened species. Not extinct by any means. But still they needed protection.'

Jones was still laughing. But there was a hollow ring to his laughter. I was not amused yet imbued by a dark humour. Jones's utterances seemed fragmented. They sprang from fabrics of Dream that floated into my Dream-book. I sought to translate them by placing them together in awkward yet pregnant collusion.

PIG rang a bell within the frame of the animal goddess as much as the torso of the Virgin of Jonestown on the Day of the Dead. Jonah Jones was a charismatic Pig within the shawl of the animal goddess and the Virgin. His brutal or coercive intercourse with nature, with a woman he deemed a whore, with a goddess who said she pitied him, was visible when he held a gun to Marie's temple.

I recalled that Deacon, Jones and I had actually begun the construction of Jonestown in the early 1970s when students at universities in the United States plastered the word PIG on campuses everywhere – not far from famous churches, famous statues of the Mother of God – in their protests at the Vietnam War.

The implicit battleground of the campus threatened to invade the premises of the Church.

I saw it translated now into the Carnival lineaments of the animal mother of surrogate Gods, the animal human queen . . .

Yes, it dawned on me that the animal human goddess had been at work through those students. PIG rang a bell in Jones's charismatic Church. PIG was the animal goddess's denunciation of charismatic politics. Yet all species counterpointed in conflictual history were to be saved to make visible in profoundest Carnival our misunderstandings and misreadings of the past and the immensity of challenges that lay ahead of us in the future.

'The early 1970s when we began to build Jonestown,' I said to Jonah, 'were a turning-point for us all. The Circus of civilization had been shaken to its Asian and American foundations. Ancient Troy and ancient Greece turned in their graves. We were still involved – if my memory in hell's Carnival on this Spring day serves me aright – in a war to save civilization from the barbarities of communism. We all had our implicit or involuntary versions of the animal goddess of humanity and the Pig whom she had thrust from her bed. We had pin-ups of film stars, emancipated queens of the media, side by side at times with bombed women and children in villages in Vietnam. Pillars of fire crossed the ocean and the air spaces into exotic pageantry upon billboards everywhere. Soon it wasn't barbarous communism that sent a chill down our spines. It was the deteriorating fabric of civilization everywhere. Drugged normality. Faster and faster cars. Illiteracies of the Imagination. It was then that we – you Jonah, Deacon and I – sought to build a new Rome in the South American rainforests within the hidden flexibilities of civilizations that had collapsed in the past. We brought all our prejudices and biases with us in half-ruined, half-intact form. How to visualize these, how to plumb innermost self-confessional, self-judgemental change in ourselves is a measure of truth that I seek in the wake of the holocaust that afflicts us all in a variety of overt or masked forms everywhere . . .'

'Human nature never changes,' said Jonah. 'And let me correct you about one thing. You talk about the brothels I visited . . .'

'I know, I know,' I said. 'I wasn't speaking absolutely of houses of prostitution but of a state of mind, a seeping promiscuity in which you hunted for fallen women and made them your mistresses. Circe became a curse. She enslaved you. Then she clung to you like salvation's uncanny plague. Why she followed you to Jonestown . . .'

'Ask her, ask her, you poor Fool, Francisco. I thought she would take me back into her bed so I let her come but she has foiled me at every turn. All this talk about the Virgin of Jonestown!'

'Where,' I suddenly cried, glancing through the window at the assembly of Carnival ghosts, 'is the boy (her child) who lay beside her in the Clearing on the Day of the Dead? Do you remember the Day of the Dead, Jonah, now that we've returned from the future to this theatre of the past? Hell hath no fury as profound as the apprenticeship to truth that it offers.'

My Skeleton-twin may have heard my question. He looked up at me. I recalled my quantum and psychical transference into the dead child beside Marie on the Day of the Dead. I was he for a flashing moment within the trauma I experienced. Some portion of myself had lodged in him then, some portion of him had come into me. The bridges of Lazarus are unfathomable. How would I know him for sure on this Spring Carnival day? Not for sure. That was plain as bone. Would he not wear a Skeleton-mask to rid me of complacency in my quest for innermost shared archetype, innermost shared identity, innermost soul? The dead grow beyond fixed frontiers, do they not? A child may wear an adult Skeleton-mask in Carnival. Or may fall back into the cradle and may wear an infant mask of soil or stone. Or may remain apparently unchanging in a void of flesh. One is twinned to masquerades of the growing, maturing dead and the unageing dead.

Jonah was laughing his hollow, confused laughter. 'Go to the Circus and see,' he said to me. 'I tell you, Francisco, human nature never changes.'

'I tell you it does, Jonah. I tell you the sacred reality of the Circus is embodied in the layered, multi-faceted mosaic of genesis and the womb in the animal goddess who may enslave us yet release us from subjection to swinish fates, to the fate of immortal cattle in heaven ruled by a queen whose dreadful beauty keeps us alive as pawns of unchanging eternity.'

Jones was angry and he thrust me out of his house into the wilderness of the Circus of civilization in the wake of the holocaust. He placed a pen in my hand and told me to continue with my heretical Dream-book. I would be punished in due course. I would be put on trial. That was my theme now of

Tropical Spring beset by many hazards, threatened landscapes, endangered species, threatened and mired riverscapes, threatened rainforests. Who was on trial I wondered? Was it I or was it civilization itself?

I made my way now to the animal goddess and Virgin of Jonestown. I recalled her sculptured torso on the Day of the Dead. But this was the Day of Living Return of the Dead or pagan Spring in the calendar of the Maya. This was a Day of dark cross-culturalities and savage, purifying humour. She was my foster-mother in Jonah's parlance of the puritan colonization of the Americas, his metaphor of intercourse with her to redeem my bastard progression into his Church of Eternity.

She was a surrogate queen, a tattooed mistress. No Virgin in his Christian, charismatic ideology but a useful frame or channel through whom to conscript orphans in his Church.

Intercourse with her was justified as a way for a puritan to absolve her of tainted antecedents, to accept unchanging human nature in himself and herself, to build the savage queen that she was in his eyes into a supreme colonial pawn or foster-wife, foster-mother of orphans, in his privileged embrace. Thus it was that an irredeemable continent was rendered sterile, it was voided of its pre-Columbian background, its legacies, its cultures, in a process of proselytization or conversion to charismatic Christianity.

As I approached her (my foster-mother) I saw her differently. His (Jonah's) supreme pawn was holy in my eyes. Her compassion for him was a glancing backwards into a numinous paganism possessing unfathomable roots *not* in the purgation or erasure of mixed ancestries that he desired (despite his propaganda against racism) but in the purgation of violence from sex. The act of the penetration of space, of Virgin space, penetration of other worlds, was not in its mysterious origination an act of violence. It was an act of creation, the creation of living diversities, the living orchestration of differing spaces, ages, realities. It could prove an exposure of capacities for genuine freedom. But the Sorrowing Wound was inevitable. One's masquerades of wholeness (the surrogacies, misinterpretations, misreadings of diversities-in-unities) fell far short of the origination of the penetrative act. So – in that exposure of numinous difficulties interwoven with the gift of freedom – violence became the price that humanity was driven to pay. It was a price that challenged the arts of the Imagination to their core. I had seen in my Dream-book the breakage of the sovereignty of violence into mystical dismemberments sustaining diversities and enlarging the capacity for disadvantaged cultures to change and grow and rediscover invaluable omens and roots . . .

As a consequence I knew I was on trial in Jonah's eyes, in the eyes of the establishment. Where the establishment sought the sterility of a conformable realism, as its absolute goal, I sought intangible but real frontiers to cross within an open universe in which my foster-mother stood as one of three Maries. She was smiling at my Skeleton-twin as I came close to her. Skeleton-twin? Foster-son? Such is the family of recovered being-in-non-being in Carnival creation.

I said to her: 'Why in God's name did you come to Jonestown to suffer a horrible death?' I stopped aghast. I dreamt I heard my Skeleton-twin whisper: 'Mystical dismemberments, mystical wholeness, is the body of the pagan Virgin through all Carnival masquerades.' I held my ear and twisted it as if it were a flute, an organ, the vagination or sheathing of sound in space. I continued quickly, repeating the question, 'Why in God's name did you come to Jonestown? I did not know you on the Day of the Dead. I saw you as Marie Antoinette (an acceptable face in European eyes for Virgins), not Circe, the terrifying, unpredictable compassion of an animal goddess such as Circe. Only now on my return from the future . . .'

The column of fire on her head had cooled. She dislodged it and placed it in the soil between herself and my Skeleton-twin who was her son, or foster-son, within the broken, archetypal fabric of the family of the Self.

She knew me instantly though she was grateful for the numinous link with her Carnival son, my twin or Skeleton in league with masked Bone, fleshed Bone. Such ramifications, or identity of Sorrows and Jests, were codes into a family of creation in the eyes of the Virgin of devastated Jonestown.

'You pay a price, Francisco, in your return. I pay a price for my former connection with Jonah Jones. He was my lover. Now he's in hell. Hell takes many forms upon the Virgin Ship that you are building. Your Skeleton-twin descended into hell. Even now he's unwilling to embrace you! He has suffered not only in the pit of Jonestown into which he fell, in your place, but in wars everywhere, in famines everywhere, from which he released you to live and eat. *You* were as ripe to appear to have perished as he, you were as ripe for starvation as he. He is intimate to you yet alien. He is your epic familiar and inner double in the grave of flesh, in the cradle of flesh. And all this is instinctive to the price you pay, Francisco! To possess such knowledge on your return to this Carnival Spring Day is to acknowledge your ignorance in the future from which you have come. Should one be wiser as one progresses into the future from the past? I doubt it. You doubt it. One needs to come abreast of the past if the past is to yield a kinship with futurity . . .'

If I did not know of her compassion I would have dreamt she was mocking me. She continued:

'I speak as a Carnival oracle, Francisco. Not Delphic oracle! Carnival oracle. Have you heard of it? Such curious speech is distressing for you I know only too well. Oracles are steeped in hidden texts that may scarcely be translated. But still translations in your own tongue (let me say), orchestrated fabrics imbued with music – are necessary. Again such translations are the price you must pay, Francisco, to see the Dead alive after knowing them Dead . . .'

I broke into the Oracle of space, as it were, when I cried: 'You said Jonah Jones was your lover. And the price you must pay . . .'

I stopped with the overwhelming impression that in breaking into the Oracle of space I stood within a gigantic brothel at the heart of the Circus of civilization. But the impression receded until I was filled with awe and terror. Awe of freedom, the terror of freedom, that the animal goddess sought now to explicate to me in the Shadow of the great phallic tree.

There was implicit truth, implicit deception, in that tree.

Implicit self-deception conceived in the notion of a mastered female nature, a tamed female nature, implicit truth in balancing Sorrow and ecstasy, freedom and licence.

It was the searing conjunction of all such ambivalences and counterpoint that gave content to the price that my foster-mother paid in returning to Jonestown in my Dream-book.

She pointed to the great phallic member within the Circus. Jonah's sweating body shone there now as he appeared to fall back into the river all over again and to climb the notched, sculpted log of wood floating above him, within him, beside him.

'Does Jonah know he's up there?' I asked. 'Is it an apparition, a Circus trick? I left him in his house a moment ago. Apparitions can be solid in that we grieve, genuinely grieve, for fleeting joys and pleasures, they can be hollow, without grief, technology without pain and grief. Does Jonah know he's up there?'

'Do you, Francisco?'

'I see him,' I said stubbornly. 'I do not see myself.'

'That's easy,' said the Virgin animal goddess. 'Easy to see Jonah the charismatic, the tyrant. Not yourself, Francisco. Jonah was once an idealist. What chance do you have, Francisco, of seeing yourself not only in him but *through* him? I can help you. That is my burden, the price I must pay to enlighten you to the well-nigh *extinct* creature that you are . . .'

'EXTINCT?' I was stunned, bewildered. 'How can a free man, a free, imaginative dreamer and writer, be extinct?'

'Tell me,' said the Virgin Oracle, 'what in heaven's or hell's name do you really know of your long-vanished antecedents, Francisco? What do you know of the worlds and spaces they occupied or inhabited before the Conquest? Precious little. What do you know of the treaties they shaped with the Predator, the Wolf, the Beast, who spoke to them at the fireside? You call me holy foster-mother but what do you know of me? You are extinct, Francisco (in areas of yourself), as a species of bird or buffalo or animal that fell to the guns of the invading puritan in the Americas since the Conquest. You are the embodiment of lost tribes, or peoples, Atlantean peoples. It's a tragedy as old as Plato's Dream. Older perhaps. As old as the fates of Prisoner-Gods on Devil's Isles.'

I knew now she was making Oracle fun of me. And yet a glimmering flock of wings – flash of wings – high on the phallic tree made me pause and consider the gravity of what I had been told.

Were those the wings of extinct, foetal organs in the Womb of Virgin space?

'I am a free man,' I insisted. 'Am I not? I can travel everywhere. I can cross frontiers. Can I not?'

The Virgin animal goddess pointed to the great bunched head at the top of the erect phallic gland or leafless trunk, shorn tree where, it seemed, Jonah's log broke into – or slid into – a belly of genesis-cloud and its flashing wings in the Womb of space.

'Free, yes,' said the Virgin Oracle, 'in that *extinction* of so many areas of yourself may be viewed ironically, or tragically, or redemptively as a *mystical unity with all creatures.*' Was she jesting, was she praying to dead Gods and living Gods in a curious sacramental orchestration of invisibles and visibles? 'Extinction that leaves you cognizant of what is happening, or has happened, to yourself – extinction that erupts backwards and forwards into rare, epic solidity and ghosts of Carnival – imbues *severances in a chain of natures*, a binding chain, with a strange, obscure, tormenting faculty that we call freedom, a freedom that needs to be weighed and weighed again and again, considered, reconsidered, for the backward glance it may bring into losses that we have suffered.'

She gave a sudden, gasping laugh as Jonah's log rose into the belly of the clouds.

'The chain breaks,' I thought I heard her say. 'The chain loses itself to create a mystical self. Does not the Christian Church speak of losing one's life to find it?' I felt the slap of her voice in my voice. A long sighing pause continued at the top of the tree and then she continued. 'Why am I telling you all this, Francisco? You write of it in your Dream-book when you emphasize *mystical dismemberments*. Have you forgotten or is it too painful to bear? Extinction of parts of yourself brings a terrifying message of catastrophe – progressive catastrophe – or of the reversal of such linear progression into changed inner lips, inner limbs, inner bodies in the evolution of the free man, the free Imagination cursed with profoundest self-knowledge. Human nature may change when it begins to comprehend the broken chains of Being in itself, a breakage that entails the gestation of freedom's body to look back into overlapping texts of the birth of time and invoke vanished but long-suffering shapes and species within the seed and orbit of freedom's self-knowledge . . .'

I shrank from the task, the trial, of Dream. *I wanted to be unfree*, I wanted to eclipse the rape of natures that freedom had imposed everywhere, the freedom of an Enlightenment (*so different from the Virgin's enlightenment*) to send into exile all voices in nature and space that differed from a human-centred cosmos preoccupied with its own vested interests in power and wealth at any price.

I saw the animal goddess's pitying eyes upon Jonah and upon me.

'The future may still mother the spectral Carnival bodies of the past, Francisco. Not by purely linear progression but by proportionalities that bring us abreast of the living past in the womb of tradition.'

She pointed up to the erect head of the Phallus in the Brothel-Oracle of space.

Brothel. Oracle. I was close to despair but something was tremulously stirring, beyond the logic of fate, that I needed to pursue within the inner limbs, the inner bodies, of the Self.

It dawned on me all at once that the Phallus had broken on its penetration of floating wings in the belly of oceanic, riverain Cloud far above me but close to Jonah's apparitional climb into self-deception of eternity's closure of time.

A red rim or slice appeared beneath the lofty erection and mounted head, mounted by Cloud, in Jonah's log. Waterfall log, rainfall log, that I saw *through* Jonah's body? I was unsure. Within the slice of log or Phallus, feathered birds, white and dark as rain, seemed to pour like a river.

It was an incalculable spatial phenomenon or omen of genesis.

A river of feathers etched its insertion into cross-sectional sliced Phallus. The feathers flattened themselves into hair at the rim of the log to which Jonah clung, intercourse with the Sky, Sky-flesh of the Virgin Animal . . .

It was but a game, a perverse and derisive game at times – as I recalled it in San Francisco (ages ago it seemed) – that Jonah played in electing me as his foster-son through the Virgin Animal of the New World that he sought to invoke as a medium or theatre in which to damn yet save, slaughter and bind my antecedents into his Church, his future Church, his charismatic Church that he entertained in his subconscious in his College days.

That the Animal Goddess would return as a formidable ghost in the Circus of civilization to illumine not only how she had enslaved him but how she came to pity him was virtually unimaginable until now when I saw the broken, mended Phallus, the notched log floating in Jonestown river, leafless trunk (devastated forest that such a trunk could imply in its intercourse with the elements) . . . The truth was that I was at a loss now in the Circus for intimate, far-flung words to translate correspondences in what I saw: leafless trunk, hell, heaven, intercourse between Sky and Earth in Churches of Eternity.

I kept my eyes glued on the Phallic tree on which the apparition of the Reverend Jonah Jones ascended.

Was the Animal Goddess jesting (as Mr Mageye would have done) in revealing to me such Carnival Cinema of the playful, monstrous workings of the psyche?

In every Oracle a play of monsters brings us close to self-confessional, self-judgemental magic by which to come abreast of the terrifying responsibilities of freedom, freedom to liberate others in ourselves, freedom to crucify others in our hidden selves.

'Look!' said the Virgin, 'the slice mends, it appears to mend or heal, it is a cross-sectional slice, it runs right through Jonah's puritan member or log (and its surrogacies in exploited woods and rivers and forests). It mends itself – let us say, Francisco – but not absolutely, for do you not see vestiges of feather and bone protruding from it, phallic wound, climactic moment?'

I was startled or I would have laughed at such a seminal Jest planted in the elements.

I looked up and studied afresh (I had lowered my eyes for a

moment when she spoke) the cross-sectional breakage, yet mended trunk, in the Phallic tree.

The vestige of wing or bone or feather within the mend, protruding narrowly at the edge of the mend, from within the mend, rushed into my mind like a sudden nest of psyche: I was privileged to see through the Animal Goddess's eyes into a sudden nest of psyche, a labyrinth of branches and cells to which – in its inscription of sacrificial sculpture – Jonah was numb. And as a consequence he was unresponsive to the intervention of grace, the intervention of the subtlety of freedom that sacramentalized the embrace of others in their own right (without forfeiting their ancestral heritage) in a nest within the mended Phallus . . .

He was numb to everything except an everlasting divide between the damned and the saved in charismatic, brutalizing sex . . .

A host of questions arose within me. I recalled the torso of the Virgin in the Clearing on the Day of the Dead. On this Spring day that torso or sculpture became a towering Ship reaching up to the nest of psyche in the Phallic tree: intervention or reach of savage grace: sudden Storm: orchestrated elements to break the unresponsive heart.

Perhaps the Oracle was angry at my questions spoken or unspoken. The climate of civilization began to change. Extinct ages began to come alive.

An ancient Storm (one would have deemed extinct) – such as I had never seen in all my life of wanderings and voyages – arose within the Circus. It arose and stood above Jonestown which lay now – in that ancient, revisited time – nameless under the sea. The Atlantic rolled far inland from the drowned Guyana coasts of South America to the base of the Kaieteuran escarpment.

The flood was as tall or taller than the Phallic tree. It was in itself a series of Phallic waves or mounds of water. I floated in the Ship or torso of the Virgin. I glimpsed the rape of Atlantis, Plato's Atlantis, far beneath me. Rape of Virgin Atlantis. It encompassed Jonestown, nameless Jonestown, in the belly of the flood.

In that flood lay the lineaments of the drowned, pre-Columbian

135

New World, since the European Conquest, in every mutilated landscape and catchment and lake.

Freedom and conquest were as old as Atlantis. Tall catastrophe.

How could such an ancient, extinct Storm be the intervention of grace in the Phallic tree of the elements? The Storm blew a leaf at last in the beak of an extinct bird. The leaf was lodged in a crevice of the flood. The flood broke, the chain of waters broke, as if to mirror a sliced, cross-sectional eruption and mend in the trunk of waters, a mound of waters, on which I sailed on the Virgin Ship from which a net descended to which Jonah clung.

Curious net! More akin to a nest that floated through the leaves of water upon which fish swam like birds that flew through the air as if defying gravity yet sustained by interleaved fractures in the body of gravity.

A chain of elements, water, earth, wood, broke. A prison of conformable natures broke. And the fate of Atlantis was laid bare as a counterpoint between rape or devastation and implicit freedom still to balance extinction with a renascence (or renaissance) of lost cultures whose vestiges and imprints could be orchestrated into the seed of the future.

I could scarcely gather together the immense orchestration of the Storm that I had evoked in the questions that I addressed, murmured questions as well as unspoken questions, to the Oracle; to the formidable ghost of the Animal Virgin who enslaves us yet pities and protects us and awaits our grasp of the nest of psyche in the broken, mended Phallic tree of universal element. Without that grasp freedom's messengers perish. Sacrificial sculpture grows meaningless and the Virgin ship itself drowns.

I should have been swept away myself in the Storm except for the Virgin torso or Ship in which I sailed. I should have been pinned into the grinding cross-sectional wound of broken, mended pillars between Sky and Earth through which one sails into the Cave of the Moon upon the Phallic gravity/anti-gravity tree.

Instead I was left to ponder the Oracle's proposition of sacrificial sculptures that break a prisonhouse of unchanging law and logic into innermost fabrics and scales on which to weigh and weigh again and again messengers that arrive and nest in the wounds of the Phallic tree.

I had seen in the Storm how those wounds grow larger and larger, steeper and steeper, when our response to message and messenger becomes adamant and insensible and numb.

On the other hand those wounds become the inimitably complex and sensitive sculptures of science and art when our response acquires re-visionary momentum and graces born of Spirit.

Freedom then turns into the servant of Spirit not the despoiler of worlds.

I was grateful to the Animal Goddess for a rare vision of equations of Chaos, mathematics of Chaos, that were in themselves profoundest, terrifying interventions of savage grace.

Not that grace was not tender and instinct with incalculable harmonies but humanity's numbness made it essential that the orchestration of the elements, abused for generations and centuries, would acquire configurations of omen, within Storm and Fire and majestic Phalli, to which cultures clung paradoxically in seeking intricate gaps or room to manoeuvre, room for the renewal of Breath, in the grave and the cradle and the nest of space.

The chain was broken within terror itself, the prisonhouse was broken within violence itself, broken, it seemed, within long-neglected inscriptions and texts of the birth of memory itself: memory's eruptive, marvellously fissured, spatial organ sprung from the unconscious into the subconscious into the conscious.

Each break was a form of primordial, sacrificial sculpture that one tended to eclipse, or lose again and again, within a proclivity to numbness, to a loss of depth and range and profoundest passion, to fixtures of bias.

The bird that nested its leaf in the flood came as a messenger of eclipsed freedom erupting again, the nested leaf broke the chain of the Storm to match extinction with the genius of recovered omen or insight into invaluable resources and species linked to us yet susceptible to freedom through us, as we were to freedom through them.

My eye was sharpened, renewed, reborn as I sailed in the

sculpture or torso of the Virgin as in genius's Ship of Breath.

A rhythm of equations linked the Ship to the Phallic tree to the leaf. Breath I dreamt I possessed – in which a leaf or a feather from long-extinct Atlantean forests and species circulated – but as the Storm subsided I was unable to translate the Oracle of Chaos and its equations. Perhaps the Oracle took pity on me.

The Animal Goddess sharpened my ears to catch the whisper of her voice on my Breath in the orchestra of the subsiding Storm.

'When one slices a chain, Francisco,' she said, 'one builds another *intangible* series of relationships. The vestige of bone and feather – you do remember, don't you – in the jointed Phallic tree is sacrificial seminal sculpture. Extinct wing possesses minute fractions that are memorialized into rocket-ships as this millennium draws to a close. Bone-Ship rocket, Feather-Ship rocket, are masks of science whose grain lies in the mended Phallic tree in its intercourse with the Sky. Rocket is *in* the bone's and the feather's hidden texts blown to us within counterpoints of creation. Simplicity itself I would say, Francisco, when one opens one's life to freedom's responsibilities but an enormous trial it remains alas that is set by me, by the three Maries, by Virgin Space . . .'

I wanted to press her with further questions. I was obsessed. But I did not wish to arouse her anger at – despite her pity for – my ignorance. The enormity of the trial was dismaying. Should I tear my Dream-book into shreds? Did not freedom signify – despite its intangible linkage with all things and species – terrorizing structures, exploited bodies, manipulated resources?

Was freedom obsolete? Had it ever existed?

Violence existed. And the ancient Gods who were steeped in sacrificial sculptures on the Phallic tree had become, it was said by charismatic philosophers, Prisoners of Devil's Isles.

Despite my misgivings – and the unspoken weight of my questions to the Oracle – the Virgin replied. Her ears were as sharp as a pointed nail's in the strangely moon-like eyes of Lazarus, Skeleton-twin Lazarus. Such is the orchestration of imageries in Oracle-Carnival to move and transfigure the numb heart of humanity!

'You need to meet the Prisoner-God of Devil's Isle, Francisco. You will quite soon. In due course. Time is sometimes vague in my mind. Better so than to succumb to the hubris of eternity in charismatic institutions. You need to experience through the Prisoner-God *not* the obsolescence of freedom but the premature gift of freedom to Mankind . . .'

'But freedom was present before time began,' I cried.

'That may be so,' said the Virgin, 'but we have come close – have we not? – to forfeiting such priorities in our misunderstandings of evolution. Evolution in its innermost unfathomable coherence within parallel universes is intangible. It serves hidden texts that we can never absolutely translate. Hidden priorities. Hidden beginnings prior to all beginnings. And these accumulate into a Jesting net that gathers up everything. The re-visionary truths of love, the re-visionary love of truth. Intangible as Breath.'

Breath

I am apprenticed to the Furies, apprenticed to Dread. How does one learn the complex arts and inter-related mysteries of the Furies across the ages yet see them in oneself and begin to turn them around by stages of incredible game into all-inclusive Love?

Francisco Bone

The Storm abated.

It seemed to arise within me all over again.

The relic of Storm within. It blew from some region within me that lay in a time before evolution was, in a time prior to evolution's wasteland. How should a pilgrim such as myself, prone to bouts of amnesia in the wake of Jonestown, spell or paint or sculpt 'wastelands' or 'gravelands' and not make them excessively newsworthy in a violent age? Perhaps I should confess again to divergences built into numinous alphabets which witness to the unfathomable premises of creation. Is 'wasteland' a whisper *Eliot* of a nether world in THE WASTE LAND or in WASTE LAND, graveland in GRAVE LAND? Is ORACLE the heightened shout of brothel-oracle in Hollywood Limbo Land?

Evolution's spectres are the pilgrims of time in Memory's flesh, wasteland flesh, yes, surreal time prior to flesh, yes, graveland time prior to resurrections of consciousness, netherworlds, constellations, subjective time, objective time, post-subjectivity rooted in hypnotic objectivity, extremities of Breath, the breath-lines infused into architectures of space in science and fiction and poetry and art.

Subjectivity is the comedy of intangible objectivity that ignites the stars into the ash of genesis, black holes, fuels the sun with greed for blood in ancient sacrifice.

On such altars of lust and catastrophe unimaginable Love is born for all creatures. And Evolution turns in its grave of space into the mystery of trial and judgement each and all must endure in Memory theatre.

Evolution becomes the resurrection of spectres to confront themselves, to indict themselves in bleak play, bleak but redemptive theatre, Memory's head on one's shoulders, limbs sculpted in ancient arts in one's limbs, dismembered Prisoners, Gods, woven into one's extinction through which – as if by another unsuspected Genesis of the Imagination – one accepts Dread and the gift of freedom to travel beyond the dice of Light in one's Skeleton-twins, the flesh of Darkness in one's Skeleton-twins, to travel beyond all wastelands and gravelands into ultimate transfigured Bone in the wilderness of space . . .

The Storm abated and I descended the stairway of subsiding waters to the floor of the Circus.

There I jested with my drowned Skeleton-twin who arose from the floor with sleight-of-Breath skill. I jested in a theatre of Breath, relic of Storm.

'Fiery customer and performer you are,' I said to him, 'despite your drowned bones. You have changed. Two deaths! One in an ancient sea, one in the sawyers' pit or grave in the land. We are ghosts of the sea and ghosts of the land in ancient and modern America. I am changed too. It's this business of relics. They bring a borderline between the oceanic lightning of the mind and vestiges of unearthly Passion that retain a spark from the blaze. One is equipped to wear another Mask on one's head and shoulders, a fiery Mask that cools.'

I tried to embrace him but he rejected me all over again. For a moment I dreamt that it was his Mask that I would come to wear in the near future. I touched the holes that had been driven into my neck and shoulders in Limbo Land in preparation for such a Mask. In his changed costume – drowned bones, sleight-of-Breath body – he acquired the air of an ancestor of mine, the air of lightning cooled Storm or Passion. He no longer breathed fire in arising from the sawyers' pit and the sea.

He may have sensed what I was thinking for he said:

'Not my Mask shall be placed upon you, Francisco. Yet to be intimate with my descent into hell may prove a necessary initiation into the angel's Mask that shall possess you . . .'

'Angel's Mask?'

'Wait and see,' said my Skeleton-twin.

'When we rode on the bicycle to Jonah's house,' I cried, 'I wondered if you would grow flames and burn me, reduce me to a handful of ashes. But now I think I know better. We are twins, yes, but you are also an ancestor of the lightning mind secreted in graves of space and in Bone (universal kith and kinship Bone) when it flashes in the Sky. Before evolution's dawn Bone flashed as a relic of Spirit in a Circus. Circus animals bounce back into lightning in the Sky. The mystery is Breath! There are different layers of Breath in the architectures of space. Imagine Circus stairways, Circus architectures, in the elements. Without peculiar rhythms of Breath one could not leap onto a frontier upon which every flashing relic of Spirit marks a crossing from pre-evolution to evolution's wasteland. And beyond evolution's wasteland to post-wasteland graves steeped in the dance and the resurrection of consciousness. One crosses the wasteland and descends into the grave. So many lightning relics descend into the grave! So many peoples, so many houses, so many dancers . . .' I stopped.

'Weigh Breath in dancing feet in the grave as they strive to leap into the resurrection. There's a key in the Breath-body when one unlocks a door into the Cave of the Moon. There's a key in the sawyers' pit and the dark moonlight fleece on the stars of the nether world,' said my Skeleton-twin.

'Let me embrace you,' I cried. 'You understand . . .'

'I understand nothing,' said my Skeleton-twin self-mockingly. 'I stand above and below. So I can teach you a thing or two about the dance.' He eyed me coldly. A faint flare in the sockets of his eyes deposited a key into the tattooed inscription of Lazarus on my arm.

How could one tattoo the Breath-key of another upon one's arm unless one invoked the cool lightning dance of wilderness space, night-dance that one's flesh could bear, upon broken archetypal fabric that one shares with those to whom one is indebted, and who begin to take one into hidden architectures, the hidden lives, in the grave of the Circus?

One needs to weigh every trickster of the cradle and the grave that one embodies yet sees as a separate entity in composite epic.

Was the Skeleton-twin a sacred trickster? He was the shared Breath of a broken archetype, heaven and hell.

We set out into the Forest of the Circus and I recalled the route that I had taken with Mr Mageye and the huntsman Christ.

He kept me at arm's length under the dark, tattooed inscriptions of the Forested Night. Skeleton-twin Lazarus! We walked on a frontier between pre-evolutionary darkness and evolutionary wasteland, a frontier that shone white with the Skeleton's glowing body, a frontier on which my dancing feet and the Skeleton's dancing feet were buried before they blazed afresh into primordial consciousness.

I now heard the surfing rasp of the sawyers' blade in the ghost-land of the grave, a wave of sound breaking on the coast of the mind, my eyes floated into that wave, I was in the wave, in the dance of the Skeleton, unable to embrace him, but in the wave, in the dance, of the dance . . .

The conversion of the ghost sawyers into architects of GRAVE LAND or the nether world into which I was descending took me wholly by surprise.

The key was in the lock as I danced and soon the glowing Skeleton and I had arrived.

Breath shone in the Sky. The sun of GRAVE LAND or the nether world was the Breath of fire.

I turned to my Skeleton-twin. 'Is this the Land of the Dead? The dancing figures before us wear the masks of Maya peasants. I know of such murals in the city of Bonampak and elsewhere. Abandoned cities flooded with murals of the happy dead . . .'

I had stopped dancing but the field before me was alive with dancers in floating apparel as they encircled a mound. They danced in the field. They danced in open spaces. They danced past houses that were lodged it seemed in a net. Had they been lodged there, drawn up there, from a lake? The rasping surf of the blade struck my ears like waves breaking on the bank of a river, or coast, or shore.

'It's also called,' said my Skeleton-twin, waving at the dancers, 'the Paradise of the Rain God.'

'Let's join them and dance,' I cried. 'Let's embrace them . . .'

'A chasm exists between you and them.'

'No chasm! They're across a field, that's all.'

I heard the rasping surf of the sawyers' blade again like the sea. But there was no sea except for the cinematic sensation on the coast of the mind, in the field of the mind beside an invisible lake or river or ocean or sea.

'There's the rub,' said my Skeleton-twin. 'You see a field, you see dancers, you hear an ocean but nothing's there. Is the field really there? They dance in elements upon a borderline between the wasteland and the post-wasteland theatre from which they seek to leap . . .'

'But that's wrong,' I protested. 'The borderline's between pre-evolutionary darkness and evolution. Did you not say so yourself when we were arriving?'

'The two borderlines look alike in GRAVE LAND. *I* am your twin now and your ancestor then in the past. Such is the comedy of relics of Spirit.'

'How do we know the difference?'

'Variations of Breath, the land that breathes, the water that breathes, are in the difference. Hard to define. For instance the sound of the sea in the sawyers' blade indicates substance that is used to build houses. Houses of the invisible sea. Houses with walls of solid water. Paradise of the Rain God. The dancers in the field then have settled for a while. As *you* appeared to settle on your Virgin Ship. Their houses are filled with the joy of rain. The Paradise of the Rain God. I would say they are primordial folk myself. Pre-evolutionary folk.'

'Who am I? What are you?'

My Skeleton-twin laughed.

'It's a good question, Francisco. You danced into GRAVE LAND on primordial feet. But in fact *you are alive, you survived the holocaust*, you possess – it is true – all the appearances of having died. But you belong to the living extremities of the WASTE LAND. You are almost in a post-wasteland grave. Almost in. Almost there. Not quite. That is why you are tattooed . . .'

'And you?' I cried. 'Where do you belong?'

'I am indisputably of the Circus. I fell into the pit and whilst you lived, whilst you grew flesh and I suffered in your place, I became a curious Skeletal animal of the WASTE LAND. I performed numerous tricks. Think of it this way. When I fell into the pit I left my inscription on your arm to remind you I was still there, I would arise, I walked in two worlds. GRAVE LAND. WASTE LAND.'

I could not help protesting. 'It,' I said, 'the inscription or tattoo, was done at Deacon's instigation. He took me to a specialist. It was a Jest, his assumption of himself as my orphaned, peasant father. We were of the same age. A game we played, Deacon and Jonah and I. I found myself with two fathers, a schoolboy rag, nothing more, but serious as hell in a land of orphans, and slave-owners, and conquistadores, and puritans. Jonah – my puritan schoolboy father – slept with an Animal Goddess, and Deacon anticipated sleeping with the Virgin of Port Mourant. For some unearthly reason he projected *me* into her, upon her, *he placed his fallen angel's Mask upon my head, the Mask of the Virgin's husband and the Virgin's son. He said my epic would redeem a relic.'*

I stopped. Shattered by the revelation. Dream-book revelation that made me into a stranger to myself, a multi-faceted stranger, a vessel of masks suspended in past futures coming abreast of future pasts.

The pain of Memory theatre, of breaking trauma in the wake of the holocaust, was great.

My Skeleton-twin reached out and almost held me but he desisted. Profoundest sympathy or empathy perhaps within which lay a chasm. Close to each other yet subject to broken archetypes that we shared but could never absolutely mend.

'Likewise myself, Francisco,' he said at last. 'I descended into the grave in your place. I anticipated the difficulty, the preterna-tural difficulty, immanence and transience combined, of *your* leaping up out of the grave to play your dual part, bridegroom-in-son, son-in-bridegroom, and beyond such duality intricate distinctions that would break a mould of incest within the mystery of freedom . . . Yes, I was aware of the immensity of the task. So I exercised my limbs as doubly supportive of you. In GRAVE LAND I suffered for you. In WASTE LAND I was close to you however apart from you. I created a chasm across which you would need to leap to fulfil your fate, to become free, to know love as you never dreamt to know it . . . Wait and see . . . A paradox of Breath-bodies I grant! You need, you see, to combine several keys into yourself. Wasteland key, post-wasteland key, primordial key. But the price you pay is the relinquishment of conquest! Your intercourse with Virgin Sorrowing space is the *intangible but innermostly supportive* embrace of many cultures living and dying upon the extremities of the WASTE LAND. So you see Francisco there are Deacon's projections that you bear and relive as a survivor of the holocaust. *Deacon did not survive in the extremities of the WASTE LAND as you do.* There are Jonah's projections that you bear and relive in ORACLE-Brothel. Jonah did not survive on the extremities of the WASTE LAND as you do. And there are my projections from within the grave and without the grave. I survived in a sense through you for whom I suffered and whom I assisted in the clothing of yourself with Flesh as you dance on the cradle and the grave of the globe. Wasteland extremity Flesh, evolution's extremity Flesh, in the Circus of Mankind . . .'

Flickeringly changing expressions swept across the Skeleton's Mask that my twin wore in the Carnival Circus of GRAVE LAND.

I swore I saw an expression of gravity. But as I scanned this it became a ripple of bones on his brow and across his high pointed cheeks like stricken sails in the Phallic tree. It may have been the Circus laughter of the relic of Storm within myself. My twin was known to ache with laughter. *I* attributed laughter to his fluid, however curiously rigid, flights of expression. But I may have been witnessing the genesis of some other nameless emotion. My Skeleton-twin caught the drift of my mood.

'You see, don't you Francisco, how mobile are other frontiers of emotion in GRAVE LAND? Am I sad, am I grave, am I smiling, am I mad, am I a fixture or a fluid personality of shadow and light? Do I sail with the turning globe, do I stand still? Am I susceptible to nameless emotions? Let me put in bluntly. Do I speak truths as clown, as trickster? All these borderlines between truth and trick!'

He paused on perceiving my bewilderment.

'Consider the key to hell within the grave. Is hell GRAVE LAND'S truths, is GRAVE LAND hell's truths? You and I entered by the sawyers' pit. We speak of a door through the sawyers' pit to which we possessed a key. But reflect! There was nothing in the sawyers' pit but a rusting lantern, some skulls, a rusting saw, rusting bolts and nuts, sodden leaves, sodden ground. How real is the key of the Imagination?'

'It is invaluable to science and art,' I cried.

'It is, I do not deny it,' my Skeleton-twin replied. 'The reach of the Imagination! But note the cautions inserted into that reach.'

'One's vulnerability!'

'Quite so, quite so,' said my Skeleton-twin. 'On every frontier that we seek to cross one needs to balance truth-makers, or truth-sayers, with tricksters. Frontiers are obdurate, believe me.'

'I know.' What did I know?, I wondered. 'I am impressed at times by such obduracy.' I stopped. 'Frustrated at times,' I admitted. 'It's a new language, a new inferno if we are to glimpse a wholly different archetype of heaven. What am I saying?'

I stood on the brink of a chasm but pulled back in time to address my Skeleton-twin.

'My frustrations are of a populist order. Is populism a new or an old conquistadorial heaven dressed up to please the greed of millions? Does populism mean grabbing what one sees and fancies and being grabbed by what one sees and fancies? You scratch my ass and I scratch yours. It's called copycat love, copycat violence, copycat predator. It lays bare the hungry and illiterate body of our age.'

My Skeleton-twin recoiled a little. But then he recovered. After all it was *I* who had endeavoured to embrace him, not he me.

He wagged a severe finger at me.

'The Cinema of GRAVE LAND, Francisco, jolts us – does it not? – even when we dream we know the blasted truth. Every blast invokes a spectre. That's all WASTE LAND Cinema is about and GRAVE LAND makes it clear. It's populist folly to think we can sleep with every woman or man in the world, we can seize or grab every dancer that we see, we can talk down each other's tongue and throat across a chasm, we can bite each other's ears off across oceans.'

'I never said we can,' I protested. But I knew I had entertained such follies in the WASTE LAND.

'Frontiers are real until Love beyond all comprehension abolishes them. Chasms between us and the dancers in the field are real.'

I protested:

'It's the obduracy of frontiers and the spectrality on the other side that frustrates and bewilders the heart and the mind. We must learn to cross . . .'

150

'We must learn to embrace the Enigma of Spirit if we are to see its relics breathe again, live again. A spiritual evolution upon every frontier, a spiritual freedom, is the task to be renewed,' said my Skeleton-twin.

He saw my incredulity, he saw my desire to relinquish the task.

'Ah, dear Francisco,' he mourned. 'You have so much to learn of the relics of Spirit. And of tricksters of Spirit. Charisma is not only the meat of tyrants, it is the meat of masses. And that's a hard and bitter truth that hell engenders. Every trickster that you encounter may well seek to embrace you. I have not. Does that prove I am no trickster? Or am I cleverer than the rest?'

It was odd. Had he not said that I might have despaired entirely of the immensity of the task that lay ahead for which I was so poorly equipped. He was eyeing me closely. He seemed to be calculating the effect of what he had said. I was glad that he had freed me to accept the possibility of failure. The genius of hell – his genius – lay in its capacity to relinquish cleverness, a talent for cleverness, in favour of sifting every obstacle to truth in the fabric of the Self.

Failure that is built into Spirituality, the uncertainties of Spirituality, may endorse every relic with incalculable momentum beyond oneself. It may deepen the Compassion of hidden figures of grace across the frontiers of one's life. It may deepen the severity of one's hidden judges as well. But some miraculous reconciliation of the genius of Compassion and the genius of severity or judgement may breathe in one's life when one confesses to failure . . .

We are assisted by powers we cannot define. We are tried by powers we cannot define. And their reconciliation is a crossing of frontiers.

'I fail to know them entirely. I fail to see them entirely. I am subject to self-deception. But they cross . . .'

'I used to play football in Albuoystown as a boy before I left for the United States in the 1940s,' I said to my Skeleton-twin in the most matter-of-fact voice. Matter-of-fact Breath! Yet matter and fact had been imbued with immensity.

151

'We played a rough game. Mr Mageye had told us in class of the ball games in the ancient Maya Circus. They played with a hard rubber ball like a boxer's fist that they bounced on a wall in the Land of the Dead. It was a hard, bruising game of Death and Life in Bonampak. I fell on one occasion and cut my lips. I wanted to go to my mother in her Leather Shop but I remembered her work-hardened hands. And I decided to bear the pain. I plastered my lips with Bread. I spent my pocket money bandaging my lips with Bread. I was determined not to worry her with my troubles. She had so many of her own. *That night her work-hardened hands added an additional bruise to my lips*. It was a dream. I dreamt that she became a judge. She could touch me across the frontiers of Dream but I could not touch her. She stood over my bed and sentenced me to leap at the ancient Bonampak wall as if I were a blunted infant in her womb. Bread was flesh-and-blood on my fists and lips. I awoke in a sweat that dripped into my mouth . . . My mother was a woman of Compassion.

'Do you know,' I cried to my Skeleton-twin, 'that I have never understood that Dream until now on my descending with you into the inner Circus of the Grave?'

We were strolling in pleasant fields and had stopped to watch the ghost-players of the Circus in the Paradise of the Rain God.

Rain bruised their lips.

A fleecy cloud descended and covered their head with Bread.

'I understand the Dream now,' I declared with Passion yet matter-of-fact Breath. 'My mother – the gentlest, most caring woman in the world – became a severe muse or judge. I could not touch her in my Dream. She was looking at me with the eyes of Marie the Judge. She looked into my heart. I had never seen such eyes before. *I* had helped to make her into a Judge. When – out of love for her (was it love or was it fear?) – I did not go to her and ask her to wipe away the blood from my lips I condemned myself to eat the Bread of her sweat. She became a severe Muse or mother of humanity. She drove me to reflect on famines, on starving peoples who mask their hunger in a cloud that rains on Paradise still where dancing peasants are happy as larks. Do they dance now or do they dance in the long ago? I planted the seed of a game that hungry generations play. Sometimes they are driven by a destructive priesthood or statehood to swarm on battlefields, to lift the game into a killing spectacle. Thus it is that the Virgin gives birth through her son to the necessity to look deep into the furies, into love's fury, into judgement day fury . . .'

My Skeleton-twin stared at me with his mourning glance. It was he who – in bringing me to descend into the depths of the Circus that he knew so well – had opened my eyes to a Passion for truth upon all obdurate frontiers between the Inferno and Paradise.

He almost regretted it now but it was too late to turn back.

'The hidden figures who assist us,' he said, 'the hidden judges who appear to condemn us, are at every wedding feast of the Virgin that is attended by the rich and the poor. They rub shoulders in hope of honeymooning in heaven. Do you recall the Animal Goddess and Jonah in the Oracle-Brothel?'

'That was no wedding feast,' I cried.

'It was an affair of the charismatic heart in which an enslaving Goddess or Judge turned into a figure of Compassion. Jonah was upheld on a log and a net and given a chance to repent. Mr Mageye will film him once again at Deacon's (and your) wedding feast. Repentance is hollow and meaningless without Muses and Virgins. Let me tell you a secret that you may have already guessed! Even as the Animal Goddess is the seer of the Brothel I am the seer of GRAVE LAND! And Francisco I *see* Kali of Port Mourant . . .'

'Who is Kali?' I cried.

'She is a pin-up Goddess for the peasants of Port Mourant. She came from India with indentured servants in the nineteenth century who are amongst Marie of Port Mourant's antecedents. She is a severe and terrifying judge who walks in the shadow of Marie. There again one comes upon a frontier between caring love and judgement shawl that Kali wears. These shall be visible at Deacon's (and your) wedding feast when you both wed the Virgin of Port Mourant: concretely (in Deacon's tragic marriage to her), apparitionally (in your retrial of the wedding and of Deacon's hubris of *immunity to pain* in planting the seed of foetal majesty and great but illusory fortune in her). These are riddling terms but

153

you shall see. A seer tests the Imagination to re-examine all "futures" in the light of "pasts". You shall see I trust.'

What was visible to me now in the Circus of the nether world was the game of PRISONERS in 'futures' and 'pasts' . . . The game was in full swing in Bonampak's Paradise of the Rain God.

The players were installed at a great gambling table in the middle of a field.

It was a sacred game set in a curiously pagan yet modern context that I could not easily define and which prompted me to ask my Skeleton-twin about 'futures' and 'pasts' . . . I heard him grumbling in response to my question: *'There's no short-cut for orphans like yourself, Francisco – born at the extremities of many cultures and civilizations in South America – with regard to "futures" and "pasts".* You are immersed in motherships, brideships, twin-ships, games of every complexion. No short-cut! Each riddle that I offer in the Circus of the Grave is a promise of immersion in experienced truth – the experience of truths to be borne by you within the blending of ages and times – *not* a recourse to formula or plot . . .'

He raised a bony cautionary finger into the air and I was reminded of my mother's work-hardened hands and of the mystery of pain. I touched my lips as though they bled in the school ground of long ago yet of which I was conscious again as an ingrained callous in this instant within my present age. Dream callous! Dream-conscience and the labyrinthine ruses of love and fear through which one may seek to short-circuit pain. Had my mother's work-hardened hands touched my lips they might have bled all the more. An extraordinary game!

One field of the past overlaps another riddling future in the Circus of the Grave when the dice are cut from Bone. Cut from my Skeleton-twin's cautionary finger.

'Cut also,' said my Skeleton-twin, 'from the bone beneath the flesh of the two fingers sliced from your hand, Francisco, in Jonestown from Deacon's apparently random bullet.'

'Do you mean,' I cried, 'that the dice are cut from *me*? And from *you*?'

'And from the Virgin's work-hardened nails as well . . .'

It was a cunning Jest of the crucifixion of the globe that Mr Mageye would have envied.

'The ancestry and progeny of the dice in the Paradise of the Rain God – in a pagan Grave as much as a Christian Grave – are the substance of new riddles of the mystery of pain and the hubris that we now entertain of immunity to pain.'

I studied the players closely as they threw the dice which bounced it seemed in my own flesh upon the table. I felt I was in danger of being torn to shreds by Maya peasants and savages. But a Prisoner came forward. He was surrounded by a crowd of dancers who shuffled up to him and touched him.

'They should be unable to touch him,' I cried in alarm.

The Game in the Nether World had now become a battle: passions, emotions, spectres, realities, crossings, recrossings, judges, graces. But by and large the Game was steeped in terrors and uncertainties. Fear lit the Circus of the Grave. And I feared for my life. Grave Land. Nether World. Uncanny Circus. Staggered identities or names of Fear. Fear ran riot on the field. I would be unable to return to the Virgin Ship. Would I make it? Would I escape? Fear cooled a little within me. The riot seemed to subside. But all the danger signals remained.

No sign of my guide, seer, Skeleton-twin.

I looked for him at the heart of the scrum but he was not to be seen. The battle that ensued was fought, or played, at the gambling table in the field of the Paradise of the Rain God.

It was a battle over the Pagan Body (its susceptibility to the elements), Pagan Sport, Pagan Riot, Pagan Economies in Third Worlds, Second Worlds, First Worlds . . .

The Pagan Body had long seemed irrelevant to Western and Eastern, Northern and Southern ideologies. Yet one caught a glimpse of intrinsic paganism in the embalmed frames of charismatic warriors or revolutionaries or saints. One caught a glimpse of a family of Skeleton-twins fleshed with natural-seeming, unnatural flesh within the gloom and the glitter of sarcophagi open to tourists: Moscow, Vietnam, ancient and modern Egypt and Rome.

Such glimpses led me to fight for Breath to save my own life. And yet I was convinced of the complexities of resurrectionary pulse within the wrappings of the Pagan Body.

I heard the sudden clamour of giants of chaos that Deacon had embalmed in a coffin in Crabwood Creek when he lassoed the Horses of the Moon and the riders on their backs. Were Third World Presidents and Prime Ministers of Guyana and Brazil in that Coffin?

Could they spring up and seize me? *They were here.* Sudden clamour, for now I knew the masked players at the table! Not only Presidents and Prime Ministers but Bankers and Peasants played at the table. They belonged to all parties across the generations of colonial and post-colonial histories. Some looked as Mayan or as Chinese as Lenin in the guise of a Pope gambling with millions of followers at the table of Latin American history. All well and good to mock them I thought, but I knew they knew me as one of the involuntary architects of the Jonestown holocaust.

It almost took my Breath away again, for they gambled with the dice of my bones, a benumbed survivor's bones . . .

Carnival has many wrappings in the Circus of the Grave and Breath becomes an essential mystery for survivors who descend into 'futures' and 'pasts'.

Politicians and Peasants – in their embalmed masquerade – are also Bankers: quite ordinary folk whom Deacon had indeed thrust into the Coffin: ordinary, extraordinary Coffin. Was it the death of politics around the globe and in Guyana?

I repeated to myself again and again: 'They are the ghost-players at the gambling table and my heart rises into my mouth.'

I fell on my knees in the scrum of worlds ancient and modern. I could not hold the players but they seemed capable of crushing me to smithereens.

I could not hold them but I was suddenly sensitive to my pagan lips bruised on the playing fields of Boyhood. I was sensitive to the Carib bone-flute within the natural, unnatural flesh that Deacon had bitten, it seemed, with his gun in Jonestown. Bitten from my hand! I was sensitive to the ground in which my mother's body lay in Albuoystown. Two or three blades of grass from my Nemesis Hat still sprang there. They resembled rain in the Paradise of the Rain God.

The difficulty in identifying the Pagan Body in Christian currencies, in Marxian money, or in any other Political or Religious cash denomination, lay – I felt – in the weight one gave to the blood of apparitions which sit on chests of treasure, embalmed treasure, that have been secured in the teeth of battle. The apparitions wave like flags on the Moon upon which Deacon and Jonah fought so fiercely on the day and night of the holocaust.

On the face of it such treasure was of museum value but blood was as real as dice. It dried (this was true) on one's lips and left its stamp there. But its imprint, its labyrinth of love and fear, was a miraculous toss of chance or fate . . . Was Breath a matter of chance or of fate? Did freedom lie between chance and fate?

I looked up at the Prisoner who stood at the heart of the mysterious battle in the Nether World. Pagan surrogate God? Solid apparition on the treasure chest of the globe? Christian surrogate God? I could not be sure. But I grieved with all my heart (as if it were the world's heart) for him. The crowd closed in on him, it touched him, they touched him, but he seemed still set apart and able to withstand assault. An extraordinary Game!

'Real rain, real blood, runs in his veins,' I cried. 'He is as real as the Breath in my body. I know only too well now – as I stand or kneel in danger beside him – how pitiless is the crowd that surrounds him. Should they succeed in genuinely seizing him . . .' I stopped. There were tears in my eyes that dropped like fluid dice in the Paradise of the Rain God. 'Should they seize him it would be a phenomenal event in the Nether World. Should they – this beastly crowd of savages – cross the frontier between themselves and him, it would be a phenomenal seizure . . .' Seizure of God, the killing of God, surrogate Prisoner-God?

The ghost-players and Bankers and Peasants and Teachers and Politicians at the table – giants of chaos they were – dressed in natural, unnatural flesh like embalmed figures, underpinning ideologies and dogmas, looked up at me. They gave an incredible smile that shook me on my knees until the pain I felt broke into

at I remained precariously whole and free to fight my
om the Nether World of the Circus.

hrew their dice at the same instant that our eyes met.
eyes. I gasped as each die revealed a limb, an organ
inted upon it, a splinter on my lip imprinted on it, eyes in my
lips. Dream Body. Pagan Body. They were gambling on behalf of
the crowds that surged around the Prisoner.

They piled the dice into a corner of the field or the table and
secured another handful from their pockets to fling again upon
table or field.

But it was the Prisoner's turn now to throw. I gasped as he
threw his lot on the table. The Players and the crowds leaned over
– they shook their heads – when each die cast by the Prisoner
proved as blank as a slate. Black slate. White slate.

'Tell him,' the giants of chaos said to me, 'that he might as well
surrender himself of his free will. Give himself freely to the
crowds.'

I was heartbroken at the price that the Prisoner was asked to
pay to reveal to the blind throng the jointed nests in the Phallic
tree of space. 'It is unjust,' I said. 'It is the mystery of injustice.'

There was a lull in the Game.

'Here in Bonampak,' they said to me, 'we secure Prisoners and
treat them as guests of heaven. If they want choice maidens they
may have them. If they want banquets they may have them. All
we ask in return is that when we bring them to trial at the
gambling table they surrender their organs, heart and limb, to be
given to the Sun. It's an honourable vocation. To serve as a
Prisoner taken in battle! In that way we light the Breath of the Sun
in the sky.'

'Barbarous, barbarous,' I cried. 'Barbarous, barbarous.'

'Is the Sun barbarous, Francisco? The Sun requires sacrifice. It's
up to the Prisoners! If they give of themselves freely – few if any in
our experience have so far – then they will be spared the assault of
the crowds (we will carve them up gently like foxes in the field,
that's all); the crowds see them as the fountainhead of fortune and
prosperity! They must give all they possess. Not only their body
but the children of their body if they have any. For one of those

158

children may prove to be a king or a saviour. If they hold
they claim that the gift of freedom under the Sun is prem
that Mankind is still unfit to carry the burden of freedom,
alas the bonfire of passion in the crowds awaits them, there is
nothing we can do but roll dice and wait. We are Bankers,
Teachers, Politicians. We please the crowds even as we make them
subservient to Money and to Propaganda.'

I was tempted – God knows! – to applaud their cynical jesting
at the state of my corrupt age but I knew I was witnessing an
unforgettable counterpoint between ancient savage ritual and
mystical dismemberment scarcely understood as the twentieth
century drew to a close. Unforgettable yet scarcely understood!
Did a chasm exist between Memory, the history of Memory, and
the genesis of mystical dismemberments as a redistributive focus
of variable supports not only for Suns and planets but for
disadvantaged cultures in need of sustenance and Breath everywhere? Such a chasm – and its reconnaissance – was pertinent to
the Nether World in which we confront ourselves, our spectral
selves, our inbuilt peasants and exploiters, prosecutors, inbuilt
victims that we are in the scrum of the Game . . .

I could scarcely speak but I managed to whisper: 'What throw
of the die from him – this Prisoner – do you wait for?'

'A moment will come,' they cried, 'when a face or a Mask will
appear on a die that he throws . . .'

'What face? What Mask?'

'Who knows? The Mask of an angel-bridegroom.' They
hesitated, then they were emboldened by the operatic mystery of
the Nether World.

'Yes,' they cried, 'this is a trial that he cannot escape. And
sooner or later the bridegroom will appear on a die: one destined
to marry his daughter whom he is unwilling to surrender. The
crowds will break him then, Francisco.'

With this alarming pronouncement they shuffled together the
dice that they had thrown and proceeded to expose them to my
gaze. My head rested on its chin at the edge of the table.

I knew of the imprinted organs and limbs but there was another
die that I had missed entirely. It was a cross-sectional exposure of

159

the Prisoner's body in which Deacon sat as upon a pillow of leaves or stone.

'Is this the die of which you speak?' I cried. I could not believe my eyes. 'What does it mean?'

At long last they replied.

'Deacon gaoled us in a Coffin. You do remember, don't you? You and Mr Mageye were there filming the event.' They spoke almost accusingly. 'He is destined to be our liberator. Gaoler. Liberator. What a paradox. We bank on him. We teach his name. Deacon fell from the stars to expose centuries and generations in conquistadorial regimes in which populations were decimated and buried yet liberated in colonial history books. The legacy is strong. It encompasses all our presidents, prime ministers, etc. It encompasses the business of politics, industry, statecraft, education, everything. Burial. Liberation.'

'Everything depends,' I said, poking my head onto the gambling table, 'on how we shoulder such legacies in order to take responsibility for our own fate enmeshed into the fate of others in ourselves. We need to go beyond politics and history . . .'

They eyed me severely as if my head had been draped in a veil. Then they put their lips against my ears which were plainly visible.

'Let us put it like this, Francisco. Deacon is a cross-sectional apparition, at one level, of our residences in the Prisoner, our fate in the Prisoner, the gift of freedom bestowed upon us by the Prisoner.'

The smooth run of their voices filled me with misgiving.

'You, Francisco,' they declared, 'may see us as thieves or tricksters but remember! we play interchangeable roles. Savage. Civilized.' There was a hiss now to their voices. 'We play voices in a crowd. We play that we fall on our knees, as you do, beside the Prisoner.' I swore they were surreptitiously changing their masks as they leaned closer to my veiled or shadowed head on the table before them. 'How can the rich save the poor,' they demanded, 'the poor the rich, the thief the saint, the saint the thief, the judge the judged, the judged the judge, unless they discard contentment, or self-righteous creed, self-righteous parasitism, and build

160

dimensions of self-confessional, self-judgemental art, that take them into recesses and spaces that may pull them *into* and *beyond* themselves? Unless this happens in the theatre of civilizations evolution remains a WASTE LAND and religion contracts into a Void. Yes, the Prisoner sometimes seems the architect of the Void in his uncertainties as to the nature of freedom in art, in science.'

Their voices grew blunt as if they had reversed their killing knives into self-confessional relics of terrifying Spirituality, terrifying necessity to change the music at the heart of the Sun, the heart of creation.

'So Francisco!' A drum in my senses throbbed.

'So Francisco!' they repeated. 'We know the danger you are in. Yet the possibilities of a re-visionary surgery of Spirit! An old/ new head. A new/old responsibility. You descended into the Grave with your twin even as we were pushed there by Deacon when he lassoed the Horses of the Moon. And believe me our protean reflections – inbuilt reflected exploiters, inbuilt reflected exploited – will pursue you should you escape from the Grave . . .'

The odd way they put it – 'our reflections will pursue you *should you escape from the Grave*' – was a blow that I could not fathom. As though they had sliced my head from my body with their sharp/blunt knives and I would need to strengthen my frame, my tissues, my muscles to replace it with another. 'Believe us!' they cried. 'You will see. We shall elect Deacon . . .' Was it a threat? Was it a promise?

A howl blotted out their operatic voices. It smote me like a calm, a howling calm that replaces a silent storm. My emotions were turned upside-down. It was the howl of the interchangeable masks in the crowds of ghost-actors, hollow shouting silent masks, around the Prisoner. He had thrown another round of dice.

I wormed my way to the wall of the Grave. Time to attempt to leave, to prepare myself, time to strengthen limbs, gain tissues, muscularity, to bear another head after a mystical decapitation.

The tone of the crowds began to change. *I swore I heard rushing footsteps.* Had they seen me? Were they intent on pulling me back? I clung to a ripple of muscularity in the wall. I clung to ribbed sculptures. The hands that sought to pull me back into the Grave imbued me with the fiercest energy to turn heaven's brow upon them. Heaven's brow in place of every skull. I flattened myself into a guest of heaven that the Prisoner had promised in the art of Bonampak.

I turned the Shadow of that brow, angel's uncertain brow, upon them as they scrambled in the sculptures around me to pull me back. They hesitated. Their outstretched, carven hands upon the wall loosened their grip upon me. They seemed to see me differently from how I saw myself. I was still Francisco Bone. How hard to conceive of myself in a pagan mural of the LAND OF THE DEAD as a guest of heaven . . . I was veiled from myself within ruses of the Imagination that I could scarcely bear. They saw the veil that topped my Nemesis Hat as it began to descend upon my strengthened shoulders. They saw the rivets and the holes as well to take the new Mask. This was the key to my escape from the Grave. I had a key in the tattoo on my arm to gain entry. Now I possessed another key in ancient/modern sculpture to return to the upper air.

Roraima's Scorpions

In the hollow of God – whether water or fire – there is
no discrimination. Everyone arrives and departs in
mutual body and mutual ghost. This is the 'architecture of pilgrimages'. The pilgrims come and go 'seven
times in a minute'.

What is a minute or a number (whether seven or
zero on the Earth)? It is above and below, it is diversity
and uncanny twinships, in the creation and fall and
rehabilitation of time.

Francisco Bone's summary and translation of the
Mayan Itzá or Izté Oracle at Chichén and other
places of sacrifice

Marie of Port Mourant and Deacon were married in Crabwood Creek in the third week of March 1954.

A week or so before the wedding the Prisoner of Devil's Isle arrived on the Courantyne coast and was promptly arrested by the Inspector of Police. It was not the first occasion that he had visited the Courantyne, been arrested and sent back to French Guyana. The first time he came an accident happened which resulted in the death of Marie's Indian parents before her adoption by the Doctor at the Port Mourant Hospital. The Prisoner – despite all this – claimed that he was Marie's true father.

On his arrest – a week or so before the wedding – I followed and slipped into the cell where he was taken.

'We shall have to ship you back in chains to French Guyana from British Guyana,' said the Inspector.

'I must see my daughter,' said the Prisoner.

'Your daughter? Who is she?'

'The nurse Marie at the Hospital.'

The Inspector pretended amazement.

'Marie is the Doctor's daughter!'

'Not so, Inspector. Not so. The Doctor is her putative father. I am her father.'

'The Doctor is a God,' said the Inspector softly. 'He runs the Hospital. He's a scientist. He sees through frames and codes of superstition.'

'I am an old God,' said the Prisoner. 'I am the embodiment of untranslated fiction, the embodiment of the Void. I need to see her before she marries a fallen angel. Angels are of the Void. They are the embodiment of an art that we should take seriously. Deacon was inoculated, wasn't he, with the bite of the Scorpion.'

The Inspector stared at the Prisoner and became indulgent. He prided himself on being a tolerant man. Poor devil the Prisoner was! One should pity him . . . He could not resist murmuring however – with a taste or rumble of mockery in his voice: 'One day I shall write a book of folk legends. You scrambled ashore with a rag on your back and now you claim to be a God. Fallen angels! Scorpions! I ask you. I have heard it all. Do you know I myself am written into the stars as the magus of the Law in these parts? . . .'

I was tempted to interrupt the Inspector – from my recess in the Prisoner's cell – and to say: 'There are prisoners and prisoners – we are all prisoners – sometimes it seems that we are all made in the image of an eternal Prisoner . . . *Except that the gravity of freedom seems so real that freedom must be true* . . . It's a matter of broken archetypes that tests us sometimes beyond endurance and yet we must continue to be tested . . . Magus of the law, Inspector! What does it mean? What does this mean? Are not law and love parts of a whole archetype which baffles us as lightning baffles the sky? And yet we glimpse it as if by chance at times, within the immensity of a cosmic gamble which weaves together a diversity of sciences and traditions. These overlap within proportionalities of "music" in the "word", well-nigh uncontainable word in music, uncontainable music in word, to revive the energy of endurance and sacrifice that would be incomprehensible *without the gravity of freedom.* Is freedom rooted in an obscure premise of evolution that bears on all being and indeed non-being, all dimensionalities (past and present and future) . . . ? Perverse Reverend Jonah Jones of the Whale – who boasted that he fucked heathens as a stick with which to strike his civilization – is twin to the poor Prisoner in this cell who claims to be the father of Marie! It seems outrageous. It seems alien. Perversity in the family of gods and humans and all species is a measure of alienation that we embrace within the gravity of freedom. Is this not so, Inspector? How else may we begin to endure the mystery of love that prompts us to see ourselves differently within a whole universe, within parallel universes, within the holocaustic, nuclear games that we play with one another? Through such alienation we may plumb some grain of innermost repentance within a fabric of hostilities that "space" itself engenders, inner spaces, outer spaces, inner bridges, outer bridges, finities, and infinities . . . We may begin to be incredibly whole, a journey beyond fear . . .'

The Inspector did not hear a syllable or a word. If he had he would have labelled me a poor Jester in the image of Mr Mageye perhaps.

His rumbling mocking voice ran through the Prisoner's cell. 'I am one of three magi at the cradle of Francisco Bone's Dream-book! Mr Mageye the Jester is another. And damn it all – who would believe it? – the Doctor in the Hospital is the other. Have you heard of Francisco Bone? I ask you, Prisoner of Devil's Isle.' The Prisoner bowed his head in consenting to the mystery of love and sacrifice that tied him to all cultures, species, imaginations in the name of the gravity of freedom.

The Inspector insisted: 'Have you heard of Bone, you god-damn awful Prisoner? He and Deacon were Scholarship Boys. It's a long fragmented archetypal narrative. Read the Dream-book! Can you read, Prisoner? They became friends in San Francisco. It's recorded, I would imagine, in Jonah Jones's log-book in the Whale of the sun in Jonestown. Francisco and Deacon returned to British Guiana every year to keep in touch with freedom fighters. A month's holiday or so. Francisco and Deacon were American Guyanese – if one may distinguish them jokingly, self-mockingly, from English Guyanese who study at universities and colleges in England. Two different prisons you see within a fabric of broken archetypes. Sometimes English law seems alien to American law and vice versa. That's how Deacon – an American Guyanese – wooed Marie. He's been in love with her since childhood. So he claims. Jonah Jones of the Whale by the way signed himself in his log-book as a Prisoner of Classics of Anger! Yes, the ramifications of the broken archetype are startling but true when you ponder upon it. Perhaps they throw some light on why Jonah Jones and Francisco Bone and Deacon sought to build a new world they christened Jonestown in the Void of Guyana. As for Bone's other magi . . . I have spoken of them, have I not? I am infected at times by amnesia from which the Dream-book suffers! I have mentioned Mr Mageye, I think, and Marie's father, the Doctor in the Port Mourant Hospital . . .'

'*Putative* father,' the Prisoner interrupted. 'Get your facts straight. Putative father.'

'Putative then. Have it your own way. The fact or fiction remains that he's another magus. The third, I repeat, is Mr

Mageye, the head teacher from Albuoystown.' He laughed to split his sides . . . And a key fell out into my hands (I was still hidden in the cell), a key to the prison of the Void. At last I was in possession of the magus-Inspector's gift. Marie's Wheel was the magus-Doctor's, a futuristic Camera was Mr Mageye's.

'Eponymous magi are the foundations of a new world that takes its variable name from magus-Law, magus-Medicine, magus-Jest. Call the new world LAW/MEDICINE/JEST in an age of injustice, of a sickness of the soul, yet curiously redemptive and divine comedy. So I am told,' said the Prisoner. 'But tell me again,' he said wryly, 'how do you *know* all these things? Is it hollow folklore or is it the universality of a collective unconscious that secretes itself in the elements that we breathe or consume, in the sun's blood as in our blood, in the elements that consume us in turn though we may be oblivious of the teeth of fire or air, of dread, dread companionships that loom unseen within us and around us until we *see* and change and become open to changes undreamt-of within the very fabric of things that we dread, a conversion of dread into a womb of imagination, moral twinships with all species and things? Such a conversion seems an impossibility yet it is the seed or grain of knowledge that anticipates unexpected varieties of knowledge, knowledge that recovers lost foundations of knowledge, wastelands, gravelands, Skeleton-twins, netherworlds, blocked they seem yet susceptible to innermost self-confessional convertibility, innermost, redemptive, self-judgemental vessel of resource . . . Yes, it is this. Such a conversion is this. Or it is nothing. It is hollow folklore. Is it hollow folklore?'

The Inspector grew uneasy all at once. He was cut to the bone by the taunt. 'How does one know anything?' he murmured in protest. Was it protest or was it uncanny, unselfconscious collusion? I wondered.

'How does one know anything?' the Inspector murmured. 'How does one know of the genesis parting of the Red Sea? Was it the genesis of blood or of rain? Or the existence of El Dorado? Was it gold or was it straw? Or the flood upon Plato's Atlantis? Was Plato a philosopher or a frustrated voyager? Or Toussaint's letters to his generals in Haiti? He was an illiterate. Did he write in letters of fire? Were the sayings of Christ uttered by him or by voices in numinous rocks and trees? Were numinous rocks and trees mass-media television accompanying him as Mr Mageye's Camera claims to circumnavigate Teresa of Calcutta? How does one travel with the speed of light that remains constant in all circumstances? Common sense falters. But the lame who extend their limbs into mystical faculties may know for sure.'

'You are the magus-Law,' said the Prisoner, 'you should know. The Law is a star for all magi. The Law is an eponymous Shadow of Nemesis against which the light of a star – long extinct – still bends. Shadow is a caveat in the *name* of Light or long-vanished stars, of whose disappearance we do not yet know, across the light-years. Eponymous Shadow of Nemesis wears the name of apparitional and concrete heartlands of Light to address the materialism and cultural hubris of our age ... Does Einstein's ghost roll dice in mathematics of Chaos?'

The Inspector looked chastened but it was his turn – in the strangest collusion of lips between the Prisoner and himself – to taunt the Old God of Devil's Isle. 'We move and have our being in a Void,' he said. 'That is all we know and hope to know. So don't knock folk legends, Prisoner, by pretending you are superior to them.'

'I thought you were doing the knocking,' said the Prisoner.

I listened with beating heart, mind and heart, to the conversation between the Prisoner and the Inspector.

Beating mind, beating heart, like a bird's in the palm of the old Prisoner or God.

Equally his heart, his mind, beat in my three-fingered hand.

Were we both prisoners of the Void?

Not entirely. But I had to confess I was a feature of shadow myself with a Bag or a Hat over my head. Had I not returned from the future into the past – from Winter 1978 in Jonestown to March 1954 in Port Mourant and Crabwood Creek – from holocaust in Jonestown to Port Mourant's and Crabwood Creek's impending wedding of Deacon and Marie?

I had been here before in my Dream-book but I had returned

again. The tragedy of Jonestown had left me stunned but I needed to revisit the scene and the entire environment – not only interior but coastal – in which it had occurred to learn of the foundations of doomed colonies, cities, villages, settlements, ancient and modern, by retracing my steps, by accepting my wounds and lameness and the speed of light with which one travels back into the past from bleak futures.

My view of the Void was different from the Prisoner's. But I was unsure. The Void for me – perhaps for him – was open to pilgrimages and to pilgrims. It was a state of affairs that witnessed to uncertainties of Home: Home as I have attempted to define it upon a variety of bridges in my Dream-book . . . Uncertainty of Home sometimes seemed a state of permanency; except that eponymous Shadow implied a womb of hope, implied the triple, quadruple, even sevenfold name of the Womb of space; implied for me three folk Maries: Virgin peasant Marie of Port Mourant and Crabwood Creek whom the Prisoner claimed as his daughter in the teeth of the Doctor's influence (and claim as well), the Doctor's aspiration to clothe Marie in gold – if that were at all possible – when Deacon became her political consort; Virgin Marie of Albuoystown; Virgin Marie of Jonestown, the Animal Goddess, with her sculpted torso. Three Maries.

I tried to slip out of the cell but the Inspectors caught sight of me and drew me back.

'Not so quick, Francisco. I saw you crouching there in a corner. You can't deceive the magus of the Law!' He was smiling with self-mockery I dreamt as he spoke. Then he turned grave and cool – not harsh – as the key which had fallen out of his split, laughing sides. 'You must confront the Prisoner, Francisco.'

I turned and saw the Prisoner's calculating and extraordinary eye upon me. He was measuring me. Already I sensed he knew me differently from how I knew myself. My best tactic was to strike out boldly, to speak boldly.

How did I see him?

'I see the Prisoner,' I said, 'as the eponymous hero of the Void which he has endured in all religions for ages. He swims, he is one-in-many, many-in-one, he is a Jester like Mr Mageye, he appears to escape, he runs, he appears to drown but he surfaces again and again. It is said that Jonah Jones is his perverse twin. Perverse, yes, that is true. He loathes cults. He is aware of the Virgin Ship and the huntsman Christ. They are new phenomena of Spirit in his aged sight I would imagine. That's my guess. So much so he fears for the peasant Virgin Marie whom he claims as his daughter. He sees her as subordinate to the wealth of civilization and therefore liable to become a pawn in the game of religious freedom.

'Let me tell you, Inspector, that I see the poor Prisoner – within the backcloth of the poverty-stricken Guyanas – as so imbued now, in my Dream-book age, with the mathematics of Chaos that some reluctant sacrifice on his part, some cruel rending sacrifice, is impending – I have a dark sensation of what it is – which bears on the fate of freedom . . .

'I say "reluctant" for the Prisoner would prefer not to be involved. He would prefer his daughter to withdraw from the marriage to Deacon. And I tend to agree. I am jealous of Deacon. But I feel it is now all too late and that the Prisoner, Deacon and I are bound together in a curious pact that resembles the pact between Deacon, Jonah and me but differs profoundly. Yes, twin-pacts they are but how they differ! The pact with Jonah led to the holocaust. The pact with the Prisoner leads I feel to an intricate dismantling of the Void.'

'Does the Void exist here,' cried the Inspector, 'on these coastlands? Great Europe I would understand as pertinent to a theatre of the Void, or the great United States, or the great Soviet Union that was and is in "futures" and "pasts". But here on these poor coastlands?"

'The Void has been here for generations. Take it at a basic level. They are deemed flat, are they not?'

'The coastlands you mean?'

'Yes, I mean the coastlands. They are deemed as flat as commonsense prose or journalism. Commonsense engineers decided long ago in the eighteenth and nineteenth centuries that the cotton estates and the cane-farming estates, the sugar plantations, were to be laid out in rectangles and squares. As a consequence they smothered the breath-lines in a living land-scape. And when the peasant rice farmer came into being he had to contend with disfigured catchments, in the coastal river systems, that would occasion excessive floods and droughts for him. The sugar barons escaped, for they had empoldered their lands into a one-sided paradise . . .'

'I do not follow,' said the Inspector.

'It's simplicity itself, but as always simplicity is a complex achievement, isn't it, for it involves us in a net of profoundest inter-relationships, re-visionary relationships. Nothing is to be taken for granted. We are at liberty now to see that the landscape is not flat . . .'

'Not flat?' cried the Inspector. 'But I still think it is.'

I paused and considered how best to explain simplicity's complexity, complexity's simplicity, to him.

'Have you heard of spirit-levelling?' I said. 'An odd term I know. Spirit-levelling encompasses the use of dumpy-levels, theodolites, surveying instruments etc. A wholly new reconnais-sance of the coastlands brought to light apparently minor but significant watersheds and drainage lines which – when per-ceived in relationship – were of extreme importance. They offered the contours upon which to build a redistributive alliance of canals, drainage, and other works orchestrated into the living landscape to provide a genuine intercourse between the art of science and the life of nature within a theatre of diverse cultivation and achievements. It has not happened, it never happened, it still is not happening. Instead the Void!'

The Prisoner stared at me with what seemed a baleful eye.

'Where in hell did you learn all this, Francisco?' he cried. 'Was it in hell or in San Francisco College? Or was it in the Nether World? You have touched me on the raw. My hands are bruised from battering against the Void. The Earth is flat in the Void. But it rears its flatness up into irredeemable structures, unchanging institu-tions, unchanging parliaments, unchanging human nature. I have battered my hands raw. So perhaps it's time for me to die.'

'So have I,' I cried. 'So have I. I bruised my fists when I arose from the Grave in Jonestown.'

'Jonestown? Jonestown?' said the bewildered Prisoner. 'Wh
is Jonestown?'

I almost bit my lip. I was *in* the past now, not in the future. I had
returned to the past from the future. I was back in 1954. I had
learnt to survey the breath-lines in living landscapes from my
Skeleton-twin who made no bones about the articulation of ridges
and watersheds and contours in the Paradise of the Rain God.

'Oh nothing,' I said quickly. 'You of all Prisoners situated in the
Void should know of mixed "futures" and "pasts". After all they
are but frames. We speak in the framed word of God but the
unfathomable Creator, the untranslatable Creator, cannot be
framed.'

'I am a framed God,' said the Prisoner. 'Have I not uttered a
dark sentence on myself? It's time for me to die!'

'Language is deeper than its frames or Gods who claim to be an
absolute God.' I stopped. Did I speak in arrogance or in
simplicity's faith in an untranslatable Creator? 'The resources of
a living language sustain a re-visionary dynamic. There is real
continuity running out of the past into the future. But such
continuity cannot be lodged absolutely in the frames and the
dogmas of the past. For then the past becomes an invalid. Even
the Doctor in the Hospital knows this if he is to see through the
masks of his patients, pigmentations, creeds, whatever, to their
essential disease . . . But he exploits them. He turns away from his
daughter's fiery glance when she plays at being a nursery princess
in a sick world.'

'What is the future, Francisco Bone? I know – or think I know –
the past. The past becomes extinct unless we *live* it in the life of the
future, freedom's future – however disastrous freedom sometimes
seems – and freedom's reconnaissance of the past. A jealous man
like yourself, Francisco (jealous of Deacon), who slips into cells,
and hides in bushes, may have something priceless to offer. Your
diminutive being is a recommendation of collective involvement
with others yet divergence and capacity to see what others – even
myself – may fail to see. What is the future, Francisco Bone?'

The Prisoner was tempting me I knew, he was flattering and
testing me I knew. He was seeking to discover whether an element

of paranoia might not reside in a diminutive survivor such as myself. Is not paranoia another wall or factor in the prison of the Void?

There were footsteps in the street below that seemed to whisper like lips of leather upon the soil. They rose to the walls of the cell with a faint, sinister momentum. They seemed to declare that the Prisoner had challenged me to become a seer, a journeyman, a prophet steeped in inventions of time, Eclipses, Bags, Nets, Nemesis, Fate.

Curious how the traffic of an age runs in one's blood with intimations of past and coming events, footsteps in the Nether World, unearthly ruins, collapsing, sighing walls and cities, a Wheel in space.

The Prisoner's life was in danger, the Old God was in danger.

I knew for I had returned from the future to the past. So I brought within me from later decades knowledge of events in 1954 associated with the wedding of Deacon and Marie. But rack my mind now as I did, a blank fell out.

Had I forgotten in the light of a wholly new element and pact that I knew – though I was uncertain how I knew – was looming between the Prisoner, Deacon and me? It evoked the pact between Jonah, Deacon and me but it was profoundly different.

Whereas the pact with Jonah signified catastrophe – and this I remembered – the *new* pact planted in the past, the *new* shape to time *within the past* (in this revisitation from the future) signified a mathematic of decapitation in the re-shouldering of past and future in my body, upon my body, through Deacon's absent body, and through the Prisoner's potential sacrifice of his body.

Mr Mageye had promised me that we would build Memory theatre. And now I began to see glimmeringly that Memory theatre is rooted in events one knows to have occurred even as it breaks the Void that imprisons one to create new pacts within lapses of memory within oneself when one revisits the past. Such strange lapses – that seem deeper than mere common-or-garden lapses – are motivated perhaps by a mystical crumbling of the Void . . . I was unsure. I could not truly say . . .

I crossed to the window and looked down from the cell into the street. Looked down a dream-ladder in the anatomy of the cellular body of the Void that I shared with the Prisoner even as it seemed to crumble . . . I remembered Bonampak. I remembered Jacob's ladder. I shuddered with the sensation that my bones walked in air with God's . . .

The dancing, ominous footsteps ceased, no one could be plainly seen in the street but Carnival Lord Death.

He was staring up at the window as if he had become a transparent reservoir of subconscious/unconscious dis-member-ment costumery and re-memberment masquerade within the Grave and the Body of Carnival.

The footsteps had ceased as if the walking dead were more cunning than one realized. They were here for Marie's and Deacon's wedding. Did I hear Marie's now, Marie's footsteps approaching mine, though I had not moved an inch in the Prisoner's cell from the moment I came to the window?

How sensitive is the mind to read a walking epitaph and a walking marriage-bed and a walking cradle in the footsteps of humanity, ghostly humanity, bodiless humanity, bodily human-ity?

All were tokens of dis-memberment and re-memberment in the air of the Void, the uncertainty of the crumbling of the Void.

Of one thing I was sure. There was danger everywhere. There was hypocrisy everywhere. There was injustice everywhere. Fiction was truth. Fact was polished and manufactured into lies. I trembled. I was a Jester of pasts and futures in the present moment. I was a Jester of chaos, I was susceptible to a transference of masks with giants of chaos, masks to be inserted within and upon familiar and unfamiliar footsteps. But I trembled. I trembled at the prospect of the wedding (Marie's and Deacon's). I trembled at the consummation of their union in the Void. This much I knew and remembered. I clung to the notion that my return into the past from the future was a phenomenon of changed time, new time, a phenomenon of the Imagination steeped in creative purpose despite every old hedge or blanket of terror.

When one returns from the future into the past, and the past becomes once again the living present day or moment or year, one sees into the womb of time, the womb of Virgin comedy, as it adventures into intercourse with Fate and Dread inscribed into a bridegroom who lassoed the Horses and their riders on the Moon and who is claimed by them now as their leader, their hero promising salvation . . . Did I remember all this or had it been inserted into Memory theatre as a new invention however rooted in past time?

Why should Time choose poor Virgin peasant Marie to marry the ruthless angel Deacon? Did one need to assess and reassess the mystery of Fate and Dread in new fictions of reality if one were to break moulds of complacency in the Void? Did Time seek to pour cold water on eighteenth-century and nineteenth-century portraits of the family? Fate and Dread are banished from such portraits in favour of a comedy of manners as the tincture or costumery of the moral family.

The Void is converted into currency – comedy of manners currency – with which to purchase the furniture of an age carpentered from felled trees and forests or spun from the fur, or the horns, or the hide of extinct species, extinct flesh-and-blood.

'A dash of cold water in one's eyes in the tears of Paradise, the Paradise of the Rain God,' said the Prisoner, 'unfreezes Memory's hollow currency as Fate and Dread revive to wed Virgin Marie of Port Mourant. *Portrait of the Moral Family* – in the novels of the past three hundred years which you were conditioned to read at college, Francisco – *cannot sustain brides and bridegrooms now who have inherited the Void and the crumbling prospect of the Void*. You see now, don't you, why I fear for myself and for my daughter?

'Let me tell you, Francisco – in the shape of the pact that you and I share with absent Deacon in this revisitation of past time – that I desire the crumbling of the Void – yes, I do – but one is not spared from scanning the Void (even as one desires a change) for the Void is in the ascendancy everywhere still masked by varieties of diplomacy in markets of culture. The dangers then that one continues to face in a cruel and hypocritical age cannot be underestimated.'

He was standing in the middle of the cell behind me, as he spoke, even as Carnival Lord Death stood below in the street.

They (the Prisoner and Carnival Lord Death) were *still*, all of a sudden, as if they had become eighteenth-century pieces of furniture in Church and State. A Jest of God. The cell and the street became an altar and an aisle. It was an odd apparition to flash into one's mind. But then I remembered. Jonah had favoured such furniture and architecture in his Church in Jonestown.

The Prisoner was bent as if in pain under a sensation – it seemed to me – of a coming blow.

Carnival Lord Death looked like a clothes-horse in the aisle of the Church or the street. He too was motionless. But the garments on his back appeared to brood in carven suspension as if they could be worn or discarded at a moment's notice in the prosecution of family rituals and celebrations.

But then suddenly, and equally surprisingly, these flesh-and-blood furnitures began to breathe in a theatre of Dread. Dread imbued them with life to oppose a system of values that burdened them with picturesque inanimation.

The Prisoner seemed to know that there was a price to the blow that he would receive in himself as an altar in humanity. Inanimation would break into genuine intercourse with Fate. He would appoint me to respond to the mystery of Fate, the trial of Fate. I saw it in his eyes as they sought to affirm the fatherhood of the Virgin. Do Prisoner-Gods pray to men to respond to a wholly different family of Being in creation?

When one returns to the past from the future, one finds that the theatre of Money in the carpentered or sculpted Prisoner above or in the altar, in the robes upon the back of aisled Lord Death, changes in emotional subtlety and passion and immediacy. The Prisoner's sacrifice cannot be measured in realistic or comedy-of-manners coin. Yet a price, involving an enormity of innermost change in all institutions, has to be paid for the gift of freedom, when Gods sentence themselves to death and pray to men to evaluate their gift . . .

I knew that I stood in the greatest danger, that the Prisoner stood in the greatest danger, that there would be a rush into the cell that we occupied.

Positions occupied by frozen actors and frozen actresses in the theatres of time move or shift and acquire a different emphasis in Memory theatre.

For instance I had forgotten in my moving to the window of the Prisoner's cell, and on looking down into the street, that I had perceived Carnival Lord Death dressed in a nobleman's robes of a bygone age.

I saw them now afresh as he stirred, discarding robes and replacing them with the suit or heirloom that my mother had given me and which I had lent to Jonah Jones. The grave-digger (who adopted the Mask of Carnival Lord Death in Limbo Land where I had met him) had acquired the suit when he ransacked Jonah's house and sought to push it into the Jonestown river. Yes, these were the robes or the suit that I saw from the window of the cell. A wind blew on Lord Death's back. I thought I heard the dead lace or fabric vibrate enlivened by Dread.

Yes, there was no doubt now that Carnival Lord Death was clothed in rich attire, in my mother's gift. The Prisoner, on the other hand, was in rags.

I glanced back into the cell and dreamt that I saw once again – in Mr Mageye's futuristic Camera – the Prisoner's bones providing a shield over mine, over my head, my face. As though God's death were my sacred life. An uncanny, almost savage, sensation! Intrinsic to Communion. Intrinsic to the eating of Bread and Wine.

Within Bread, within Wine, is the mystery of Bone: Bone adorned with Flesh.

I was subject to a dazzling glory and terror that I was unable to translate. Bone is a hieroglyph of sacrificial Phallus, sacramental sex, and contemplation of a honeymoon with the bride of humanity.

Were these signals of the crumbling of the Void? Perhaps they were. But I had a far way to go to insert a key into the many doors within the Prison of the Void, a key – that one could so easily despise – for it had fallen out of the split, laughing side of the Law.

Comedy is chastening therapy when one scans the Void, the intricate theatre of the Void, as one begins to unlock a variety of doors that are relevant to the pact between the Prisoner, absent Deacon and me.

ABSENT DEACON. I had said it before but unthinkingly.

Now the full force of his absence came home to me. *Deacon had not returned for his wedding day*. Did I hear the echo of laughter as the Law split its side all over again?

Comedy is chastening therapy. Comedy sometimes portrays consequences born of hubris.

Deacon had died in Jonestown. I had seen his body on a rock under the Waterfall beneath the Cave of the Moon in which I had sheltered on the Night of the Day of the Dead when I had fled into the Forest and narrowly escaped plunging headlong into the sawyers' pit.

Deacon's body lay on the rock beneath the Cave. I saw it distinctly when daylight came.

No laughing matter. Why then the echoing tracery of the laughter of the Law? Such laughter sometimes jars, it seems inappropriate, it seems irrelevant. But then for no graspable reason it becomes a shuddering music, it may break one's heart. Deacon's heart broke in his last moments, broke with inexhaustible tenderness, inexhaustible love for Marie, inexhaustible hope of heaven's forgiveness . . .

He (Deacon) had overcome Jonah when he fought him in the Mask of the Eagle and the Vulture Knight in Maya style.

No one knows what circumstances of remorse brought such a winged career to its apparent close. Had it been a straightforward accident as my death in the sawyers' pit would have been? Had he tripped into the ravine – as I nearly did – under the Cave at dead of Night?

Heroes run in parallel sometimes with the vague footsteps of hapless multitudes murdered on the battlefield, or in concentration camps, or in Jonestowns around the globe, and are on occasion the victims of obscure Fate upon ladders and stairways into the Void.

Deacon's flying, falling ghost was alive I was sure within the crumbling of the Void, exposure in the Void, but he (or it) had not returned to Port Mourant to celebrate a replay of the wedding to Marie in Memory theatre. And yet in choosing an actor to play the part the Prisoner knew how compelling was the life of the ghost in the actor's revisitation of truth. In choosing an actor to play the part – an actor such as myself – the Prisoner knew the turmoil of his or my emotions, my jealousy of Deacon, my love for Marie, my insight into his last moments when he slipped through space onto the rock. However apparently fictional those insights were they could make all the difference within imaginative truth to the motivation of the life of the ghost in me. I was to play absent Deacon in Memory theatre. I knew the ghost was alive in me, with me. I was alive, it was alive, in a strange concert of understanding to be sparked by the Prisoner and a multitude of shuffling footsteps around the globe.

I suspected that though Deacon had not returned his ghost in me was also in Mr Mageye's Camera . . .

Absent Deacon – played by me as Present Deacon – would prove a formidable engagement with humanity, re-visionary spectralities of humanity in heaven and upon earth in myself . . .

He (Deacon) had dreamt of immunity to pain. No wonder he got along well with the Doctor and turned his back on the Prisoner on the day when a bonfire flared and the Prisoner was consumed and broken on a Wheel of revolving arms and legs set in motion by Deacon's constituency.

Immunity, Deacon declared, should be a factor in godhead when humanity turns violent. Immunity was consistent with the humour of falling angels, perpetually falling, but immune to pain, because of inoculation with the political and economic venom of the Scorpion Constellation.

No wonder Deacon possessed the ear of the very constituency he had buried in a Coffin but which arose from the Nether World to lift him shoulder-high on his wedding day.

I did not believe a word of such immunity but it was a joke of sorts that raised a laugh in a gathering of tricksters who tricked Scorpions into play, biting play, with no ill effects. It was akin to walking with bare feet upon coals of fire. It was akin to feats of conquest upon earth and in heaven. Above all it was a foretaste of the Sleep of the Virgin on honeymoon day and night, a Virgin inevitably surrounded by tricksters of every culture and pigmentation, by furies real and deceptive, true and false, that climb into her arms and the arms of her bridegroom when she lies with him.

Deacon's investment in such humours of immunity empowered him, he declared, to go anywhere, to do anything. He was committed to climbing Roraima (which is infested with Scorpions) in order to unearth a great treasure for Marie's first-born child and for his constituency. This was his boast in 1954. My mind was a furious, tormented blank about Marie's first-born, my mind was tricked into lapses of Memory in playing the role of absent Deacon. But of one thing I was sure within the information that I received from Deacon's ghost.

Deacon, in his last moments, had experienced the *pain* of laughter in the body of the Law. And this filled him with Dread, filled him as well with an immensity of love for the child Marie had borne and whom he had equated with a great fortune or treasure to be secured by strategies of venom within his veins.

He saw the hollowness of such power. It seared the mind in his wings. It seared the wings in my mind. For the shock seemed – in some incalculable way – a part of my own trauma when I narrowly escaped the Grave in Jonestown.

Did I – when I flew up the wall in Bonampak with winged feet – touch Deacon's mourning, sorrowing wing perpetually falling?

Perhaps I had been equipped then to wear Deacon's terrible brow or Mask in the theatre, the brow of heaven inscribed into Eagles that soar and plunge into the Void.

The Prisoner knew and when I knelt before him I felt his hands confirming the holes and rivets, flesh-and-blood miraculous rivets to take Deacon's Mask in my shoulders and neck.

I would take Deacon's absent place. I would share his torment and remorse and tenderest grieving love which his ghost had conferred upon me. I knew the pain of laughter in the Body of the Law, the pain that had stricken Deacon when he lóst his way in the black Forest and fell into the ravine beneath the Cave of the Moon.

Such is the transference of roles that chastening comedy confers when falling heavens converse with diminutive survivors upon Earth.

*

I rose from my knees and moved again from the Prisoner to the window of his cell. A wedding – not Marie's in Port Mourant – was taking place in the street or aisle of a Church in Carnival land.

It was an absurd affair but I was in no mood to laugh.

I had witnessed Jonah's affair with the Animal Goddess or the Virgin of Jonestown. That was a kind of wedding . . .

Now I was called upon to witness my mother's apparitional wedding to the ghost of an eighteenth-century slave-master. She acted the part of her great-great-grandmother who had slept with a French aristocrat and owner of *La Pénitence* and *Le Repentir* estates. He had owned her as well.

It was his money that had paid the fees for my scholarship to the United States. A ghost's money to endow scholarships for orphans or for disadvantaged poor families with only one parent.

Were I to meet him in the street he would – despite his largesse – not know me or scarcely wish to know me.

Yet Money was the heart of morality in any eighteenth-century *Portrait of the Family*. So my mother reasoned. It was necessary to legitimize the legality of scholarships – bestowed by past slave-masters upon their future progeny – in the Carnival theatre of the Church.

My mother's apparitional flesh-and-blood was ripe to play the part of the wife of the Frenchman in the legitimization of Money and Scholarship.

The Frenchman himself had long vanished and there was no one coming forward on his behalf in the *Portrait of the Family*.

Carnival Lord Death however solved the problem. He draped my mother's arms and breasts with the heirloom or suit or robes of a nobleman that the Frenchman had left in Albuoystown with his favourite slave-mistress.

What in God's name, I wondered, was the object of such theatre of the Absurd in the Void of a Colony?

'No theatre of the Absurd,' my mother cried. 'A *Portrait of the Moral Family* is relevant to your age, Francisco. Is it not time to claim your inheritance on all sides of the blanket?

'Suppose for example that you went to London or Paris or Berlin or New York as a High Commissioner or an Ambassador, it would be morally sound, would it not, to secure a Swiss Bank Account for your family. Suppose a coup occurred in Guyana or Trinidad or Brazil or Nigeria! Where would you be without Money? Money ensures that wars on foreign soils, famines, etc., won't touch you. You would be as safe as a character in a Jane Austen novel or in *Madame Bovary*.'

I was stunned by all this. It seemed out-of-character with the memories I possessed of my mother in Albuoystown. True, she had a passion for Carnival theatre and had read English and French eighteenth- and nineteenth-century novels which she borrowed from the Carnegie Library. She was a Virgin never-theless – a sacred mother of beggars – not a Madame Bovary. But Virgins are also furies. They embrace the longings of fallen women from all areas of the globe, they embrace poor and rich wives within the glitter of structured romance so unlike the waste land of their own existence. They embrace idyllic churches and manses and middle-class homes in England in which eligible suitors woo ladies and plot with sophisticated strategies of behaviour to advance their prospects in the marriage market. Was Madame Bovary a prisoner-Virgin in such idyllic Portraits of the Moral Family?

Carnival Lord Death was laughing – Carnival Death sometimes mimics the laughter of the Law – but my mother was grave. A hidden smile on her lips. She held the nobleman's robes close to her breasts. Music was playing in the aisle of the Carnival church in the street. They were a talented lot: Carnival Lord Death and his crew. They could have easily staged Hollywood on the backs of painted, black, Southern plantation slaves. Hollywood Limbo in black Carnival.

'Imagine, Francisco – God forbid!' my mother said, 'a coup in Guyana! Imagine yourself as a High Commissioner or even a President. Imagine that you have been shrewd enough to salt away sweet money in a Swiss Bank Account. Your wife – let us say – for the sake of Carnival argument – is a French woman or a Dutch woman or an English woman. You wash your hands of the wretched politics of your country. And why not? You buy an abandoned country manse in a quiet village in Europe. There are

183

guard dogs. Or perhaps you settle in a villa on the Mediterranean. You send your son or daughter to Yale or Harvard or Princeton or the Sorbonne or Cambridge. Your family is safe. You gamble discreetly on the Stock Exchange. You have a number of discreet affairs. Money is the central moral in your existence. Money banishes tears. Indeed you write books about the horrors of the Third World. They sell well. You are knighted. Not a Maya knighthood. A Birthday Honours knighthood. Money is morality in your villa or converted manse.'

'It's not true,' I cried. 'It's not true. What difference would there be – if it were true – between my hypothetical Swiss currency, Money without tears, and Deacon's immunity to pain?'

'Dread,' said my mother. 'Deacon's immunity turns into Dread Love at the last moment within perpetually falling heavens, tides of refugees who envy the security of the sick in rich countries (as medicine prolongs the life of wealthy populations). Angels become signals of perpetually falling heavens and their re-visionary spectacle of Love, the pain of Love, a re-visionary spectacle that we scarcely understand though the message is interwoven into every wedding to a sacred Virgin.'

The aisle in the Church in Carnival street threatre appeared to narrow as my mother walked away from me in Mr Mageye's Camera.

I followed my children's children's children as they streamed into the future. They loomed but I grew increasingly indistinct to them, remote from them.

I heard my mother saying: 'No one knew it but he loved my great-great-grandmother.' She lifted the suit or heirloom then pulled it back upon her breasts. 'He loved her with all his heart but he never really knew until it was too late. An ocean and the Grave divided them when he returned to Europe and was killed by a Jacobin who wore his brother's Mask.'

Her voice seemed to be fading. I saw myself now at the far end of the aisle within the loom of my descendants. I stood in my great-great-grandfather's suit, my mother's gift for my coming honeymoon with Marie. I stood in that suit at the window of the Prisoner's cell.

'You do see,' my mother whispered in the midst of the shuffling footsteps of Carnival, 'that you shelter many ghosts in Memory theatre within your Mask, Francisco. You are my long-lost husband's son. And he has returned to witness your coming trial though you may not see him as I do. There is pain in the Body of the Law. Your Swiss Bank Account topples. Jonah's Bank Account toppled. You grow wings. You shall fall. But with a difference. I cannot say more.'

She touched my lips at last as if to heal them. I recalled the games I played at School. I recalled not only rough-and-tumble soccer but sonship games, fatherhood games in College which seemed now to have happened a century ago in past futures, future pasts.

'Farewell, fare forward, dearest Francisco.' She had vanished.

This was the cue for the footsteps that I had heard earlier to resume their pitch, their curious dark ascent and descent upon the ladders and stairways in the crumbling of the Void. The crumbling of the Void was living Bread. The crumbling of the void was living Wine. The crumbling of the Void was Rice, but a Drought persisted everywhere despite a key that one possesed to the rehabilitation of living landscapes.

I turned into the cell. The Prisoner had sliced a loaf of Bread. He gave me a thin slice which slid between my Masked lips. I felt a new current of flesh enlivening them as I ate the Bread.

He gave me a sip of Wine.

There was a bowl of rice which sweltered under an electric bulb in the cell.

There was a newspaper on the floor of the cell with the following headlines:

DROUGHT HITS VILLAGES UNDER THE SIERRA MADRE
MEXICO
AN EAGLE'S FLIGHT FROM BONAMPAK
MOON LANDSCAPE
DECADES WITHOUT RAIN
CALL FOR A SAVIOUR

185

I translated SIERRA MADRE as ancient mother of the Americas and consort in bygone ages of the Prisoner-God of Devil's Isle. The expression MOON brought my heart into my mouth. Heart of Bread. Was not MOON an arena of duels between Eagle-knights and Tiger-knights? Had not Deacon lassoed the Moon Horses and their riders (giants of chaos) and lodged them in a Coffin in the river dam of Crabwood Creek?

My Dream-book – I perceived now – was a net of associations of 'pasts' and 'presents' and 'futures' in which one could trace an immense and subtle transference of Masks such as I had glimpsed in the Nether World, in Limbo Land, in the Cave of the Moon, and elsewhere, in the aisle or street beneath the window of the cell. Its ramifications could never be absolutely seized but it brought into play a wholly different epic fiction from conventional European fiction, an epic net which embraced Europe as well – an epic net conversant with the European Conquest of the ancient Americas but antecedent to European models. Thus one could sense uncharted equations between the Prisoner-God of Devil's Isle and a vanished Prisoner or husband of the Mother of the Americas whose body lay in mountains and valleys and rivers even as it reappeared in peasant Virgins and Animal Goddesses . . .

My heart was filled with sadness. 'I speak with a sorrowing, inner tongue,' I said to the Prisoner, 'born of the coming wedding feast and a Drought of Spirit that hangs over the occasion. Deacon first met Marie at the end of a drought in the Courantyne savannahs when the rains came as if to ward off the perennial sickness of the globe that would erupt again and again in the elements. A Drought of Spirit affects the ancient peoples in the Americas: a Drought as well in the elements, a Drought in space.

'Memory theatre fictionality is the life of the Mind to create "pasts" and "futures" into an uncanny cellular net in Body and Womb and Brain to ignite self-recognition in the recognition of a saviour amongst us. For if one is spiritually blind one cannot see. Mind entertains the creation and re-creation of a saviour . . . And Drought cannot be taken lightly – wherever it occurs – in Memory theatre. Drought is a bonfire – if not Bone Fire – to illumine skeletons of Dread, to illumine other bonfires of genius and grace, that flare in the cells within us and around us. We are on fire with grace sometimes, with dread sometimes. We are fever and drought. We are sick. We are well. We are the genius of the Rain God when we respond to interventions of fire, and differentiations in the fabric of fire, in the keys to rain, the harvesting of rain, that we may possess in the body of the Law of heaven.'

I had seen the Pagan Body in the Nether World. Now I sensed – in the comedy of the Law – differentiations in the Body of heaven.

Where was the Inspector, the laughing Inspector? Did he not hear the shuffling footsteps that had begun again and were swarming into the Prisoner's cell? Had I unwittingly inserted my key into the lock of the cell with the crumbling of the Void? I was unsure. I was uncertain of my own responsibilities in this moment.

Had I brought them (those echoing footsteps) with me from the Orchestra of the Nether World? Were they solid ghosts clad in familiar leather? Were they agents of sacrifice in ancient art and modern science summoned by me and by the Prisoner in the cellular chemistry of life-in-death, death-in-life?

The half-shuffling, half-dancing footsteps ceased. The pause gave me a chance to attempt to scan the crowded room around me which seemed hollow yet full. The cell had become a seminal bubble and the ghost of Einstein was reflected in it. He rubbed shoulders with the newspaper headlines that had blown up from the floor of the cell into a ballooning SIERRA MADRE or mother of the ancient Americas in the Shadow of a bonfire lit by ghosts.

I thought of concentration camps in Europe – during World War Two – which Einstein had escaped in coming to America. But the ember of flame in the cell was the first signal of the coming death of the Prisoner. What a differentiation between murder in Nazi cells and a sentence that a surrogate God or Prisoner passes on himself to justify the genius of fire, the genius of the Atom, to which Einsteinian mathematics had been an invaluable key.

It was over at a stroke.

Einstein had vanished, the Prisoner consumed. His bones overshadowed me as though they were the architecture of ancient mothers and fathers, young brides and bridegrooms.

The crowds were upon me now. Would they tear me limb from

limb? *They knew me.* No, they did not. They saw me as the tyrant-angel Deacon. They lifted me shoulder-high and bore me out of the room through the fire.

On one hand history would say that they had liberated me. On the other hand I knew my escape was the result of the Prisoner's deed or will or legacy in electing me to play the role of Deacon.

I did not trust the swarming members of my constituency whom Deacon had once locked in a Coffin. They had seized their freedom. Or had it bestowed upon them by a reluctant Prisoner-God whose ashes were now the celebrated robe of the furnace. How strange! I wore the heirloom or suit my mother had given me: the robe of august slavery.

I knew they saw me as the one to bring a fortune to the land when Marie conceived. But still I was out in the open air and the ashes glittered like stars in broad daylight, stars from which I had fallen.

I saw the Doctor waving at me in the Shadow of the bonfire as though he stood on the Constellation of the Scorpion.

I saw Mr Mageye waving a banner of Prometheus. It was one of the props that he intended using in the showing of a film he had shot of Deacon and Jonah and tricksters associated with Virgins and with august slavery and with wars in heaven.

Supreme entertainment!

He would show this in the Banqueting Hall that the Doctor had provided.

Marie was painted black as she lay in bed. But when I touched her *black* became the feathers of heaven. Deacon had fallen upon her with the outstretched wings of a Vulture. Each feather was the imprint of their original embrace. As though the Vulture was the primordial Scavenger of the flesh of burnt Gods and Deacon knew – beyond a Shadow of doubt – that she was the Prisoner's daughter. Not burnt flesh was hers but sculpted thighs, born of fire, to match a beak of lightning that brings rain upon the parched earth. She conceived Deacon's child in that instant.

I was in a quandary now. Yes, I was playing a part, a mere peasant role or part in Memory theatre. *But it had become real.* Not that I was possessed by a ghost. No, I was driven by the prayers of a ghost in my Dream-book. A mere book! Does it matter? Do fallen angels matter which pray to survivors of holocausts?

A curious transference of ghostly – sometimes aggressive, abusive – prayer had begun on the lips of Deacon far back in boyhood and childhood. It insinuated itself even into my jealous passion, my jealousy of him when he and Marie got married in 1954.

The events of that year were so stark I had suffered from lapses of memory. But on the Night of the Day of the Dead in Jonestown – when Deacon fell to his death under the Cave of the Moon – that prayer to me in him (in all its ribaldry and tragedy) had revived.

I was required by him to write a book in which Memory theatre would take me back across the years to revisit the scene of his wedding, to embrace Marie in Dreams, that were more real than broad daylight dream, to *see* through his *blindness* when he had forfeited a true intercourse between heaven and earth.

The Prisoner knew. The Prisoner knew how terrible freedom is when one is at liberty to re-imagine the past, to enter changed spatialities in the past that were more real than the real world; to do so with the permission of surrogate Gods and fallen angels and yet to suffer the inmost bite of moral conscience. Was it adultery – or sacramentalized adultery – to sleep with Marie *when her dead husband in my Dream-book was still alive*? I was reliving the year 1954 – however changed in shape and spatiality – and Deacon was alive then! I had taken his place in bed with her. I slept with her on the honeymoon night.

It was a Play of Fire, a Play of the oldest authority. It had happened in the Cave of the Moon and upon remote mountain-tops where figures of ancient tradition sought to arrive in the future – even as I sought to re-enter the past – to bring news of a cellular chemistry of love (threading together re-visionary wed-dings of heaven and earth) which humanity had long forfeited until a Drought of Spirit presided. Fire had become an enemy. Rain was becoming an enemy. The elements were becoming enemies.

All this Deacon had seen – at the last moment – when he found himself perpetually falling to his death yet suspended above his death in a net that permitted him to communicate with me as if his voice, his multi-faceted shapes as bird and soul, had been salvaged to hang in space.

Deacon fell upon her with the wings of an Eagle. Each feather was silver-ash when I held her in my arms in his place. The silver fell away yet curled simultaneously into mutual passion within our bodies and flesh and skin. It was the ash and silver of Moon landscapes upon the Earth, scorched landscapes that glow against a black, winged sky. It was silver and gold feathers of the Eagle as he dipped his beak in fire. Marie strengthened the original seed of conception that the fallen, falling angel had planted.

As I held her in my arms I sought to evaluate Deacon's *blindness* in my *seeing* intercourse without her, within her. Exterior body, interior body of the Virgin. But I knew I would need to see without always seeing, experience without always understanding, the cellular transferences of involuntary desire that brought misreadings into the masquerading features of love within ourselves that lay far back in the uncharted genesis and genius of imaginary time. I was but a minor apprentice of such ghosts and Gods and furies which were themselves major apprentices of an unfathomable Creator.

As I held Marie in my arms I knew – peasant bride though she was – that she was the daughter of science and of ancient art, the Virgin of modern science and of ancient tradition. Peasant widows, dressed as brides, had accompanied their ghost-husbands onto funeral pyres in ancient India. Modern India as well. They were to be seen again in the traffic of hell in modern Europe in World War Two. The tragedy of humanity – in its blindness, in its misreadings of the genius of fire – had become visible to Deacon, the perpetually falling angel, in his last suspended moments on earth.

Visible to him, yes, but the fact remained that he had been a ruthless hero, a tyrant, and I was still clothed in his blindness. Not entirely, for I had also inherited the suspension of death that he endured upon a rock beneath the Cave of the Moon. No wonder the ghost of Einstein – from whom fallen, falling angels draw some of their mathematical equations as engineers – had arrived in the Prisoner's fiery cell through which I had come.

The riddle of celestial mathematics occupied my mind as Deacon fell upon Marie again and again in their honeymoon bed and I embraced her simultaneously. How was I to account for a strange lameness in Deacon with each successive fall upon his bride? Angelic potency should keep one perpetually whole, or uninjured, or beak-like in each encounter with fire.

I seized upon Deacon's lame member. It gave me support as a mere mortal survivor still unequipped to die and yet not die, to fall and yet remain perpetually falling. I recalled my Lazarus-arm – as if it were indeed separable from my body – as I seized Deacon's member.

The truth was – the mystical extensive wholeness of the Body that one tended to misread and misunderstand – that he had fallen upon her so continuously and wastefully and lustfully that a portion of Breath in his body and mine tended to edge into uncontrollable flame.

The member that he used in penetrating his bride tended to cut loose in the Void. Sex became senseless, predatory, the equipment of rapists. It became nothing but technology, technology in the conquest of love.

The *conquest* of Love was Death's immortal ambition . . .

I glimpsed such hideous perversity as I seized Deacon's member. I was filled with Dread but at least I knew what I was, where I was. I was visited then by a knowledge of technology's deprivations in the human prison of love. I knew that love could easily become a mass-media technology and that freedom – so-called freedom – could conspire with a liberty to chain millions into the exhibitionism of their grossest appetites.

The fascinations of lameness in sexual encounters were legion. Especially in the light of the orphanage of angels, the orphanage of humanity by sundered generations, separated parentages. Thus one's cousins, one's unacknowledged or unknown brothers and sisters, were legion.

Hephaestus – the ancient Olympian God – was lame. He was the father of technology. He was Deacon's cousin. They had

191

fought shoulder to shoulder in wars in heaven prior to Deacon's fall to Earth. He had armed Achilles – another of Deacon's cousins – with a shield Carnival Lord Death would have envied. He deceived millions with promises of eternal peace inscribed into the shield: pastoral scenes, running brooks, sheep, lambs, grazing . . .

I had seen Hephaestus falling from Heaven on many an occasion when Deacon and I and Jonah had quarrelled in the construction of Jonestown.

And now I saw him again in my Dream-book as Deacon netted his bride again and again. A perverse net. A curiously impotent net. Not the huntsman's net which had saved me from the Predator in Limbo Land! A jealous net. Was I jealous of him or was he (his ghost) jealous of me, though it was he who had urged me into bed with his wife?

Deacon, in his blindness, was shrewd enough nevertheless to seek to deceive Marie. He elevated her in bed into a tourist madonna who fancied Poverty as a realm inhabited by giants of sex. Anticipation was enough. Anticipation became a refuge in which the madonna waited, as it were, for the coming of her giant.

He adopted the walking stick of a Vulture in the shape of the prestigious giant Legba of Haiti.

Legba's brand of exotic lameness had long secured a large constituency in the Caribbean and the American black South. He was a tourist attraction. Voodoo was a giant's business.

The penetration of the Void by Legba was a feat that appealed to Hephaestus. How could an apparently poverty-stricken giant secure a Lingam to match that in Asian temples in India?

Sex is a religious industry in the Third World. Vast crowds of tourists flock to pay tribute to the technology of the Lingam. The Third World is no superpower in Western eyes but Legba closes the gap on the crossroads between Haiti, Africa and India.

He is able to solicit dollars and pounds and francs and currencies of every denomination. Poverty becomes almost glamorous in the eyes of rich, frustrated wives. They take Poverty's giant into bed with them when they sleep with their husbands. When he appears too black they paint him golden-brown or white. Lame Legba is susceptible to varieties of paint as he dresses the wounds of his people and offers his back as a seat for the globe. Poverty's Atlas – upon which the globe rests – is blind sex with heaven . . .

I could not help laughing as I pushed the ghost of Deacon out of bed and embraced Marie. But Deacon was back. He was shrewd enough to return with his blandishments of the madonna.

Lingams – Marie had been told – were the property of the giant Siva but Siva was Legba's cousin within the orphanage of humanity.

I saw a wicked flash in Marie's eye as she pulled a shawl over her breasts and sat up in bed.

On the shawl were inscribed the features of Kali, a pin-up for Indian peasants in Port Mourant.

Kali was a guardian for Marie, she was a dangerous Goddess in her own right. She scoffed at lame giants yet relished their long-standing trickeries and inventions. She knew they were virtually divine in the tales they spun, the promises they gave of renewed potency in suspended intercourse between heaven and earth, the anticipations they nourished that the gap would close between rich nations and poor nations.

She knew of Marie's love of the Wheel but sorrow that the Wheel had been a toy in El Dorado (the richest kingdom of its age) and that it had never been employed in quarries where brutalized labour broke its body toiling for rocks and stones in the construction of palaces and of pyramids of the Moon and the Sun.

And as a consequence wheeling arms sprouted from her body as if they originated from the luminous circles of Marie's breasts. *She was not Marie*. She was one of Marie's guardians. She was the many-armed Goddess of antiquity that indentured peasants from India had brought to the Guyanas in the hope of finding El Dorado and renewing the potency of gold.

She placed Legba and Siva upon the Wheel in the Circus of trade everywhere and expectation of an economic miracle.

Thus in the re-visionary dynamic of Marie's Wheel – as I rolled in bed with her as if such intercourse with fire were nothing but exhibitionist trade – I was able to set up a stall in the bedroom of the Virgin on which to sell a variety of wares and relics under the Drought of heaven. When heaven suffers from Drought, a variety of occult, sexual, technological practice alerts us to a vacuum in existence, North, South, East, West.

I was able to set up the mechanics of a scrutiny (Mr Mageye's Cinema, Lord Death's Carnival) of the natures of the rich and the poor, the gullible and the cynical, the hopeful and the hopeless, the strong and the weak, the trickster and the truth. In some incongruous consistency they supported each other, rich poor, poor rich, strong weak, weak strong, trickster truth . . .

They implied latently, sometimes openly, sometimes subconsciously or unconsciously, that a mystical Body was still alive however absurd its manifestations in a blind age, not wholly blind yet seemingly blind to originality, to the life of the Imagination and its ruses and unpredictable humours as well as its implicit collaborations between music and science and art.

At the heart of a bloody-minded age lay nevertheless a new semiology of concordance and dissonance and orchestrations of intimate and alien imageries in the quest for truth within the prison of human, aberrant love. Prison, yes, for freedom (in a profoundly self-questioning sense of a cellular chemistry linking apparition and concretion) was beyond a purely individual grasp. There was a community of selves akin to individual self *yet other than individual self* in the genesis of the Imagination. The stress on purely individual character was an impoverishment of tradition. No wonder the cult of individual freedom was fast becoming a Lingam tourist rope around the globe. And yet that symptom of malaise in the rope was convertible in the huntsman's net into the orchestration of gravities and anti-gravities in the salvage of institutions and bodies fallen, perpetually falling . . .

I arose from bed and moved to the window of the bedroom. I had heard Mr Mageye's urgent voice. Our eyes met.

'It's time to visit the Banqueting Hall, Francisco, time to consider our grasp of Memory theatre that we have been building or salvaging. Nothing lasts forever in the mystery of time and yet the net is there even when it seems to elude us or deceive us. Time to see my film, Francisco. Time is upon us when I shall leave . . .'

'No, no, Mr Mageye,' I cried.

'It's time, Francisco. We have covered some ground. Even as the Prisoner left you I too must go.'

'But why, why?'

'Dread has arrived, Francisco. You are in bed with the Virgin. And you must pay the price. You must look into the heart of the womb of the Camera. You must touch the seed of a conception that humanity has well-nigh forfeited. You must approach it by indirections in the labyrinth of space and time. My Camera is such a labyrinth, as you know already. And now it seeks to net the Whale afresh as a temple – shall I say – of Jonah's repentance. That's one inadequate way of putting it to draw you into this (shall I say final?) entertainment before I go. Remember, Francisco, there are linked signals, symptoms and convertibles in your Dream-book. The Prisoner is consumed. I shall vanish. There are the three Maries, three weddings. Linked motifs. There is the pact between Jonah, Deacon and yourself. Remember? You broke that pact. You converted the pact into other realms, the Nether World, Atlantis, the Waste Land, the Paradise of the Rain God . . . Another pact came into play. Do you remember? A pact between the Prisoner, the Mask of Deacon, and yourself. The Prisoner vanished as a signal of sacrifice and the convertibility of sacrifice within Phallus and Lingam. The lame Gods became divine spinners of tales *still awaiting another conversion into truth*. For the genesis of the Imagination remains perpetually unfinished and open to unpredictable spheres of otherness.' Mr Mageye was smiling. The most wonderful sacred Jester and teacher that I knew. Yet I wondered. Did I truly know him?

'Francisco,' he cried. 'There is another pact to consider. Now that you have slept with Marie in the name and head of Deacon – now that *you* transgress into a sublime trickster – you need to weigh transferable masks of truth and trickster in my film; and that involves you in a pact between me and yourself and the ghosts of Deacon and Jonah and Kali and Anansi and others. Anansi is Legba's cousin. I have another card up my sleeve, Francisco. It's the Sphinx. But more of that later before I take my leave of you . . .'

195

He turned. I stood at the window as though I were falling into the street. It was a most curious premonition . . .

A great banquet was launched by the Doctor on the Day of the Wedding. It taxes me now to remember the places where everyone sat, even though I had sailed from the future into the Banquet, sailed with the Memory of the past that one stores in the future. Sailed with the architectures of the future back into the past. It was necessary to extend the dining-room in which Jones and Deacon and I had eaten our last meal together, in Jonestown, on the eve of the holocaust November 1978, into Port Mourant 1954. Such an extension was rooted in Memory's holocaustic fire and changes in spatiality within the crumbling of the Void. A submerged dining-room I felt in deceptive elements. It began to lift nevertheless backwards in space into the banqueting hall. Such is the architecture of Dream. I sought as well to bring the Prisoner's cell, where I had eaten a slice of bread, into the banqueting hall.

Such sailing architectures in Memory theatre are a medium in which to dislodge closed structures within an open universe born of the arts and sciences of concentrated Chaos and its rebuttal of catastrophe and bias as all-consuming.

It was a tall order and laughter therefore – the involuntary laughter of the Law – could be aroused into a serious, cosmic asset.

There are intricate winding stairs within the lower anatomy of an upright Boar or a Pig and the Inspector sat under these in the banqueting hall enjoying the flavour of black pudding. Someone said that that seat had been reserved for Jonah Jones, but it did not seem to matter as Jonah sat somewhere else.

The Boar grunted like a base instrument, base instrumental laughter as the Inspector turned and dipped into curries, pepper-pots, roasted beef, dishes of rice and sweet potato and yam. A meal fit for a Roman emperor or a medieval king.

On such a day, or sailing coronation, the populace was prepared to fall ill in consuming a multitude of dishes. They sought medical aid and in so doing stuffed dollars into the Doctor's pockets to pay for the banquet.

196

The Doctor possessed a prosperous private practice on the side. He advised his son-in-law Deacon to build a hospital in Jonestown that would be similar to the Port Mourant public hospital but in private hands. Perhaps also a great Cinema Wheel through which patients would slip on the day that they died. I thought of the huntsman and his dog slipping through the Wheel but this raised a serious ingredient in the Doctor's half-joking plans in my Dream-book!

A hospital in spectral Jonestown in 1954?

Jonestown lay still submerged in the collective unconscious! It had not yet been built in 1954. This was true but I could see it lifting onto a wave of the future. Deacon and Jones and I were already taking fiery soundings with regard to a new Rome a star's blaze or throw from old Devil's Isle.

'We shall build Jonestown in honour of Deacon's first child. We shall print on its portals IMMUNITY TO PAIN.'

I felt an ominous shuddering sensation run through my limbs as the wave of the future struck the banqueting hall. But the magus-Doctor adjusted himself in his seat. He sat cross-legged like a Buddha under the prospect of medicine's advance into IMMUNITY TO PAIN. The magus-Inspector sat under the Constellaton of the Boar and the Pig. Magi are susceptible to royal pageantry and to greed – royal illusion, royal greed – in order to know and to resist temptation. I saw at a glance that the Inspector had abstained from over-eating though he had had his fill. He sat in sober fear perhaps of the Jovian split in his sides . . .

The magus-Doctor agreed that soundings should be taken with regard to a new Rome in spectral Jonestown. The very spectrality of Jonestown, its existence yet non-existence, its cinematic river and forests, was an apparition of fire (as if one were visualizing a wave of light arriving from distant space as a star unseen begins to reveal itself on the back of the light-years). Such revelations could be profoundly challenging and creative or they could be riveted into complacency or Drought. Light-year Drought!

He looked around for me since he knew I was fearful of a liberty to break with the regime of Public Hospitals and to foster the practice of private Medicine or profit within escalating malaise in the settlements and cities of South America. I was a Fool, I was a captain of Jesters in Mr Mageye's fleet. I sat under the Constellation of Prometheus. An eagle gnawed at my side as I recalled the honeymoon bed of the Virgin and the seed of conception planted in her by Vulture or Eagle. But no one truly saw me for I hid within Deacon's lofty, fallen, perpetually falling Mask in the Circus of the banqueting hall.

The Doctor was relieved at my absence. It was not I however who was absent from the banqueting hall. But that was a private joke that I entertained with the ghost of Deacon who was to appear in Mr Mageye's film. Time plays tricks in the womb of the Camera and the Cinema when one returns from the future into the past dressed in another body's acting clothes. Hollow Masks act. Hollow clothes act when faces and hands and feet are daubed upon them, beside them, beneath them.

Jonah Jones was sitting across the hall under the Constellation of the Whale and the Tiger. But beneath these stood the Spider Anansi and a Goddess of India with several hands that sprouted from her side. He had arrived from San Francisco that very morning for the wedding in Crabwood Creek. Was he a ghost? Had he in fact sailed in upon a light-year star from his grave in spectral Jonestown?

The Whale was exquisitely painted as though it had been beached against a wave of the future and it seemed to shudder gently at times and to send a vibration through the limbs of the Spider.

Every grave and sensitive captain in Mr Mageye's fleet scans the insides of Whales. Stand on the top of a wave with Captain Cook in 1770. Fallen, perpetually falling wave.

Cook was astonished when he fell around the globe to come upon Whales painted by Australian Aboriginal Old Gods in which had been sketched Spider houses. Jonah was to be seen. The houses were *in* the Whale, they were organs of the Whale, coal-black organs. The houses were inhabited by futuristic immigrants from Newcastle or Leeds or Liverpool or London. At first sight they were similar to the cell of the convicted Prisoner or Old God in French Guyana's Devil Isle. But each splinter of coal glowed and enlarged itself into bedrooms, dining-rooms, draw-ing-rooms, and closets with Bibles.

The insides of Jonah Jones's Whale were a theatre of Memory's fire and I glued my eyes into Mr Mageye's global Camera in order to see the detail of Aboriginal genius in sculpting the evolutions of mutated holocaust, altered spectres of holocaust into the sacrifices (voluntary and involuntary) that humanity makes in striking a chord linking Devil's Isle to Botany Bay to Port Mourant to dread Jonestown.

Jones would look for a blazing woman in Port Mourant or New Amsterdam after the wedding. 'They all love an American to put out the fire,' he said. And it was true.

I held my Breath. A house in the Spider Whale was a Camera shot of Jonestown. The house stood on the river bank. I remembered the web of the past in the future. A high wire in the Brain, in Mr Mageye's Camera, sends one sailing on a wave, sailing on fire.

Two cyclists were approaching the house in Mr Mageye's curiously Aboriginal film. I swore I was one Aboriginal survivor (Aboriginals have been decimated on every continent around the globe) and that my Skeleton-twin was the other. It was the bundle of newspapers that we carried on our heads. But in fact the cyclists were Carnival Lord Death and his twin or likeness the grave-digger.

On arriving at Jones's house they dumped the newspapers into the river. Then they turned on the house itself. They began to push. The house slipped inch by inch, foot by foot, towards the water's edge. As it gained the bank I knew it would fall. But as it came upon the brink of toppling it was held or salvaged in the huntsman's net; seized and converted into a play, fallen, perpetually falling Aboriginal theatre of the globe.

Mr Mageye's humour was as unpredictable as that of ancient Jonah who adventured into the Whale in the Bible and from whom Jones borrowed his first name.

'It is necessary, Francisco,' said Mr Mageye, 'to see that the perpetually falling Aboriginal globe promoted a dialogue between Deacon and yourself when it catapulted you (and

Deacon before you) into the head and form of an angel (as old as Methuselah) even as it catapults Jones into a perverse dramatization of Jonah. I tell you this in order to make clear some of the premises of Aboriginal theatre in any area of the world. Kali – the many-armed Indian Goddess and guardian of Marie – is more, much more, than an individual pin-up or film star. Populations have been catapulted into her. They reside in her at various levels of perversity and virtue, danger and the promise of salvation. The same is true of black Anansi (an actor, as you shall soon see in my film) who arrived in the Guyanas with African slaves. The same is true – as you no doubt realize – of immigrants from Leeds and Liverpool and London who were bundled together into a faceless Prisoner and transported to Australia where for better and worse, in perversity and virtue, they confronted their Aboriginal Twin from whom they began to sculpt the resources of a new Paradise tainted alas by racism . . . I mention all this to make clear some of the intensive/extensive ground of my film as it proceeds . . .

'Look, Francisco! Look into the womb of my Virgin Camera.' Mr Mageye could not help laughing, despite the gravity of humour in his expression.

'Look, Francisco,' he cried. 'Deacon approaches within or upon or beneath the back-bone of the Whale. He now embodies the elemental furies of many an adventurer and explorer. He's the solid ghost who hangs under the Cave of the Moon. He's a submarine commander about to launch a hidden torpedo. He bundles his constituency into himself. He arrives at Jonah's house . . . It took me ages to film that bit . . . His face is black as thunder. He thunders at the door and sweeps into the dining-room where Jonah sits. Look and listen, Francisco.'

'What in God's name is the matter, Deacon?'

'News from home. Have you read last week's papers which arrived today? Bloody November is upon us I tell you! How can you stomach the end of the world, Jonah? This Whale has no back door into the Bank of America.'

Jonah crossed to the window and looked out upon the river.

'There they are,' he said. 'Floating high and dry. I knew there was something in the air. My house gave a slight tremor a

200

moment or two ago. Earthquakes do shake the region once in a while. Water is floating ash.'

Jonah was clearly disturbed. He felt the turbulence of dying fish in himself within the vista of futures. He felt the rape of species. He felt as if he were being choked by stocks and bonds.

Deacon was mad, Deacon was angry. 'The papers say you have broken the law and defrauded the Bank, Jonah. The Inspector is on his way.'

Jonah moved – turbulent stomach and all – to the dining-table in the middle of the room and polished the shining table-top that the sawyers in the Mission had prepared.

'It's as bright as a coffin,' he said. 'We shall dine on table-top coffins, Deacon. Bring your constituency.' As he spoke Spider Anansi crept delicately out of the coffin. He danced upon coal.

Human Spiders, Anansi tricksters, were once the saviours of slaves transported through the Middle Passage from Africa. They secreted runaways in graveyards, in coffins.

But an irony came into being within the play of populations, the irony of sweet-tasting power that the political firebrand began to enjoy in himself as he roasted his followers.

Picture him dining now on the fish in Jonah's stomach: fish reserved for dignitaries in the banqueting hall.

'What more intimate picture may I paint,' said the Jester Mr Mageye, 'than to give Anansi access to his master's delicacies, stomach, temple? They are apparently equal now in the sight of the state. It's a figure of speech, mind you. Nothing sexual. I'm talking, remember, about populations that these archetypal tricksters represent, the epic embodiment of populations in crisis. Not individual indulgences. We know little of the collective, hidden ambivalences within mixed or heterogeneous societies, the inner trophies that one group may secure from another, the haunting sense of loss or retention of privilege or power, the greed, the longings, the ruses, the strategies, behind the façade of establishments.

'When Anansi becomes as much a ruling appetite – in the banqueting hall of history – as the former missionary or ruler or master with whom he contended – then the establishment and the trickster are equals. Listen, Francisco, to what Jonah is now saying to Deacon.'

'There is some consolation,' Jonah said slowly, 'in the thought that – as the end of my mission approaches – blacks and whites are equals. I have converted Anansi, have I not, to cast aside Doubt. He can trust me. His growing appetite for the good things of the world may kill not only revolutionary originality but bitterness at the injustices of the past. We are equals now, black and white.'

He knew he was lying in Deacon's teeth. Deacon wanted to say: 'You are a bloody liar, Jonah,' but he kept silent.

Suddenly I was confronted by the ramifications of the Trickster in Mr Mageye's all-inclusive film. I was down here in the hall looking at Deacon, looking at myself acting up there. Was it Deacon's ghost up there, or was it me feeding upon his lips as he stifled his words?

Was it politic to sustain a traffic in lies?

I touched my flesh-and-blood Mask in order to sift the power of lies within the art of the Camera, lies that bear on Conscience, the trickster-Capacity of Conscience to question itself openly (yet hide itself all the more effectively), to spy itself in the speaking yet self-gagging roles that it plays in Aboriginal, archetypal theatre.

How integral is the lie in every evolution of collective theatre to know the truth yet kill it?

Jonah was lying to Deacon. Deacon accepted – or appeared to accept – the lie out of political necessity or fear. I was masked in Deacon in watching myself on the screen. Not myself! I had no desire to lie. Did the screen lie then? Or did I lie? Who am I? Where am I in a mass-media reductive age that Mr Mageye seeks to illumine and transform through the cellular chemistry of interwoven spectralities in others built into unique dialogue and response in oneself?

My head was spinning but I kept the Mask firmly in place as Mr Mageye's portrayals continued to unroll down here in the banqueting hall and up there on the screen.

'It's a question of pride,' said Jonah. 'Pride in God's will. I must win, Deacon, don't you see? At all costs. Nothing counts but winning. Even if I have to drag Jonestown into the grave. I must teach Anansi to forget. Anansi populations must fuse into eternity. Eternity is a realm of forgetfulness. I shall persuade my people here in Jonestown to eat or drink whatever I dish out. Poison is palatable when it is braced with projected dominion over all species in a coming paradise or eternity when we shall be millionaires in devouring the planet. Not only doomed fish but doomed species of all sorts. It's not just cyanide in Coca-Cola or milk or champagne or whatever. It's the conquest of the lower orders. Don't you see, Deacon?'

Deacon wanted to shout NO but he lied to himself and nodded. He pretended all was well but he knew he would have to break the pact and shoot Jones on the Day of the Dead. Perhaps not before but certainly then. He would strengthen his fingers on the trigger by slicing mine off to assist his. Thus he would generate in me the sensation that when he fell under the Cave of the Moon I would shoulder his ambivalent, angelic, ruthless Mask and begin to play *him* up there in the sky or screen and down here in the soil of the banqueting hall.

The troubling dimensions of the lie were as pertinent as celestial mathematics. Mr Mageye knew that the self-confessional, self-judgemental arts of the Trickster were essential in laying bare a fallen, perpetually falling humanity. He prodded Deacon – as he swung in the sky between heaven and earth and under the Cave of the Moon – to make visible the Virgin Goddess Kali from whom sprang a multitude of arms that were reminiscent of the cosmic Spider.

'A most challenging aspect of my film this is,' said Mr Mageye. 'Look! There she is! A kind of lightning dance instigated by an angel.' He eyed me with his quizzical humour. Was I sufficiently paranoid (as brilliant actors need to be) to believe that *I* – in the Mask of Deacon – had invoked the slow-motion, lightning-shawled dance of Kali in my Dream-book embrace of the peasant Virgin Marie? The question staggered me in the dance, for my Dream-book was more real than the real world.

'As you see, Francisco,' Mr Mageye continued, 'Kali dances with you. A dread Goddess. But do not fear. She has conscripted you as another lame – shall I say inoffensive? – giant. She wheels you around with Legba and Siva. But look . . .' he paused. I was horrified at what I now saw. Kali was also wheeling in her numerous arms strangled female infants.

'Good God,' I cried. 'It's impossible. She is the guardian of the Virgin.'

'She is,' said Mr Mageye. 'We all are, aren't we? Up and down streets and highways and in the byways – in planes that sail in the sky, in trains, in buses, in saloons, in brothels for that matter – the Virgin resides protected in someone's handbag or pocket or wallet. Is it superstition, or is it a promise of welfare, or is it an insurance? Yes, we are all guardians . . . But economic necessity is a plague. Hell is everywhere around us despite heaven. Kali kills out of brutal economic necessity. The male child is privileged, the female is sometimes a liability. I know it's hideously perverse. *Kali is associated with the guardianship of the Virgin yet kills infant females! It's a bleak parable, civilization fuels Kali, civilization sustains her, when economic necessity incorporates violence into itself and Love, the Virgin's Love, becomes an ornament.* The chasm between necessity and love needs to be bridged ceaselessly . . . Unless it is bridged the male child freezes into stone, the saviour-archetype is blunted. All this runs deeper than gender. Archetypes run deeper than gender. Their manifestation is partial at the best of times. We need to read them in their broken fabric, we need to read differently. Remember Herod slew *male* infants in panic and cold-hearted self-interest at the thought of the coming of a saviour that might shake the walls of his kingdom. When one reads reality differently from slavish alignment to literal frame or code, when one reads by way of indirections that diverge from formula or frame, by way of weighing another text (a hidden text) in a given text, *then* the privileged male discloses privilege as a form of perversity, a trauma, that cracks open to hint at the saviour-archetype dressed in partialities and biases that civilization should never absolutize or it is forever trapped in the venom of history.

'Likewise the pathetic female infant on Kali's wheel may still break the shell of brute economic necessity to reveal the Virgin-archetype on the Cross of the Wheel. The chasm between gender, male and female, is momentarily bridged . . .'

I listened silently and was nudged by my Dream-book into contemplating American Indian peoples that were decimated since the Conquest. Was this decimation driven by brute economic necessity?

'God help children if we succumb to the tyranny of gender and expunge mixed origins in the body of the archetype, saviour-archetype, Virgin-archetype.'

'Children? What children, Deacon?' Jones demanded.

Jonah Jones was a naturalist in accepting changeless vice, changeless virtue, the naturalism of the charismatic pulpit, the charismatic preacher pledged to incorrigible eternity.

He seemed oblivious of the cosmic Spider (the Carnival attire of a Child) on the dining-room coffin. He seemed oblivious of its subtle Carnival metamorphoses as it hopped on the floor and crept out of the room onto the riverbank and into the fabric of Mr Mageye's Camera. Its eyes gleamed, light-year eyes within the cradle of humanity in the soil of the Earth; light-year eyes *sensitive all at once in a peculiar and unexpected way to the wheeling presence of Kali*. I felt my phantom fingers move on *my* hand that had been despoiled by Deacon's bullet on the Day of the Dead even though they were alive now, it seemed, in the cosmic Spider.

Jones's addiction to changelessness made him oblivious of such *sensitivity attuned to a changing nature of natures* within myself and within a cosmic Child or saviour-archetype or Spider quest in the stars and upon the Earth.

The Spider knew how unprepossesing it was, it knew the terror it could infuse into others. He (or It) knew it had edged itself into the lineaments of the nightmare guardians of the Virgin. But, on the other hand, its attunement to the mystical technology of the Gods, exercised in my phantom fingers, gave it a grasp or hold on the Virgin's *unconditional love* . . .

Outcast from heaven it seemed to be (yet so was Prometheus). It dined at its master's table in the rafter of coffins, it instigated worms and fishes to transmute themselves into stars beside the Scorpion signature of lightning that breaks the door of the tomb.

I could scarcely believe the multi-layered, redistributive focus of Carnival which I dreamt or thought or visualized in my Dream-book. Spider-metamorphosis enveloped the cradle and the grave and a resurrection of consciousness through the door of space, a resurrection steeped in caveats, bitter counsels not to be deceived by lies (an age of lies) even when nature appears to change, when human nature in animal natures appears to change, to acquire attunement to a redemptive, evolutionary capacity within a universal creation.

There was craft, there was daemonic, self-mocking humour in the Spider's Eye, Spidery ape of Christ, ape of Prometheus. And so – in becoming aware of lies as I gazed into the depths of cosmic Tricksters reflected in a Child's masquerade in the womb of space, Spider Carnival masquerade in earth and in heaven – I was seized with sorrow, with a conviction of truth one must pursue within the innermost recesses of the living Word.

I was suddenly aware of the magnetic charm and beauty of the Predator born less of the Virgin and more from the shamanic lore of Tricksters. The Spider itself was unprepossessing and without apparent beauty. Except for his brilliant Eye that mirrored the door of the tomb split asunder by lightning.

I looked up suddenly as though lightning indeed had flashed through counterpointed immovable and movable doors of the Void. LEAP . . . LEAP . . . But I held my ground in fear of counterpointed imageries and spaces, orchestrated paradox . . . I was fearful still of my capacity to leap backwards/forwards in space and time.

I looked up at Mr Mageye's Cinema where I was playing the role of Deacon (Masked actor Bone as Deacon's ghost-flesh on the screen). I was confronting Jonah in the whale of the sun upon the screen or stage.

A terrifying role to play, terrifying Mask to wear on my sculpted yet frail shoulders. Was Deacon satisfied with my performance? Was he pleased with my split performance as I sat in the banqueting hall and looked up at myself/himself up there in space, in the Void of cinematic heaven?

Such conflict of conscience on my part (which led me to breach or cancel the pact with Jones), such conflict in Deacon's psyche (which led him to duel on the Moon with Titan Jonah) did not appear to arouse Jonah Jones's apprehensions. He was firm in his allegiance to unchanged natures since time began, in his mind, its slippage into eternity.

As such he was less tormented – if at all – by the lie that I had perceived in the perversity of saviours which haunted the womb of space. How to accept responsibility – I asked myself – for a lie (an age of lies), which taints creation, yet submit oneself to the trial and judgement of truth one still (however precariously) embodies . . . ?

I sat and dined now under the constellation of Trickster-Prometheus in the banqueting hall as if a coffin had been raised over my head from which I would awaken, or had awakened, when I ascended from the Nether World.

Prometheus, quite rightly, broke a pact with the Titan of eternity. But in so doing – out of fear perhaps (fear such as I had felt when I broke with Jonah Jones) – he invoked the lie in the Trickster's heart. Deacon and I had lied to Jones on the eve of the holocaust. We had pretended to be one with him when we dined . . . Prometheus lied to cover his rebellion. He lied in order to conceal himself, in order to plot. Violence was born out of apparent necessity, necessary rebellion, necessary lies. Why did he lie? Why had he not rebuked the Titan openly and inscribed his heart as a token of life in outer space, a token of therapeutic angelic blood to revive creative spirit in a fallen, human race? *He saw his chance to rule.* That was it! He would rule with the gift of fire though fire was an incalculable element and from its ash would spring birds of prey and predators and all the extraordinary – sometimes nightmare – guardians of unconditional love; from its ash would spring the Predator, the magnetic beauty and charm of the Predator clothed in bars of shadow and fire. So was the Predator born in the vein of species, in the wake of a lie which would convert fire into ammunition and self-injury for humanity. The stress of counterpoint appeared within an inimitable haven (hoped for, longed-for) between fire and fire, therapeutic heart of fire and injurious ammunition of fire that humanity employs. A chastened and chastening music was born (within Love itself) whose sublimity, whose toppling precipice of sound was pos-

207

sessed of harmony and complaint, earthquake, lightning, storm, concordance, dissonance.

I was possessed of a glimmering perception of the sacrifice of the Prisoner of Devil's Isle, the sentence that he passed on himself in conceding freedom to Deacon's constituency, the sentence to remove himself to another plane of re-memberment and self-understanding beyond predatory coherence. I began glimmeringly to perceive why Mr Mageye would vanish. The sentence he would pass on himself needed to be translated onto a page on the Predator's skin if one were to leap backwards and forwards into the music of space . . . I perceived why the huntsman Christ held the Predator in his net when he saved my life. The dread, beautiful Predator needed to be stroked by a Child. Its markings and hieroglyphs and signatures needed to attune themselves to changing natures of nature, memorials of catastrophe, therapeutic Bone-fire, and the ultimate hoped-for withdrawal from lies in the ambiguous technologies of Prometheus.

The surrender of frames of language to inner frames and still inner frames – in plumbing the illumination of the innermost Word – is the music and the variable orchestra of reality.

The ghost of Deacon suddenly stood on the stage. A ghost from within the framed ghost that had previously informed me of its wishes in my performance in the Mask I wore. It was tall and thin and dressed in a coat like the flake of rock. It stood in my Ear. It was an inner cloak within a cloak. I saw it. No one else did. I had never seen it before, though I knew Deacon well and wore his Mask. It was inner flesh within a flesh-and-blood Mask, inner ghost within an outer ghost that had previously informed me how to play the role. And now the role I was playing began to reveal an inner role, an inner flesh, though no one else saw it as the ghost-within-a-ghost spoke in the labyrinth of my Ear.

It was a Voice in the phallic tree of space.

'There's a leaf in my side,' said the Voice, 'a leaf shaped like the face of Marie's Child. Marie's Child is both inner and outer seed. Your reconception or reconceptualization of the Child must release it from my outer grasp. That is why I now address you as a Voice that haunts your Ear. The Ear is the labyrinthine invagination of music. And my ghost-within-a-ghost tells of the song of the seed everywhere. Watch for the song, watch for the coming of the song and save the Child.'

'The Child sings amongst ghost-children in the Dark,' said the Voice. 'On the Night of the Day of the Dead I followed you Francisco into the Forest. I contemplated the narrow shave that you experienced at the edge of the sawyers' pit. I followed you to the Cave of the Moon with borrowed eyes that I had plucked from a Cat, from Jonah's Tiger's head. No wonder my eyes shone in your back and you turned for a moment fearful of predators but did not see me when I pulled the lid of the Night over the stars in my head.'

The Voice within my Ear stopped again. I had no way of defining its innermost tread or illumination of the fabric of the seeing/hearing Brain. It was Deacon, I knew. I was sure now in the labyrinthine theatre of the Ear and in the muscularity of my back riven by starlight – through the dense ceiling of space – on the Night that I fled into the Forest.

It was Deacon I was sure. And yet he came from *within* the familiar body or shape I knew, familiar ghost I thought I knew . . .

Such is an actor's torment when the role he plays becomes abysmally, spiritually true . . .

'I was about to follow you up to the Cave, Francisco, when I received a blow. Imagine that blow! It was frail, it was the leaf on the wing of a tree, it was a Child playing up there! A Child's blow. A frail wing of darkness in a tree. I stopped. In bodily hell I cannot describe. No! Let me qualify what I have just said. Not hell of the body, not that, pain of the Spirit. Is Spirit Body, Body Spirit? I do not know. *You*, Francisco, now wear my Mask, you act in my shoes. But remember the inner Mask, the inner shoes, the inner dark. For those are messengers of Song.'

He was gone.

I made my way across the floor of the banqueting hall. A swirl of dancers swept around me, a river of Spirit running through a Church.

I was a floating shell on that river, paper of flesh-and-blood. I was swept uncrushed into the arms of Kali, the wicked princess. She spared my head but broke female dolls on the brow of lame giants in her wheeling arms. It was a new style of entertainment to make the populace laugh. But laughter sometimes breeds sorrow and I extricated myself from the Wheel, from her wheeling arms.

Kali's embrace had imbued me with the substance of laughter and sorrow.

In cracking the brow of lame giants with wheeling dolls, children, beggars, thieves crept out from the heart of such union into the banqueting hall.

I was reminded of the Inspector from whose split sides of the Law laughter crept forth in the shape of a key to the Void.

I was reminded of the Spider trickster who crept forth from a coffin-top table in Jonah's dining-room.

They crept from the brow of a lame humanity – in all its surrogates – when Kali wheels the living and the dead into her arms and appears to crush them all into nothingness (as she threatens the infant female or the nursery of the seed of future life, but relinquishes it despite all appearances of ultimate cruelty, ultimate violence).

'The archetype of the Game, in the games of childhood, is disturbing,' I murmured to the thieves and beggars around me. 'It is fractured and broken in crises of civilization. Kali's terrorized infant dolls are a species of the obscurity of the womb, the mourning lament that arises from the womb, as it contemplates, through Kali's terrible eyes, the lost and the abandoned on the Wheel of time. Such are the games that children play who seek, in the dance of death and life, the archetype of the saviour-Child, Marie's Child, my Child, the world's Child.'

I sought by indirection to converse with Kali through the children in the banqueting hall. But her lips were closed as if they were parallel eyes of Sleep. She spoke to me through a wealth of imageries that seemed paradoxical at times on the Wheel of death and life. She spoke in a forgotten language or chemistry of the re-visionary Word one needed to relearn step by step. Such wealth of imageries seemed light at this moment in contradistinction to material fortune or power.

I was swept along with the children to Mr Mageye, who greeted me with his jesting, quizzical smile.

'I see you are impressed, Francisco,' he said, 'by the new Computer, the Kali Wheel, it's magnificent.'

I was stunned by the news. I had not seen the Wheel as a Computer.

Mr Mageye chided me gently. 'Your Dream-book is a numinous Computer . . .'

He saw my amazement and inability to reply.

'Flash up any page, scan the imageries with care, flash up another, scan the selfsame imageries, selfsame I say but note the re-visionary dynamic (if I may so put it) that informs them. It's a question all the time of the inner – the innermost – resources of the language (a living language) to address a framed, commanding surface that it is so easy to reinforce into an absolute. A Dream-book is a numinous Computer in this peculiar sense that the life of a language, its capacity in depth, empowers it to reflect upon itself, to re-vision the frames or dogmas that have such a commanding grip . . . Even as I say this – the very issue I have just raised – I am taken back to the nature of freedom that the Dream associates with the Prisoner of Devil's Isle. Freedom, in this context, does not mean that anything goes or may masquerade as re-visionary dynamic. Not at all. For the Dreamer (or surrogate creator of all systems and universes) is pulled into profoundest concentration upon concretion and apparition. It is an extraordinarily demanding task. Such is the true work of freedom . . .'

I was incredibly grateful to Mr Mageye, for his kind word, his encouragement. But I felt sad all the same. I sensed he was preparing me for his departure from the Dream-book of which he had been an architect as much as I was, indeed more so than I . . .

'Are you sure, Mr Mageye,' I asked with a kind of lameness in my voice, 'that Kali – in this banqueting hall – is a Wheel-Computer? I have not seen such mechanics of Spirit before.'

'I am,' said Mr Mageye with a gleam in his eye that sprang from the depths of his hidden laughter.

The children – some wore greybearded masks – and the beggars were somersaulting and leaping in imitation of the Kali Wheel. Others hopped on sticks like Legba. Others shaped themselves into agile Anansi legs. Still others created a broken brow or cavern – streaked with the straw of dolls' blood – through which they leapt.

'These children *live* in Dream-computers, Francisco,' said Mr Mageye as he turned *his* Sphinx-like brow upon me. The ghost-children achieved such leaps at times that it was as if he occupied a foothold or a handhold at the very base of the Wheel where nothing moved.

'Yes,' he said, 'they live in computers as the twentieth century draws to a close. Their soul occupies computer games. They mimic wars in heaven and on earth in computers. They climb spiders' web, they visit dragons. They fondle serpents. They are cycled and recycled in computers. They are children of the Wheel who die to themselves upon Venus and Mars and in the Milky Way. In an age when it is said that the ghost has fled the machine they are the returning ghost, the thieves and the beggars and the clowns who now inhabit the spirit of the game in the machine.'

'What do they see from the Moon?' I asked.

'They see a black-out wilderness Sky above the Moon. They see the universal unconscious or the collective unconscious (as some Jungian bodies would put it).'

'It's alive, that unconscious,' I said and felt like a Fool.

'It's alive,' the Sphinx that resided under the Wheel confessed. 'Yes, it's alive for it is possessed of the rhythm of the spheres, or the music of the spheres, black-out music or song – if you like – in the rhythms of an apparently unconscious universe. We hang, don't we, upon every flare for a signal of life from a far distant light-year planet.' The Sphinx was jesting, it seemed, to imply bridges of space across vast distances between light-year suns, light-year planets, and planet Earth with its star or sun. 'We hang, don't we, upon orchestrations of death and life. For who knows whether light comes from extinct stars whose death or resurrection we are still to prove. The music of the spheres – as the ancients used to put it – is now *black-out song upon the lips of living ghosts which blend concretion and apparition . . .'*

I was stunned as if I myself were unconscious yet inhabited in the great Dark of myself by singing ghosts as the voices of the children woke me and brought me back to life in the wheeling games that they created.

I saw their black-out lips in the blistered shoes that they wore at the door of my mother's Albuoystown shop. Their flesh crept through those holes, through their patched garments, as they stood on the Moon and sang with a hidden choir in the crumbling Grave of space.

'They are children of a lame humanity in the computer of the Moon,' said Mr Mageye, 'on the Wheel of time.'

'Do they seek a new Church,' I asked, 'a new Rome?'

'They are possessed of a *virus of Spirit*,' said Mr Mageye. 'Make no mistake about this. They are *involuntary* explorers of numbers in every machine, joy-riding machines and fast computers, involuntary mathematicians of Chaos, lottery populations on the Wheel. Who is to live, who is to die, upon an overcrowded planet?'

'Virus of Spirit?' I demanded. '*Virus is poison.*'

'Ah, Francisco,' said the Sphinx Mr Mageye, 'you startle me out of my wits.' The children were bouncing upon him now as if he were Atlas with the Moon on his back. It was all he could do to recover his breath and speak.

'Love is an ailment,' said Mr Mageye at last. 'We all know that, do we not? Love is ill. Love has become a kind of infection of the nerves, a disorder. *We make love.* What does it mean to make love? The nerves of lust become active. *Love your enemies* is the supreme commandment that breaks all other commandments in that one exposes oneself to be bombed, or blasted, or ridiculed, or loathed, or labelled a vile hypocrite. To love one's enemies tends to signify that one desires their wives or husbands, that one is plotting to steal their possessions, their ass, their horse, their sacred property. To love one's religion is to blow oneself up in a car in order to kill as many on the road as possible. To love one's faith is to crusade that one's faith is the only true faith and all other faiths misguided. To love one's friends is a pretty hazardous business at times. Caesar loved Brutus. Brutus loved the people. He was a patriot. Love then is tainted by treachery and patriotism. When I speak of the virus of Spirit, Francisco – let me make this clear – I am implying a capacity in Spirit to endure torment in the name of Love, a Love that unravels tainted systems to orchestrate the illnesses that plague humanity into a numinous dispersal of fanatical absolutes.'

He paused and I dreamt that I could perceive a curious *fraying* within the garment that he wore, as if threads had been loosened in his tussle with the children who still swarmed upon him, or clung to him, when they were not upon or in the Kali Wheel.

'Deacon alas,' said Mr Mageye – as he plucked a thread from within his garment – 'equated the virus of Spirit with inoculation with the venom of the Scorpion Constellation when he fell into the folkloric Imagination of the people. He saw such inoculation as a shield against the bite of pain, he saw it as the shield of power. Whereas the virus of Spirit is a measure of access to the profoundest unravelling of the charisma of power, access to acute and innermost tormenting self-knowledge . . .

'I prefer to die now, Francisco, than to become a vegetable institution on the sick-bed of the humanities . . .'

'You are no vegetable institution, Mr Mageye,' I cried. 'How in God's name could you say this? Stay with me.'

'Perhaps not,' said Mr Mageye, 'but the Sphinx in the desert of the Imagination that we tend to witness on every hand is becoming a Vegetable, and if one could begin to unravel that supreme Vegetable, to pass sentence of death upon oneself in Play or Dream-book, then, who knows, we might salvage a future from the ruins of the past. It is a worthwhile sacrifice, is it not Francisco?'

The banqueting hall was now veiled in the mystery of past futures, future pasts, open to originality.

Jonah Jones was now crossing the hall from the seat that he occupied under the Constellation of the Spider Whale and Anansi Tiger. Or so it seemed in the darkened hall. Constellations rise and fall and change their shape in black-out orchestras and music and song.

'Jonah,' I cried. 'What has happened to you – I scarcely know you now – in the Grave of space? I knew who you were over there. You were large as a Titan. Now – as you cross the floor – you have shrunk. You're a dwarf. You are – it's difficult to describe it – a bubble which a child blows from bone or flute on the Moon into space. There's a precipice in space that is black, but when it sings one dreams of universal repentance. Do dwarfs repent more easily than Titans? If so you are truly welcome, Jonah, to join the band of mischievous children that you see around you.'

'Alas,' said Mr Mageye, 'society never forgives transgressors. One knows how obdurate one is. Repentance remains a bleak task in the face of one's own obduracy and within an unforgiving world.' He plucked a number of threads from his unravelling robe. I was reminded of the threads that had fallen from my Nemesis Hat upon his grave in Albuoystown and upon my mother's grave. Was Mr Mageye an apparition, a solid ghost that had begun to shed its cloak? Of course he was. I had long been aware of this. What was astonishing were the bodies within the bodies, the ghosts within ghosts, tree within tree, that addressed one within black-out music of dissolving spheres, resurrectionary spheres. Deacon had trespassed into my Ear as ghost within ghost to inform me of the face of the Child within a leaf upon the phallic tree. Mr Mageye had spoken of the Vegetable Sphinx in the desert. Titan Jonah had become a dwarf . . .

'Society is adamant. It rarely forgives. One has to start from within in order to bestow – as each garment falls – another page in Memory theatre's Dream-book on which to assemble new traces or traceries of repentance in the fictionality and actuality of the Dark soul. That is why, Francisco, I shall leave you the skin of the Predator when I go. *Write upon it, Francisco.* Write the last (or is it the first?) epic of repentance. Society tends to be unforgiving. Murderers never change, do they? They must be punished to the end of time. Under lock and key if not on the gallows or the electric chair. None exists to convince the social animal that the heart of the wild is susceptible to change! None except the Predator whose repentance is our only hope. I know in my innermost self and so do you. I am the Enigma of change. I live with predators. I am the Sphinx. The Lion is my dress and so is the

Tiger and the Eagle and the Vulture and the Serpent's grace and gentleness of the Dove. You are a diminutive survivor, Francisco, in whom live multitudes, prey and predators and victims alike. We are reflections of the Vegetable encounter with all species within paradoxes of evolution which may lay bare a resurrectionary, innermost consciousness which breaks the mould of the everlasting tyranny of the unconscious. We are unconscious of the debts we owe others in history, we are unconscious of the crimes that we have committed in ourselves or through our antecedents. No medium can help us except *life* in the Precipice of the Dark mind. No word can help us except another music that we blindly see or hear in the computerized grave of the globe or cage of rhythmic numbers.'

Mr Mageye turned his gaze on Jones. He signalled that he was about to depart, to take his leave of us. He had been in contradistinction to the tyranny of the unconscious – a supreme teacher of unravelled obduracies that gave way by stages to meaningful sacrifice within my Dream-book.

Every supreme teacher wears the Mask of Enigma, Jest and Compassion in ruined banqueting halls, ruined Colleges, ruined legislatures, senates, in Brazil, in the Guyanas, Mexico, the Yucatán, everywhere . . . Perhaps a state of ruin had been hidden but present all along, misconceived beginnings, misconceived empires, doomed Colonies, doomed Jonestown, Bonampak, Chichén Itzá.

He tossed the skin of the Predator to me.

I scarcely knew him now. He was devoid of his robes. The Skeleton-twin of all creatures! But that could prove to be another masquerade in some other dimension, some other universe.

'Write upon the Skin,' he said. 'Use quills plucked from the Eagle or the Vulture. Write upon the walls of rotting, colonial institutions, test every fragment of a biased humanities, break the Void by sifting the fabric of ruin for living doorways into an open universe. This is my last gift. Remember me, Francisco.'

'Francisco? Francisco? Where is he hiding?'

'In my Mask, in my head,' I said. But Jones looked at me, at Deacon (whose Mask I wore) with scorn.

My first task – as Mr Mageye began to leave the hall (I knew I would never see him again, and I wept) – was to collect the scraps that littered the floor of the banqueting hall. Scraps of an orgy on my wedding night. I thought of civilization's sacrificial supper which Leonardo da Vinci had painted. I had once dreamt of buying this for the Virgin Ship but could not raise the requisite millions in gold.

Was it possible to build a Ship of Bread from the scraps in the banqueting hall? Was it possible to sail upon this to seek a fortune for Marie's first-born? The Play in Memory theatre, my revisitation of the Day and the Year of the Wedding, required me to sail in Deacon's footsteps to Roraima, to wear his Mask, and to return with a fortune. But black-out music made me conscious of discrepancies in Memory and of a changed spatiality in time as I contemplated the journey. I felt I was under the eye of judges whose faces I could not discern. I looked hard but they vanished.

The shattered banqueting hall – shattered across forty years from 1954 to 1994 – was littered with trampled crumbs of bread, meat, fish, rice, sugar . . .

'Guyana is poor,' I said to Jones. 'Is it not time to contemplate a new Economy for the North, Central and South Americas? Guyana is shackled to an accumulation of negative dollars and interest on "futures" as obdurate and solid as Atlas and the globe on his back. Brazil is shackled to inflation. Destitution is starkest when seen backwards from discouraging futures *within flexible generations nevertheless* and a Waste Land of Politics; generations that need to ask themselves profoundest questions about the life and death of the Imagination, the limits of materialism and realism, the necessity to transgress boundaries into the hidden caveats of ancient civilizations, to leap beyond conventional codes of racial or cultural individualism, and into cross-cultural epic born of diverse re-visioned legacies and inheritances . . .'

I began to assemble buckets and baskets of bread scattered everywhere on the floor after a riot, a century of riots, a century of hunger and orgies.

I stopped and mounted a rostrum under the screen on which Mr Mageye's film had appeared. Jones came close and waited.

Perhaps – I was unsure – he expected me to pay him a tribute. He had forked out a lot of American dollars to make the banquet a roaring success. Poor people's fees to the Doctor and Jones's American dollars (Jones had been attached to Deacon in San Francisco even more than he had protected and favoured me) were not to be sneezed at. Jones saw himself as a giant back in 1954, but now that he had returned to the year of the wedding across fifty years, the disguises that he had worn, since his death (or deaths) in 1978, had perversely accumulated or subsided into the head of a mighty dwarf.

'I am steeped,' I said to the audience in the banqueting hall, 'in a bottomless sense of sorrow at Mr Mageye's departure. In olden days, it is said, humanity mourned the passing of a golden age into a silver age. In later days nostalgia seemed to feed upon despair. Gold and silver had declined into lead or bronze or coal or oil or bauxite or whatever.

'Each age and its passing – whether golden or bronze or bauxite – was neatly labelled as fate or fact within history's unswerving plot, unswerving closure of the lives of labouring men and women.

'But Mr Mageye taught me differently. He sought to unshackle history and fiction from predatory coherence or closure that reduces communities to a desert . . .'

I stopped. I was aware that Jones was listening intently but a cloud overshadowed his brow. He listened but did not wish to hear what he heard. As if it were a book he turned each page but did not wish to read what he read. 'Deacon is inventing a new language,' he said silently to himself as he confronted my Mask. 'But no,' I replied as silently as he. 'I am drawing upon dynamic resources within a living language that we could so easily imprison and forfeit.'

The hall had darkened as if the faintest mist of dust were raining from the rafters.

'True,' I continued, 'I am sorely tempted to say that the age of the Virgin Ship in my Dream-book is over and is passing into the age of the Ship of Bread built from crumbs that fall from rich men's tables.

'I am tempted to say this because my mind is flooded with acute sadness, with oceanic misery, on Mr Mageye's going. Not his passing but his going. A gleam of hope remains in that – as he left the hall – he seemed to hint at complex layers of repentance. He broke apart the investitures of the Sphinx. Not to imply finality to theatres of cruelty . . . Not at all. I have inherited the Skin of the Predator upon which to write . . . The Skin illumines the Carib, cannibal morsel which one must digest and transform in oneself within the cellular organs of a new body. Do you remember, Jones, the Carib morsel that we ate on the eve of the holocaust?

'Why should Bread – however trampled – be inferior to the horror and grandeur of Gold and the crimes that the conquistadores heaped on themselves when they ransacked the treasuries of ancient America?

'The defect lies not simply in the constitution of Bread or Gold but in our difficulty to discern the innermost ghost of Bread, the innermost spectrality of Gold that can haunt us with excess.

'Ask King Midas, enthroned by greedy cultures as an immortal. His twin was the Golden Man of Guyana's El Dorado. Midas starved himself to death (his first death or his second?) when the Bread he ate turned to Gold in his mouth, when the gospel of materialism he preached in charismatic palaces and churches turned to hell on earth . . .'

'You bastard,' cried Jones. 'You are not here to sing praises to Mageye . . .'

I hesitated but sensed there was still time to complete my eulogy or address in praise of my teacher.

'Here's a quick snapshot of voyages we have made, voyages – God forbid – that are closed or over, voyages susceptible to revisionary perspectives. We sailed from the age of Jonestown (1978) back to the age of Albuoystown (1939) and also to Crabwood Creek in the same year when Deacon – a mere child – lassoed the Horses of the Moon, a feat comparable to the seizure of serpents by Heracles in his cradle.

'On our voyages we glimpsed Alexander and Genghis Khan and the Golden Man. Marie – a nurse in the Port Mourant Hospital – played the role of a princess of El Dorado and minted a range of currencies in the Bank of history: some were possessed of the head of Lenin and Marx, others were imprinted with the bust of the queen of France who herself loved theatre and played at being a milkmaid and a nurse in the revolution until the axe fell down the precipice of the guillotine.

'I glimpsed that precipice in the torso of the Virgin of Jonestown, another Marie Antoinette in the Carnival theatre of sorrowing mothers and peasant queens, and milkmaids, of dispersed humanity around the globe.

'Some legends claim that the Prisoner of Devil's Isle arrived in the Guyanas in the age of Reason forged on that precipice of the guillotine. But this is untrue. The age of Reason was the golden age of the Void. The Prisoner himself was a native of the ancient Americas. He anticipated the coming of nihilist Reason long before it plastered itself on banners of freedom, dread freedom.'

'Stop, stop, Deacon,' cried Jones.

I started. I was Francisco Bone. Not Deacon.

'How dare you stand there and overlook me in praising this Mageye? This hybrid? It's outrageous. And what you are saying is barbarism.'

A beggar crept out of a cardboard box and touched my hand. I bent down and he whispered in my ear. 'Mr Mageye, the huntsman and another rider have ridden up on horses from the Moon to bring you an urgent message. They are waiting outside by the river.'

I was overjoyed. I descended from the rostrum and made for the door. Jones climbed up and began to voice his annoyance at my behaviour. No sign of the horsemen outside but I dreamt I could perceive the phantom hoofs or prints in the dust. And the Ship of Bread lay at anchor in the river!

'Where are Mr Mageye and the others?' I turned to the beggar. But he too had vanished. And then there was a crash. The roof of the banqueting hall had collapsed entirely. The walls of the building caved in entirely. And yet some obscure, hidden salvage persisted in a black-out net in my Dream-book.

'Jones is dead,' I thought to myself. 'Jones is dead. But he lives, he will re-emerge from the salvaged banqueting hall in space in another charismatic crusade. Poor Jonah! The road to repentance is a long, long one.'

A key fell at my feet and I unlocked a door into the Ship of Bread and began to sail for Roraima. Epic hoofprints of the leather of horses (such was the jest of the unravelled Sphinx in translating hide into hoof) metamorphosed their grain into human footgear, uncanny footsteps, Deacon's footsteps in a space age, footprints in space, upon water, upon air, upon fire, earth, upon the Moon, upon Mars, upon space stations, upon distant planets . . .

Such is the logic and illogic of a Dream-book mirroring the breakage of trauma after a holocaust. Outer space and inner space begin to respond to the folklore of remote localities upon planet Earth in which angels fall from the stars and require profoundest fictionality of origins. Remote localities become a theatre of counterpoint between outer spaces and inner spaces. They cease to be remote. They are here and now, they harbour past and present and future voyages. They bring home the gamble of life in all its immediacy, pressing appearance, elusive character, uncertainty, arrival, departure, trial, judgement . . . They bring home the gamble of resources, the gamble with resources, across an ocean of Spirit trailing itself into one's Masked blood . . .

'All this is rhetoric,' Mr Mageye would have said, 'the rhetoric of cosmic Jest.' He once hinted to me that a rhetoric of Jest was native to twentieth-century epic; a rhetoric of Jest – which seeks to embrace inner spaces and outer spaces – was a form of repentance for theatres of cruelty implicit in nature, a nature in us, in our consciousness, that recognizes its kinship to hostile and deadly environments close at hand and far out in the universe, in parallel universes that whisper in a flicker of lightnings . . .

I sensed that such kinship is an enormous caveat, it illumines our apparently natural proneness to savage the planet on which we live; it invokes the mystery of universal repentance that runs in our blood interwoven with dread. Universal repentance perhaps, but one remains largely blind, largely deaf . . .

What is repentance?

Does repentance invoke shared extremities, shared with all creation, extremities inner and outer? Do extremities imply a counterpoint between parallel universes, a well-nigh untranslatable counterpoint harbouring and nursing unconditional Love despite brute appearances, despite one's spiritual blindness, one's spiritual deafness? In the counterpoint between all extremities resides the music of a haven, an archetypal haven one never seizes though the extended Shadow of the imagination is nourished there.

One is naturally blind, it seems, naturally biased and deaf, it seems, to insubstantial premises of counterpoint in the music of space, insubstantial counterpoint between extremities. One clings to the extremity of wealth or fortune as a natural fortress of economic salvation in a cruel world . . . Wealth seems real; it is, is it not, a trustworthy appearance. It blazons and embellishes the apparition of Bread in a hungry age. Saint Francis of Assisi, on the approach of his death, dreamt that the Bread he held in his fingers (*I dreamt of my phantom fingers sliced by Deacon's bullet*), with which to feed his flock, began to crumble . . .

It was a poignant parable of appearances. Why Bread? Why should poor Bread speak for gold, or diamonds? Why should a parable of brute appearance not dress itself up in august, imperial robes, why ride on the back of weak Bread? Unless Bread itself is susceptible to predatorial instincts and needs the administration of a saviour-Child as much as a saint?

These are riddles of evolution I am unable to solve except that Bread leaps, even as it crumbles, fish leaps, fire blazes and leaps even as a waterfall evolves through fossil apparitions of Rock in cosmic and geological theatres of appearance . . .

Long before Jonestown, November 1978, Marie of Port Mourant and Deacon were married in Crabwood Creek on the 24th March, 1954.

Curious, it seemed, to recall such detail, the exact date, and to forget so much, to be in the Dark about so much, to remain in the Dark about the journey which lay ahead of me in my revisitation of the past from the future.

Deacon set out the morning after the honeymoon pregnancy.

He had no time to waste to secure the bountiful appearance of a fortune to place at the feet of his unborn, soon-to-be-born son, the promised saviour of his people through whom he would rule. The saviour-archetype is universal, however hidden. It is as much the promise of salvation as it enshrines, or appears to enshrine, wealth and prosperity. I myself had no time to waste as I boarded the Ship of Bread to voyage along the course which Deacon had taken on the day he set out. I voyaged in Memory theatre. I saw now as never before that Deacon's eyes were blind on that morning when he set out and that I (in his Mask) would need to see *through* his blindness. Seeing *through* was the art of Memory theatre, the dispossession of implacable appearance. To be blind therefore may prove a curious gift, the gift of the strange ghost Deacon had become in me, the gift of epic theatre, the gift of the voyaging part I played, the gift of seeing *through* . . .

Deacon was deaf when he set out, deaf to the splintering crash of the banqueting hall. But his ghost within a ghost – that I had encountered on the stage of Memory theatre – inhabited my Ear in the Mask and I heard the sound of black-out salvaged lives myself in the orchestra of space. Yet my mind was still a blank with regard to the journey I was making and my return to Port Mourant or Crabwood Creek and the newborn Child. Deacon had returned to greet the infant in December 1954. Deacon had returned nine months to the day that he set out. I knew all this in a kind of calendrical, mechanical version of colonial fortune, religious as much as ideological expectations of El Dorado. But abysmally enough – much as I exercised such expectations in the Play – I could not see myself returning in the Mask of Deacon.

Commonsense Memory theatre declared I was required to return within the ground of the Play. Even as the saviour-Child was called upon to manifest himself. After all (I touched the solid, fantasy, theatrical or dramatic *persona* and Mask I wore) I possessed lines, did I not, to utter to Marie – lines of greeting as I bore great wealth in my hand – on seeing her newborn Child in the Play. But even as I touched the Mask, and sought to confirm the wealth of El Dorado, a shudder ran through my frame and I knew (without knowing how I knew) that some peculiar hidden text or change in the Play had been inserted into my dangerous revisitation of a past year I should have remembered in all its details. Dangerous revisitation of past times!

Past time carries within itself (when revisited in numinous truth) hidden textual crises relating to debts left unpaid by those whose Masks one wears. Those debts may incur facing – in this instance – Deacon's judges which would then become *my* judges in the altered textuality of the Play. Why judges? What crime had Deacon committed for which *I* must pay in standing within his shoes and his Mask? Ghosts are real in Memory theatre as the frame one inhabits gives way to undreamt-of apparently *immaterial* truth. Such immateriality is a challenge to the core of materialism one takes for granted as the real world . . .

A shudder ran through my frame as I felt myself ageing. The Mask had aged in the grave of space, cradle of space. Grave and cradle were extremities in counterpoint to assert a medium of epic, well-nigh untranslatable ghost one seeks nevertheless to translate through hidden, eruptive texts within the Play of civilization. I was curiously alive at the heart of untranslatable counterpoint between all extremities.

How old was I in cosmic humour, cosmic theatre, in revisiting the past? In 1954 I had been twenty-four years old. In 1994 (when I was on the verge of completing – or apparently completing – my Dream-book) I was sixty-four years old. Deacon was also twenty-four in 1954. I had sailed back in time from 1994 to 1954 and should – as on all previous voyages with Mr Mageye – have resumed my youth (or the youth of Deacon whose Mask I wore) in the Play of Memory theatre. I should be as old as Deacon was on his wedding day and on his departure for Roraima. Surely the matter was simplified by the fact that Deacon and I were the same age.

Was there an outer textual age, an outer textual ghost – which Deacon and I shared in the music of space – even as he had inhabited my Ear and released the invagination of anatomy infused to leap into well-nigh indescribable counterpoint between all ages?

Mr Mageye would have laughed at such dread yet comedy. Divine comedy ages stars or imbues them with paradoxical youth in the astronomy of science upon the immense depth and canvas of space.

So perhaps light-year comedy in theatres of archetypal time brings characters into play which are vessels of simultaneous age and youth. A Jest! Think of the grey-bearded children in the banqueting hall. But on this occasion it was an omen of mystical terror, cloth of hair and flesh, unravelling attire that I scarcely relished. Would I disappear, would I vanish soon, as Mr Mageye and the Prisoner of Devil's Isle had done? Yet I enjoyed (if 'enjoyment' was the term) a curious lightness as if Mr Mageye were raining cards upon me which he had kept up the sleeves of his robe as he discarded his dress. They fell on the Skin of the Predator that I had spread upon the Ship of Bread.

At last the crumbling yet resuscitated Ship – crumbling, salvaged Ship – arrived beneath an apparition of Roraima, as the great Rock of ages may have been geological aeons ago, when Roraima pulsed and rolled in space in the form of a giant waterfall, a giant card of transience and transition and appearance from Mr Mageye's deck. Transience and solidity are interchangeable features in the Carnival gamble of resources which we need to approach with sacramental identity and care . . . I felt the necessity to measure such sacrament by leaping into space myself (as if I had fallen out of God's pack of cards) but was held in check by my desire to secure a fortune for Marie's Child . . .

From the hills around the Apparition of Roraima I saw the natives of this Sky-region descending. They moved at a slightly awkward pace attuned to the lame who voyage upon the comedy of light. Light-year feet tend to stumble upon nursery ladders in space.

Was this the Sky-river which Deacon had entered in his travels in 1954? I felt awkward myself as my feet and limbs aged into unpredictable youth and vice versa in a counterpoint of concordance and dissonance. I turned the riddle of age once again around in my mind. When I sailed back to Albuoystown from Jonestown I had assumed the age of nine (rightfully mine it seemed in 1939) except that two fingers were missing from one hand. And that was a signal few – if any (except Mr Mageye) – perceived as the mystically changed age of the body when it revisits the past in numinous character and truth. One slips into elusive frames akin to a deck of cards raining in space when one revisits the past.

A deck of cards (celestial mathematics Deacon would have said) fall apparently randomly, haphazardly, upon the Skin of the Predator in Memory theatre. My body is amongst them now, old, young. The Ship of Bread is amongst them now. Eclipses appear within the Sky of the past (Eclipses of Memory) which one revisits and sees *through* historic blinds or curtains: such Eclipses have immediacy in the Dark of the Mind, the Mind of Memory, the Mind of history. Memorial stars appear over the cradles of humanity and arch in the neighbourhood of Eclipse. Such curvatures of light were apparently non-existent in the past to the Eye of history.

When the alterations in spectralities of time, in the bristling life of the Predator that one touches in oneself, through oneself, beyond oneself, appear negligible, as negligible as a smashed, ghostly finger that one brings from the future into the past, one is (I am) inclined to dismiss or underestimate one's trespass in space in the body of dreams and the scars that remain after every encounter with life in space. Such encounters slip from dream-memory but are revisited upon us in the fierce games that we play on Earth, games that sometimes shatter us into a revelation of inner, textual bodies, outer, textual bodies, inner tongues, outer tongues. But one misreads – in the flat, mechanical word – the intensity and the extensity of the Game, the Game of resurrection within and beyond the Grave of space. That is my Play of staggered yet orchestrated imageries . . .

Every misreading on my part stirs the Breath of the Predator into the pulse of another random fall from a deck of cards. In addition to a ghostly, sliced hand (that may attempt to sort the cards I receive) I suddenly find incalculable time imprinted on the gaol of flesh, the youth of flesh that I treasure. Imprinted on my Mask! On Deacon's Mask when he fought as an Eagle-knight, an Eagle-angel, with the Titan Tiger Jonah! And still one may seek to deny an orchestration of self-confessional, self-judgemental imageries and their inevitable counterpoint but changing roles of appointment with the Predator whose claws are visible everywhere in a wounded universe. The epic repentance of the Predator takes us beyond the framed and flat word into the Virgin-archetype and the rhetoric of intercourse with reality shorn of violence in the illimitable (however apparently black-out) music of counterpointed universes into which we may leap.

Giant rocks and waterfalls and precipices on the Virgin deck of space intermingle with the Predator's random, chastened pulse. Such is the riddle of my Play (my Play, Deacon's Play, Mr Mageye's Play?) in its Virgin transgression of frames of terror.

I turned at last to confront the Apparition of Roraima in geological time. I felt the scars of rock and waterfall and fossil grain in my bones and upon my skin in their eclipsed encounters with apparently inhospitable space, inhospitable grave.

Diamonds and gold seemed to bubble at my fingertips as I reached into the inhospitable grave of Roraima in its long and dangerous sojourn through geological ages to acquire a perch, an Eagle's fierce perch, within and upon the watershed between the floodwaters of the Amazon and the torrential rapids of the Orinoco.

On the Eagle's beak I saw a glistening network of Scorpions that seemed to aid me – within eclipses of Memory – in the acquisition of gold from the rock of ages, the waterfalls of ages in great Roraima.

Extraordinary plants and flowers shone with teeth and brilliant flowering, repetitive lips in the Shadow of the Scorpion Constellation . . . Yet when I reached again nothing was there. Nothing itself was a fossil apparition in space. Much depended on the apparently random fall of the deck – its corresponding imprints upon oneself – if one were to reach into time past in the present relived moment for an incalculable storage of wealth that had evolved and accumulated. The hazards and dangers varied with apparently random imprints that made time past accessible in tangible form when one rifled secret hoards in fire and rock and water and space.

I had clearly no apparitional key – in this instance – to secure a fortune in apparitional diamonds and gold from apparitional Roraima. Were I to return in a hundred years or a million years I would then perhaps be able to trespass into fire and rock as if I had arisen from the Grave. I would have conversed with life in the universe for the necessary key. Or perhaps I would fail again, be driven to retreat again, and return again through eclipses of Memory theatre . . .

Scylla and Charybdis were Clashing Rocks but there were Swimming Rocks in Roraima or fossils imprinted with Vegetable gold that I tried again to reach but it seemed to reside on the sick-bed of the Predator and within some unfathomable music or orchestration of the powers of Love within the Virgin . . .

I knew I could not seize the Vegetable gold but my mind and heart were light in my ageing body . . .

It was then that I was seized by the natives I had seen upon the hillsides. They were masked judges and I was unable to tell who they were. Their slightly halting, awkward pace made me wonder whether they were as old or young as I, lame or leaping as I.

It was a consolation to dwell upon such thoughts. Surely they would question me and let me leave. But they seized me roughly and bore me up a hillside towards a cliff-top above the Waterfall.

When we arrived they took the Skin of the Predator from me and spread it on a table.

'We caught you red-handed,' they said, 'with your hands in the Roraima till, Deacon.'

I wanted to laugh as if their utterance was a joke but I knew it was no joke. I flung out my hands from my body.

'Nothing,' I said. 'I tried to reach into what I saw. There was something there. It seemed at one stage to nestle in my fingertips but it melted, one assumes, for there was nothing there though I swear there was something. It was like a sunset and a sunrise within the breaking, crumbling Void of the universe. They are nothing, but when they harden yet run within volcanic space they become a black river of gold.'

I tried to brazen out my predicament in the light of the severity of their veiled faces, veiled eyes, unsmiling, bitter lips.

'Liar,' they cried in unison. They seized me and pushed their fists into my pockets. I felt their fists opening like roses or crabs and in an instant they came forth with gold and diamonds that were strewn on the Predator's Skin into neat piles and heaps.

'Liar,' they repeated. 'Where did you get this?'

I was utterly astonished and unable to reply.

'Soon you will tell us, Deacon, that you were born with a silver spoon in your mouth and that you sold this in your infancy, infant unconsciousness, for a fortune.'

'Mockery is not proof,' I cried. 'I tell you there was nothing there. *You have framed me.*'

'*We have framed you?*' They spoke with fury and deliberation.

'Well you must have done so,' I cried. 'For there was nothing there. *And I am not Deacon.*'

'Ah! we were waiting for that. We knew you would deny it all.'

'Deny what?'

'Deny that we have caught you at the scene of the crime. You couldn't keep away, could you, Deacon?'

Where and what I wondered was the scene of the crime? I stroked the Skin of the Predator. In the dying afternoon light it shone with disturbing beauty. There were idyllic portions in the Skin where sheep and lambs seemed to graze and birds flew. There were portions that gleamed with swords and shields and armour. There were portions that appeared to invoke the launching of ships, the arrival of Cortés and Pizarro in ancient America.

'Where is the scene of the crime?' I demanded.

'You are a cunning devil, Deacon. You would distract our attention from the fact that we assisted you to garner a fortune from Mount Roraima forty years ago.'

'I know Deacon was here forty years ago,' I agreed. 'But I am not Deacon. He was seeking a fortune for Marie's Child through whom he intended to rule his people. It was a kind of folkloric contract with the stars. They were savannah people. Up to all sorts of tricks and bargains. But Deacon was marked out from the day he was found in the savannahs and adopted by the entire community. A fallen angel! I know all this. I know that he fulfilled, in the eyes of the peasantry, some expectation of leadership if not kingship. He was pretty ruthless. His betrothal to Marie, for instance, was a national event. A small nation, needless to say! But does size matter? Does the size of Bonampak or Rome or Jerusalem or Bethlehem or Tula matter upon a deck of raining cards in which a kingdom or a hamlet may become the eye of a storm? The truth is I suffered from partial amnesia and severe trauma after the Jonestown holocaust. I slowly began unravelling the trauma as I made my way through Limbo Land to New Amsterdam, where I was well enough to begin my Dream-book and to sail in the company of Mr Mageye.'

'What are you up to, Deacon? Do you think you can deceive us again? What Dream-book?'

'Please,' I asked. 'Come to the point. Tell me why you have arrested me and what this trial is all about.'

'You live in and out of your Dream-book, Deacon,' they said with a harsh voice and humour like keys grating in prison locks. *'Well it's time to come out and stay there.'* They were mocking me I knew.

But there was more to it than the bite of mockery. There was a long and incredible pause in which Silence entered my voice as I confessed.

'Yes,' I agreed, 'come out, it's true, on the other side of Dream, the other side where Dread stands. The trial. The judgement. On the other side of Dream. *Not* the other side of the grave. On the other side of Dream one lives, one *is* beyond all "beyonds" within a measure of measureless counterpoint between all extremities.'

My judges remained severe, unrelenting. Even as my Skeleton-twin had rebuffed me, but I knew now that rebuff and severity were part and parcel of extremity. How else would the immensity of counterpoint between all places, all extremities, prevail if one's judges were less than severe?

'We tell you straight,' my judges cried. 'Forty years ago, Deacon, we helped you to gain a fortune.'

'I have no fortune. I am poor.'

They ignored my remark.

'We helped you to gain a fortune,' they insisted. 'Roraima is the mother of Scorpions. The dread and fourth Virgin . . .'

'On the other side of Dream,' I confessed. 'There she teaches me that Love can scarcely be borne, it is so infinite. It is Compassion, yet beyond all riddles and expectations of Compassion.'

'We do not know what she teaches you, Deacon – you who claim to have fallen from the stars – but she taught us that without inoculation with the venom of the Scorpion you would be unable to climb the Rock . . .'

'A misreading of the Scorpion Constellation,' I said. 'On the other side of Dream Roraima, the dread mother of Compassion, heals Mankind with and through all creatures in whose obscurity of soul repentance is the farthermost evolution Mind – despite its addiction to cruelty – may begin to contemplate . . .'

My judges were smiling now at the Fool I was.

'We see you *do* recall the folklore of your region. So much for your plea of amnesia.'

I was stung into protest. 'I never said I had forgotten everything. Partial amnesia. I had not forgotten *pain*, mental pain, and this was enough to keep me going and to give me the impetus to put myself in the shoes of the people of Jonestown on the Day of the Dead in a Play of extremities that sought to come abreast of their and my predicament. They were alive in me. So was Deacon in a variety of particularity. And Jonah . . .'

I stopped for an instant under the veiled gaze and unsmiling lips of my judges.

'Deacon,' I said, 'was the father of Marie's Child. This I knew, this I remembered. But – here's the rub in eclipses of Memory that I had to endure – I suffered a void or a blank as to what actually happened to their Child, what illness. Child mortality throughout this century and past generations has been high in the Guyanas! Malaria is a species of predator. The building of Jonestown I knew was a kind of memorial for Deacon. But even there the circumstances grew vague for me after the holocaust. How to blend a memorial to a Child with the inferno! On the other side of Dream perhaps where I now stand . . . Jonestown was a memorial for me too when we started building . . . A memorial to my mother and the beggars and children she cared for in Albuoystown. Once again how to blend a memorial dedicated to care with hell or the inferno. On the other side of Dream where we may arrive in the life of the Imagination . . . So you see there were

231

eclipses and gaps in Memory theatre that I sought to fill within an original enterprise back into time yet forwards in changing dimensionalities of past time. *I am not Deacon.* Can you see?'

'You are Deacon. We won't be deceived again. We helped you . . .'

'How did you help me? How did you help Deacon?'

'We helped you by arranging for an Arawak Doctor or shaman to inoculate you with the venom of the Scorpion. Roraima is infested with scorpions. It is also a garden of rare treasures, exquisite plants, leaves, exquisite fossils of the soul of living landscapes. You were at liberty then to climb the great Rock, or mother of the Guyanas, to climb with scorpions riding on your back, on your limbs, at your throat. You were immune to their bite. Immune to pain. Their bite was nothing. It was as if you reached into and climbed Nothing. You climbed the greatest living fossil Apparition that takes us back to the rock of ages. You rifled it. You secured all you could carry. You secreted gold in your mouth, in the crevices of your body, everywhere. *We helped you and we warned you.'*

'Warned me?'

'We warned you, Deacon, that inoculation with the venom of the Scorpion forbids intercourse with women, with your Virgin wife Marie, *it forbids your touching an infant in the cradle.* It's the curse of El Doradonne Midas secreted in Roraima . . .'

'Oh my God,' I cried to heaven. *'I remember now.* I see now through Deacon's blind eyes in the Play on the other side of Dream. He forgot the shaman's warning. I remember. I see through his blind eyes in the Play. The Play's the thing, the real world beyond all real worlds. *That is the innermost, outermost, vocation of trial and judgement in fiction.* Or else fiction is dead. One must re-imagine death as a live fossil apparition. Imagination Dead Imagine. Deacon returned on the day that the Child was born, he lifted it into his arms. He felt himself superior to all curses. And the infant stiffened in his arms. A stone leaf grew where its face was, the face of the Child at the edge of Roraima. I saw it yet I did not see it in the exquisite garden of treasures, the most precious treasure of which is the soul of living landscapes which we abuse at the drop of a hat. Nemesis Hat! How can I bear it? How can I bear such knowledge in the Play? On the other side of Dream where a measureless counterpoint exists between all extremities . . .' My eyes were light but I was weeping.

'When the news of the death of the Child,' said my judges, 'seeped through to the waiting populace they turned upon you with a vengeance. They sought to tear you limb from limb, Deacon. *You* had become their Prisoner. But you escaped with the Titan's (Jonah's) help. He was able to bar them out. He was an American! We warned you but you forgot or ignored the curse.' They stared at me with a veiled but savage humour. 'Did you suffer another Eclipse of Memory, Deacon, when you lost the Child and were driven from your wife? You hid in the Shadow of a great Cat that covered the sun. Rich folklore, Deacon, but you won't deceive us again. We have brought you out. Out into broad daylight in the setting sun . . .'

'I am not Deacon,' I cried for the last time in the Play.

'Who then is to be tried and judged? If not Deacon, who? Does no one claim the part? Is everyone innocent, no one guilty or responsible?'

I was still. I was a mere Colonial. Not an Imperialist. My limbs had aged nevertheless under the burden of Eclipses of Memory. Are Colonials the only potential creators of the genius of Memory theatre? I was weak but I had gained the other side of the Dream.

'Who then are we to judge?'

'Judge me,' I said at last. 'I am here before you. I have nothing. I am poor. Judge me. It is no accident.'

They took me without further ado to the edge of the cliff. The sun was still high though setting on the Skin of the Predator. It shone there, it was imprinted there. It was alive. It fell with me, the Predator fell with me, when their hands, the judges' hands, drove me over the edge of the cliff. Black-out music. Black soul music. I fell into a net of music, the net of the huntsman Christ. The Predator peered through me, in me, but was held at bay in the net. We stood face to face, Dread and I, Predator and I. Old age and youth parted and I was naked in the lighted Darkness of the Self. The Child rode on the Predator's groaning back. Lightness

233

becomes a new burden upon the extremities of galaxies in which humanity sees itself attuned to the sources and origins of every memorial star that takes it closer and closer – however far removed – to the unfathomable body of the Creator.